Izzy's
Cold Feet

Sarah Louise Smith

CROOKED
CAT

Printed for Crooked Cat by Createspace

First Red Line Edition, Crooked Cat Publishing Ltd. 2013

Discover us online:
www.crookedcatpublishing.com

Join us on facebook:
www.facebook.com/crookedcatpublishing

Tweet a photo of yourself holding
this book to **@crookedcatbooks**
and something nice will happen.

For Chloe,
my sous chef

The Author

Sarah Louise Smith lives in Milton Keynes with her husband, two cute cats and a loopy golden retriever. She has an extremely lovely twelve year old step-daughter and a passion for reading, cooking and travel.

Sarah has been writing stories ever since she can remember and this is her second novel. Her first, Amy & Zach is also published by Crooked Cat and available in both paperback and e-book formats. Read Sarah's blog at: www.sarahlouisesmith.com.

Acknowledgements

A huge thank you to you, Reader, for buying this book, and to all the people who have sent me lovely messages on Twitter and Facebook. I love hearing from you so please keep getting in touch.

Many thanks to the following people for all their amazing support and encouragement: Chloe, Mum, Dad, Val, Steve, Nan, Dan (co-inventor of "Ring, ring"), James, Katy, Sarah, Dave, David, Serena, Deborah, Becky, Emma, Susan, my Chick Lit Goddess friends (you ladies rock!), my fellow Crooked Cat authors (what a talented bunch you are), and all my other friends and family who have been so enthusiastic about my writing.

Special thanks to Laurence of Crooked Cat for everything you've done to get me here and the fab cover, and to my fantastic editor, Jeff: this book is so much the better for your efforts.

Most of all, thank you to Nathaniel for providing me with time, patience, encouragement, glasses of water, inspiration, feedback, and much more so that I could write Izzy's tale.

Sarah Louise Smith
Milton Keynes, July 2013

Izzy's
Cold Feet

Chapter One

Saturday. One week before my wedding day.

I opened my eyes and stretched. Then I remembered what day it was. Well, it was too late to cancel now, with only seven days to go. That settled it. Too much time and money had gone into planning the wedding. Most guests would have bought their outfits and gifts; booked hotels; not to mention how much the wedding itself was costing - which was thousands.

I had let this go on for too long and now I was just going to have to marry him.

So I took a deep breath and tried to get my body to relax. He wasn't a horrible person. I mean it wouldn't be that bad, would it? Spending my life with someone as lovely as him? No, not bad at all; there was plenty to be grateful for.

But ... did I really love him? Surely I shouldn't marry him if I wasn't sure of that?

My mobile vibrated, making me jump. A text from my best friend:

OMG! You're getting married in one week! ONE WEEK! See you soon. Amber x

I sat up and sighed.

Don't get me wrong, I knew that Greg was everything any woman could want. He had whisked me off my feet like something out of a classic romantic movie. He was, quite literally, perfect.

Amber and I had gone over the list of reasons he'd make a good husband several times:

1. He was handsome. I mean, really, *really* good looking.

2. He was wealthy. Not that I was marrying him for his money, you understand, but it meant I'd be financially secure for the rest of my life. Up until now, I'd been pretty much living on my overdraft since I graduated university, so this would be a good thing; an end to my money woes. I would have a comfortable life.

3. He had a wonderful family, who could trace their lineage back several generations to Lords and Ladies who mixed with royalty. I mean, how romantic is that? My future children would be a part of that line.

4. He loved me. Despite the fact that I was just plain and ordinary. Although I had a 'nothing' job, and I wasn't rich or stunning to look at, Greg loved me. I was lucky. Very lucky indeed.

Whenever I considered the women he knew – those he grew up and worked with; daughters of his mother's friends who met him every year at her annual summer party - I realised that there were at least several eligible women known to him, and perhaps even dozens of women, who *must* have a crush on him. Who wouldn't? He was funny, charming, intelligent, and *very* good looking.

Greg had already demonstrated during the time that we had been living together that he'd be a perfect husband; he spoilt me all the time with little surprise trips out, and cared for me. He would give me a very happy, carefree life.

Despite realising all these things, I had been unsure about

marrying him, ever since he'd proposed six months earlier. Sometimes, when we were alone together, I thought I was crazy to doubt. But then other times, and more and more lately, I'd wanted to run away as fast as I could. It wasn't the commitment; I wasn't scared of being with someone forever. In fact, I thought that sounded quite wonderful. It was Greg. I loved him, but was I *in love* with him?

Something was missing, some sort of spark or passion that I'd felt before. I missed that feeling. I wasn't sure I wanted to go without it for the rest of my life.

"Passion is overrated and burns out after a while," Amber had told me. I'd sighed and nodded at the time, admitting defeat. Either way, there was no backing out now.

It was time to get up. An idea had formed in my mind. Without giving myself the opportunity to hesitate, I got up and went to the shoe box I kept in the bottom of my wardrobe and pulled it out. I'd guiltily stuffed it behind all my shoes when I'd moved in six weeks earlier, not really expecting to ever want to look at it again, but not quite ready to dispose of it either.

I'm a hoarder. I keep stuff. Somewhere in my parents' attic are several boxes full of mementoes from my youth: toys, books, letters, postcards, cassette tapes, scarves, my old school tie and a bunch of photos. Those things meant something to me and I couldn't throw them away.

This box at the back of my wardrobe contained somewhat different, more adult memories. I sat on the carpet and stared at it for a few seconds, knowing that it was a bad idea to open it, and yet knowing that I couldn't resist it anyway. I may as well get on with it.

Slowly, I slid the lid off the box and picked up the envelope resting at the top. It contained photographs, and there, ready to seed the doubts even further, were the faces of all the men in my life before I met Greg.

First, there was a photo of Ewan, with his stupid straggly

long hair, broad shoulders and sexy smile. Oh, how I'd loved him. I sighed again. I wondered what he was doing now. Did he ever think of me? There were a few photos of him: sitting on a beach showing off his muscular chest; another where he was standing in front of a mountain with a thoughtful look in his eyes; and then one of us together in Verona. My heart ached at the sight of us, side by side. We looked so happy. Until the day we'd split up, I was happy. I had never doubted my feelings for Ewan, like I was doubting my feelings for Greg. What did that mean?

Next, my eyes fell on a photograph of Jason, looking serious and sophisticated in his dark grey suit. I tried to remember which wedding it had been taken at. I looked closely into his dark eyes and felt a tingle inside my chest, remembering how he used to make me feel whenever he looked at me. There were several more photos of him cooking and of us together with other people. I was always smiling in those photos. I'd been happy with him. Why had I screwed that one up?

I quickly pushed the photos of Dexter to the back of the pile. Every time I saw his face I still felt the humiliating wound he'd left. If he hadn't hurt me would I still be with him now? I'd been asking myself this ever since I last saw him. It was no good. I'd never know. I'd probably still be with him. *But he doesn't love you*, I reminded myself.

I put the photos down and looked at the other items I'd saved: a beautiful platinum engagement ring, which I realised now with a shudder of guilt, I preferred to the one I was wearing; a post-it note that said 'I love you!' in Jason's neat handwriting; a pen from Venice; a shell from a beach in Pembrokeshire. Each object held a memory of the man I'd been in love with at the time.

I put the lid back on the box. This was stupid. It would do no good to look through the memories of the men who were no longer in my life. It would only add to the 'what if' question that was burning through my mind. What if one of them wanted me back? Would I marry Greg then? Who would I choose if I had the choice? Who had I loved most?

I told myself this was enough. I couldn't keep doing this to myself. Anyway, what was I going to do after all this money had been spent? Jilt Greg at the altar? I could never do that. And just think of all those new dresses and hats and suits that'd been purchased especially. All those presents maybe being wrapped right at that moment, as I sat on the floor.

Yes, the presents! I hate to sound shallow but, really, I didn't want to make people have to go to the effort of taking them back. If you think about it, marriage is just a piece of paper. If it doesn't work out, we'll just get divorced, right? Lots of people were divorced. It would be no big deal.

All I needed was positive, happy thoughts. Think about the gorgeous dress, I told myself. And the beautiful house you live in. And Greg's handsome, lovely self. And how wonderful life with him might be. If only I could make the effort to stop over-analysing and think of something else.

I imagined my dad giving his speech, nervous in front of all those rich people that Greg's mother had insisted we invite. Then, I thought about Greg's mother and wondered for the umpteenth time what she really thought of me. I had a suspicion I wasn't considered good enough to be her daughter-in-law. I recalled her shocked face when we told her we were engaged.

With one final sigh, I put the box back in the wardrobe, wondering if I'd ever get it out again. Maybe one day I'd stop thinking about all those past loves and just throw the box away. I smiled at the thought, got up, pulled my dressing gown on and went to the kitchen to make a cup of tea.

I'd been delighted when I'd moved into Greg's house. I love to cook, and he had everything I could ever wish for: a brand new oven; gadgets and utensils; pots and pans; and recipe books his mother had bought him that he'd never used. There was a solid oak worktop and one of those islands in the middle. The kitchen was my favourite room in the house. I wondered if I should add 'great kitchen' to the list of reasons to marry him.

I looked at the clock and realised with surprise that Amber was about to arrive and fulfil the role that my sister Helen should have, if she hadn't been taken from me.

Chapter Two

My first memory is of my sister Helen and me putting lipstick on each other's faces when I was four years old, which means she was about six. I've tried so hard to remember back before that day; to picture us playing or fighting or doing anything … but I can't. I stare at the photos of the two little girls, and I wonder what we meant to each other. I try to work out what impact she had on me because, since she's been gone, I've felt like something is missing. There's a hollowness inside which sometimes makes me catch my breath.

My mother had a lot of makeup, back then, which she kept in a fuchsia pink vanity case next to her mirror. Helen snuck into the room first, and I followed. I loved my mother's room. It always smelled of lavender and talcum powder. We sat on the soft, white duvet - my mother always, always had white bedding - and went through all the delights within the case. There were fake eye lashes which we stuck to our hands: nail varnishes of every colour; mascara and eye liner. We picked it all up and played with it. We smeared brown lipstick all over our lips, and drew on the mirror. Helen drew a huge spiral in thick waxy pink, and I was just about to attempt the same when our mother appeared in the doorway, hand on hips.

She smiled and whipped us both up, plonked us in the bath, filled it with bubbles and scrubbed our faces until we cried.

Life was pretty simple for Helen and me back then. Sometimes we got on, sometimes we argued. It was probably fairly normal. No different from the average family, I guess - to start off with at least. We saw our cousins a lot. I was always closest to Jade who was born the day after me. We used to lie on my grandmother's bed every Christmas, talking about cartoons and books, and then when we were older, we would dream about the boys we liked. I remember wishing that Jade was my sister, instead of Helen. I feel terrible about that now.

When I was twelve and Helen was fourteen, she told me that Mark Jones, a boy from her class, had asked to be her boyfriend, and she'd said yes.

"Yuck," I said, picturing Mark's cute little face.

"What?"

"Who wants a boyfriend?"

I did, that's who. It wasn't fair; just because she was two years older, she got to do all this stuff first.

"I do," she said. "I want a husband one day. I want to live like Mum and Dad. You see how happy they are? I want a cottage by the sea, with a blue front door, a chimney and a big garden. And a dog. A big, lovely, friendly golden retriever. I'll live happily ever after."

"With Mark Jones? Really?"

"You don't like Mark?"

"He's alright. I just didn't think you'd look for a husband until you were like, I don't know, at least sixteen."

"Are you jealous?" Helen laughed.

"I'm *so* not."

"Are too."

"Why don't you just go and die?" I said, not realising how much I'd regret it only a week later.

Of course, a week later I had no idea if Helen was dead or alive. No one did. All we knew was that she had vanished.

It happened on a Tuesday and I was the first to realise.

It'd been raining most of the morning and the ground was wet as I walked home from school. I was thinking about Helen and her house by the sea with the blue front door and wondered if I'd be able to come visit her and her husband very often. It sounded nice.

Helen had a flute lesson after school, so I'd walked home alone, thrown my bag down in the hall, grabbed a packet of jammy dodgers from the cupboard, and sat on the sofa watching TV.

Helen had told me that morning that she and Mark Jones had kissed behind the fence in the school field a few days previously. I found it disgusting, and yet I was curious. Would I want to do the same thing in a few years? I somehow thought that maybe I would.

After a few hours of television, I realised Helen hadn't come home. Mum was in the kitchen, stirring pasta. I popped my head around the door.

"Dinner's nearly ready," she said.

"Where's Helen?"

"I thought she was in there with you," Mum said, putting some garlic bread in the oven.

"She hasn't come home yet." I looked at the clock again to be sure I had the time right.

"You sure?" Mum asked, still calm.

The next few hours were a blur. We never did eat our pasta and garlic bread. We walked to the school and back, looking down all the side streets, quickening our pace. Mum grew more and more frantic, asking me more and more questions about Helen, like who she might have spoken to and where she could be. I kept saying I didn't know. I couldn't imagine her sneaking off without telling me.

Mum called various people: mothers of friends we knew at school; my grandmother who lived within walking distance. But no one had seen or heard from her. Dad got home from work, asked a bunch more questions, and then, with a pale face, he called the police.

The police seemed too calm when they turned up. One male, one female, sat quietly taking notes on the sofa, asking questions about Helen. Like did she have any reason to run away? No, we told them.

Mum gave them photos and Dad sat there quietly, staring at the floor, looking horrified.

"Aren't you going to look for her?" I suddenly shouted.

And they did go out and look. For months, actually. There was no trace.

I don't remember much about that time. I went around in a daze. The first few nights, I didn't sleep. I just lay there in my bed, wondering where she could be. On the third night I went and got in Helen's bed, and somehow managed to drift off.

After two weeks, my parents urged me to return to school. Everyone stared at me, and I kept myself to myself. Dad would walk me to and from the gate, which drove me crazy. He was afraid, I know. But I kept almost hoping I'd be taken too; at least then I'd know what'd happened.

Of course, over the years I'd suspect almost everyone.

There was Mr Richards, the school caretaker, who used to stare at the girls in summer in their short skirts. I found him creepy. He'd always wear the same green overalls and had a grumpy expression. He particularly stared at me a lot but then everyone did after Helen was gone.

My mother went around in a daze, taking sedatives and barely talking. I survived on sandwiches and crisps mostly, though sometimes my grandmother would come round and cook to make sure we had a proper meal. Dad somehow held it together, going back to work after a while in an effort to give us all some sense of normality. After a year he suggested we move house, go somewhere where no one knew us; to start afresh.

Mum didn't like the idea at first, and they argued a lot. I think she was in denial - convinced that Helen would just walk through the door one day. Eventually, when it seemed most of our hope was gone, she agreed. We packed up the house and we moved to a new one, where there was no bedroom set up for Helen. It got a bit better after that.

I started a new school, which suited me just fine as no one knew I was the one with the missing sister. Somehow, some sort of normality returned.

Chapter Three

Saturday. One week before my wedding day.

"I wish Helen were here," my cousin Jade said, as Amber painted my toenails.

"Me too," I said, smiling. Amber squeezed my big toe.

Jade and Amber had turned up an hour after I'd rifled through the box containing all those past memories. Tonight was my hen night and we were spending the day lounging around Greg's living room, pampering ourselves and watching girly movies. Greg had left the night before for a weekend in Amsterdam. A dark, sick, hidden part of my mind was hoping he'd return with some weepy confession about a prostitute and I'd have a reason to call the whole thing off, but I knew that was a horrible thought and also slightly twisted wishful thinking; he was too nice to do something like that.

I watched Jade flicking through a pile of magazines she'd bought with her. She had long, chestnut hair, much like mine, except hers always hung nicely, with a few waves at the bottom, whereas mine always seemed to be a frizzy mess.

"So how're you feeling today, you know, about the aristocrat?" Amber asked casually as she moved from painting one toe to the other. She had been referring to Greg as 'the aristocrat' ever since I'd met him.

"Fine. Great. I'm going to stop over-analysing," I said, hoping I'd convince them. And myself.

"Do we need to go over the list again?"

"Nope." I smiled but knew they'd see through me.

"If you're not sure ... maybe you should talk to Greg," Jade said, without looking up from the magazines.

"I'm fine. Really."

"I'd be nervous too," she continued, "with all those rich people turning up to see you in your dress. But you'll be stunning."

I smiled again and nodded. I hadn't even given that part much thought as I couldn't really imagine the day happening, somehow. Yet here we were, preparing for my hen night.

Pamela, my mother-in-law-to-be, had organised most of the wedding, for which I was incredibly grateful. It was taking place in a big country hotel in Surrey, with over three hundred guests and all the usual big-wedding trimmings. I had no idea how much it was costing because she'd insisted on paying for everything, but I knew it was a lot. More money than I'd ever had in my life. My dad had bought my dress for me and he'd had to insist on doing even that. So I couldn't back out now, not with other people's money spent, could I?

I might as well drink plenty of champagne and enjoy the hen party.

The day passed by quite quickly. We watched some girly films, gave each other mini-facials and talked about old boyfriends.

Okay, I admit I deliberately swung the conversation that way, as we were right in the middle of a chick flick when I paused it and said:

"You never forget your first love, huh?"

And they fell right into my trap, the poor darlings.

"Your first love was Ewan, right?" Amber said, getting up to top up our bowl of snacks.

"Oh yes, Ewan!" Jade laughed. "I can't picture him but he was gorgeous, wasn't he?"

"He was sexy and sweet," I reminded them, "and very... interesting. He gave me an adventure, remember."

"That's true," Amber laughed, popping an olive in her

mouth.

"How do you know that Greg's the one?" Jade asked. She'd never been in a relationship that lasted more than a few months.

"I don't know," I hesitated. Amber glanced at me, ready for yet another pep talk if I needed it.

"I think that every time you fall in love, it's different," I told her. "And I'm just ready now, to settle down, you know?"

"I think I know what you mean. Like you're at the right stage in your life right now?" Jade asked.

"Yes. And each person I've been in love with has led me to who I am today. They each make up a part of me."

"So there was Ewan. Jason..."

"Dexter," I said, too quickly. Amber glared at me again.

"Oh, yeah, how could I forget Dexter? And now Greg. The Aristocrat."

"My point is that each one was different. I was in love with each of them. But now I'm older and wiser, and just ... ready to get married."

Is that really true? I wondered.

"I get it," Jade said, "but I was hoping for something more romantic."

I wanted to talk about them some more, to really delve into the complexities of each of those relationships, to analyse my compatibility which each of those men. Because I'd never felt as unsure about any of them as I felt about Greg now. Why was that? Had I loved them more than I loved Greg?

But there was no time for that now. It was gone six and we were meeting the rest of the party at seven thirty. So we got dressed up. I put on a little black dress I'd bought in the sale a week before; Jade did my make-up and I did Amber's. Finally, when we all looked gorgeous, we headed out of Greg's house and into a waiting taxi.

Half an hour later we were at my favourite restaurant, The Orchid, greeting a small group of my closest relatives and friends. There were fifteen of us all together and we bumbled into the restaurant and took our seats. They made me wear a sash to let everyone know I was the bride and hung a big plastic willy around my neck. We ate delicious food and drank plenty of wine and then we moved to the pub next door.

I was having a great time, talking and laughing, when I noticed Amber frown, then get up and walk through the crowd. I couldn't see where she'd gone or why so I got up to follow her, wondering if she felt ill.

I pushed through the crowded bar to see Amber chatting to someone in the corner. I peered over someone's shoulder, saw his face, and felt myself miss a heartbeat.

There before my very eyes was Jason.

Should I go over? Would he want to see me? Did he hate me?

If I'd been sober, I think I'd have avoided him. But I had that drunk, invincible feeling, which gave me a confidence boost. I went over, forgetting about the sash that was actually twisted, and the willy around my neck, and the fact that I would be married this time next week. I walked over, feeling bold.

He was wearing a blue shirt with a black v-neck jumper. I thought I recognised it, and stared at it for longer than necessary. Then I glanced up to his face and saw the two dark brown eyes I'd almost melted into when we first met, look at me again.

"Jason!" I said, almost too enthusiastically.

"Hello Izzy," he said, smiling as if he was genuinely pleased to see me, and reminding me how much I loved his voice.

"Amber tells me you're getting married. Congratulations! I'm very happy for you." He leant forward and kissed me on the cheek. He smelt good. A little tingle ran through my chest.

"Thank you," I said quietly. My mind went blank. I wanted to think of something to make him stay, to start a conversation.

17

"Nice necklace," he said, gesturing at the willy.

"Thanks."

A woman returned then. A tall, skinny, blonde thing with a perfect face, like she'd just stepped out of an advertisement for perfume or makeup or some such. I hadn't realised people could look air-brushed in real life. To my annoyance, Jason put his arm around her.

"This is my girlfriend, Anna."

"Hi," I said, wondering if I'd ever hated someone so much on the first meeting before now.

"Hello," said Amber, smiling at Anna. "I love your dress."

Thanks Amber. You Traitor!

They began a conversation about where the above-mentioned dress was purchased. I smiled and nodded then glanced at Jason. He was staring at me. I looked back at Anna and Amber, but didn't listen to their conversation. I just imagined pulling Jason into the bathroom, ripping his clothes off and letting him devour me. I was just at the delicious point of my fantasy where Jason had pushed me up against a cubicle door and whispered "I think of you whenever I make love to Anna", when Amber said:

"We'd better get back to the others."

"Well, it's really nice to see you." Jason smiled awkwardly. Our eyes locked for a second and my pulse quickened. I felt myself blush.

"You too. Of all the pubs in London, what were the chances?"

"Yes, what a jolly coincidence, huh?" he said with too much cheer.

"We'd better get back to the others," Amber said again, pulling my arm.

Jason nodded and smiled. I loved his smile. He always looked cute yet nervous, in any given situation.

"Well, congratulations," he said and kissed me again, just lightly on the cheek. Wow, he smelt divine.

"Thanks. Goodbye Jason."

Amber pulled me away.

"You okay? It's a bit weird isn't it?"

"Not really," I said. "He lives nearby."

"Izzy," she said, looking at me sternly, "do not tell me you suggested this place on purpose. Does he come here often?"

I ignored her question.

"He seems so ... happy," I said looking back at him. Amber smiled.

"Yes, bless him. I'm glad. I always liked Jason."

"Hmm..."

"What does that mean?"

"I don't know, I just ... I guess ... I miss him sometimes, you know?"

"You're just feeling weird about getting married. Stop over-thinking."

"Yes. You're right. I'm going to the ladies."

She nodded and walked off to join the others. The bathroom was very different, and much dirtier than in my Jason sex-fantasy, which was kind of disappointing. I did the necessary, washed my hands and as I was coming out I almost bumped into someone leaving the gents.

"Oh my god, Izzy!" he said, grinning from ear to ear. I thought I might pass out as I looked into two eyes I thought I'd never see again.

Ewan.

The first man I'd fallen in love with.

The man I'd once thought would be the love of my life.

Chapter Four

I met Ewan when I was twenty. He was the exact opposite of what I'd have looked for in a boyfriend, and yet he captured my attention from the first time I saw him. You see, he rescued me from a slightly embarrassing situation.

I was a student, and I'd not had a lot of experience with men. I'd had a few dates, a few sexual encounters, but nothing serious. I wasn't even looking for anything serious.

Then one day I was in Sainsbury's and I dropped a bottle of wine on the floor in the alcohol section. It was a rosé, intended to be a present for my housemate Zoe, who was having a big birthday party that weekend. I was also attempting to carry a box of chocolates and some flowers, and it all landed on the floor with a loud crash, spraying tiny shards of glass and pink bubbles over the floor and, to my horror, my brand new suede boots. I froze for a couple of seconds, unsure what to do and felt my face flush hot with embarrassment as the pink liquid spread all around me.

Ewan swooped in, just as your typical hero would, clearing the mess and even picking up another bottle and handing it to me. He had long side-burns, rough stubble, straw coloured shoulder-length hair tied into a messy ponytail, muscular arms and, as I later told Amber in dramatic fashion: "his eyes were the colour of a tropical ocean."

I started going back about the same time every week on a Friday afternoon when I knew he would be working. Amber had laughed at me and called me a stalker. I didn't care, even though it involved a bus detour on my way home from my

Friday afternoon classes.

The second time I saw him he was stacking shampoo on the shelves, and I went over to offer my thanks for his assistance the week before. He looked at me vaguely for a second, trying to remember and then said:

"Oh you're the rosé lady. No problem, no problem at all." And he winked, and turned back to his shampoo stacking.

The week after that I saw him tidying up the toothpaste shelf. I'd carefully picked out my outfit that day; some old jeans and a baggy top. I'd put my hair in a deliberately messy pair of pigtails and was attempting to look scruffy as I figured he seemed a little scruffy himself and this might appeal.

I walked past about five times before he caught my eye, smiled and winked again.

"Alright?" I muttered.

By the sixth week we were making polite conversation and I was delighted to discover he only lived around the corner from me. On the seventh week he asked me if I'd like to get a drink when his shift ended.

By this point, I'd already made up several details about him in my head. He was an art student, I'd decided, because my stereotypical view of art students was that they were cool but a little untidy, and he'd be interested in poetry, and liked to sculpt. None of my imaginings were true.

We met at a pub on the corner of his street and there Ewan told me that he'd recently quit college, because he "couldn't be arsed anymore" and was sharing a small three bedroom house with two total strangers, who I later found out barely spoke a word to him or each other. He worked full-time at the supermarket and had no further studying or career ambitions at all. He seemed fascinating to me. By contrast, I'd planned my whole life out:

Step One: Finish degree and get a job. Probably something in an office, maybe as a personal assistant to someone very important and/or famous. Prince William had been a possibility when I'd first decided that personal slavery was the way to go (although I hadn't considered it slavery at the time; I thought it'd be quite glamorous). By this point, when I met Ewan, I had set my sights a little more realistically, or so I thought, at someone like a television presenter or small-time movie star.

Step Two: Buy a small apartment in as nice an area of London as I could afford, and start dating eligible bachelors.

Step Three: Date, become engaged, and plan wedding (perhaps at the church near my parents' house, although I wasn't religious at all. I just liked the glass windows and the majesty of it all). My husband-to-be would be a caring person, maybe a doctor or a vet. Someone who saved lives.

Step Four: Get married and buy a bigger house by the sea. Just like Helen had wanted. Get a golden retriever, to complete her idea of "happily ever after". If she couldn't live her dream, I'd live it for her.

Step Five: Maybe have some kids, and let life serenely pass me by with annual trips to hot, white sandy beaches.

It seemed pretty simple, straight forward, and achievable. It seemed normal. That's what I wanted: normality.

"So what do you do?" Ewan asked me during our first date.

"I'm studying for an English degree."

"Cool." He took a sip of his beer and I fiddled with my wine glass.

"What about you?"

He laughed.

"What do you mean? You know I work at Sainsbury's."

"I know, but… is that *all*?"

He laughed again. "Yes. For now."

"Okay, so what's planned for the future?"

"I'm not really a making plans kind of guy, you know?"

I didn't know actually. I planned everything. I wrote lists. I was highly organised. I was going to make a *great* personal assistant.

"I'm just enjoying life, having fun, and I'll see where the wind takes me. I'm a bit of a drifter."

"That sounds … wonderful."

He laughed yet again.

"It is. You're cute, Izzy. I think we're going to have fun together."

He had me right there. Having fun. Seeing what happens. Why did life have to be so serious all the time? Suddenly I realised that I'd been a serious, have-to-set-my-life-out-ahead-of-me-girl, ever since Helen had gone. The idea of switching to a 'no plan' plan seemed liberating.

"What inspires you?" I asked him. He grinned at me and thought for a moment.

"Travel. Seeing amazing places. That's what I'm saving for. I have this long list of places I have to see before I die."

"Like?"

I suddenly saw us standing at the top of the Eiffel Tower together, at sunset.

"Everywhere. The Alps. Nepal. India. Japan. Australia. New Zealand. All over the Americas."

"Paris?"

"I've been to Paris, but I'd love to go again."

"What's it like?"

"It's an incredible place. You should go."

I smiled and sipped my wine. He'd bought me a rosé (obviously remembering the broken bottle incident) but I wasn't really a fan of it; it'd been a gift after all. But I didn't like to say. In fact, I drank rosé for the remainder of our relationship.

"Who's your favourite historical figure?" he asked me, coming back from the bar a little later with more drinks and a bag of cheese and onion crisps. He split open the bag and put it in front of me. I took one.

"Elizabeth the first," I told him, munching on my crisp.

"Really? Interesting. Why?"

I panicked for a moment. Elizabeth I was my favourite because I'd just read a book about her and felt the most knowledgeable about her at that exact moment. I didn't have an answer as to why she was my favourite.

"Who's your favourite historical person?" I said, taking more crisps and avoiding an answer.

"I like the Tudors, too," he said, "but I like the Romans best, I just find them so advanced and ahead of their time, you know? I love reading about Caesar, Octavian and Mark Anthony..."

He continued to tell me quite a fair amount about the Romans, and I was impressed. He seemed so knowledgeable, so full of opinions and ideas. The rest of the night went much the same way, asking random, trivial questions about likes and dislikes. He had an opinion on everything whilst I really had none, so it was easy to be agreeable. I found him quite intimidating.

I'd been living a fairly boring existence up until that fateful day in Sainsbury's. I shared a house with Amber and two others. I had liked Amber from the first day I met her. She was confident, straight-talking, and knew what she wanted. She had long, curly red hair, green eyes and a full, curvaceous figure which she showed off with low-cut tops and A-line skirts. She and our other housemates, Zoe and Tanya, were always meeting men, dating them for a few months, then moving on when the guy wasn't long-term material. They were always searching for something serious. I wasn't particularly bothered about having a serious relationship until I met Ewan.

Compared to the life I had before I met him, which was all about my studying, and planning for the future, Ewan seemed light-hearted and easy-going; somehow he provided fun to balance out all my good sense and lack of imagination. With Ewan, instantly, it was just relaxed. He was so cool and calm. There was no need to daydream and plan, he told me, but just live in the moment and have some fun. We ended up kissing on that first date on my doorstep after he had walked me home.

"Dinner tomorrow night? Pick you up at six!" he said, winking and walking backwards down the garden path before I had a chance to accept or to invite him in.

"So what's he like?" asked Tanya as I floated into the living room. She was applying dye to Zoe's hair.

"Well, he's kind of a free spirit. He's so laid back about everything. I really like him." I flopped down onto the old brown sofa, suddenly unaware and uncaring about how uncomfortable it really was.

"A free spirit?" Amber asked.

"Yes..."

"Doesn't sound like your type. Don't you want to marry a doctor or something like that?" Tanya laughed, separating Zoe's hair into sections.

"Sounds more like my type, actually," said Zoe. She always ended up with wild, no-hoper guys who were on the verge of being arrested or doing no good.

"He's not a loser," I told them, slumping on the sofa. "He's just letting the wind take him wherever it takes him."

"Right."

They giggled as I hiccupped.

"Anyway, I'm not looking for a serious relationship. I'm not about to certify if he's husband material. Just a boyfriend will do for now."

I'd never been out with anyone that gave me the spark I was feeling now. None of them made me want to see them more than once or twice. I went to bed thinking about him, wondering if he was thinking about me.

I had no idea what to wear for our dinner date. Ewan didn't seem the type to turn up in a suit and tie. I didn't have his number so I couldn't call to confirm the time or where we were going. So I settled on a white cotton dress with small red flowers. It was casual and summery but not too formal. I put a little makeup on and Tanya helped me pin my hair into a messy but chic bun. When he rang the door bell she ran down to answer it and mouthed the word "cute!" at me as she turned and I passed her to greet him.

"You look amazing," he said, kissing me on the cheek. He was in dark jeans and a pale blue shirt - smarter than I'd imagined.

"Here you go." He passed me a helmet and started walking back to a scooter parked in the road.

I'm quite sure if anyone had asked me if I'd be willing to get on the back of a scooter with a man I barely knew a few months earlier, I'd have said no. But I didn't question it; I just hopped on the back, making sure my dress was covering everything it should, and wrapped my arms around his rather firm torso.

Ewan zipped in and out of traffic, and I held my breath and closed my eyes. He stopped after what seemed like a long time and I realised we were parking up near a lake.

He grabbed his bag and my arm and led me to a spot by the water. There, he laid out a blanket and produced a picnic consisting of sausage rolls, strawberries and two bottles of warm beer. I found this so sweet, I was pretty much half way to falling in love with him, even though I hated strawberries and wasn't too keen on cold, let alone warm, beer. I didn't say anything though but ate and drank happily, smiling as the taste of the beer slid down my throat, making me want to cough.

I asked him about his family and he told me about his

parents, brothers and sisters. He seemed to have several and I couldn't quite keep count.

"I'm the disappointment of course, the one who's just a drifter. But we all get on alright."

"I'm sure they're not disappointed in you. That's cool, anyway, nice to have such a big family."

"What about you, any siblings?"

I looked away for the first time in several minutes.

So I told him a bit about my parents, and then I told him about Helen. Not the details - just that she had gone missing. That we had no hope.

He sat up and hugged me, perhaps tighter than anyone had ever hugged me before, or since.

"I'm sorry Izzy, that's awful."

That was the only time I talked to him about Helen. Ewan didn't talk about intimate feelings, or sentiment. He did fun. His way of helping me was to make my life more enjoyable.

After another slightly scary ride on the scooter, he came back to my room, where he undressed me and threw me on my bed. It was fun; fast and intense and exciting. For the first time, I enjoyed sex.

He slept at my house that night. And the night after. Then I stayed at his. After that we were together all the time. He made friends with my friends. He bought me cups of tea or orange squash when I was studying. I cooked for him when he was working late. We went to the pub and we watched a lot of films.

He gave me confidence and I wanted to be more like him. He seemed mature and wise and had an opinion about everything from political issues to music or art. I didn't realise it at the time, but I adopted all the same opinions too. Mostly, I think, because I didn't really have that many opinions of my own, so I just agreed with whatever he thought.

He said the Liberal Democrats 'rocked', so I voted for them. He said Blur were the best band in the world ever, so I bought all of their CDs and listened to them until I knew every lyric. He thought *Star Wars* was boring, so I declared it was overrated and pointless. My whole world was Ewan. Even what I liked and didn't like was because of him.

Somehow, even though he was a little spontaneous and zany, he brought some calm to my life. He allowed me to forget about the plan for a while, to stop fantasising about the house by the sea with the blue front door ... and I only wanted to be with him, every minute of every day. It kind of simplified things. He didn't always talk a lot, and never about anything meaningful or personal. Conversation was usually about the news or ideas about travelling and where he'd like to go, but just being in his presence, holding hands on the sofa or reading while resting my legs on his lap, or walking about town, was calming. He was like a drug, and when he was at work, or I was in a lecture, I felt a little lost and forlorn. I'd only feel calm and relaxed again when I was with him.

The only two negative things were that a) I was aware of the fact that I loved him more than he loved me, and b) he kept talking about travelling. He wanted to take off and see the world, and the only thing that appeared to be stopping him was lack of cash. So what would happen when he'd saved enough?

I was afraid of losing him so I never asked. I decided ignorance was bliss.

Chapter Five

One weekend, Ewan went to stay with his parents down in Kent, leaving me alone to mope about like a lost puppy. I spent the whole Saturday absorbed in a book I was reading, but I finished that around dinner time and then sat around feeling low the rest of the evening. I didn't like not having him with me, or nearby at least, and that's when I realised it: I really was in love with him. Up until that point I'd known I liked him a lot and I wanted to be with him all the time. But I'd never thought it would last forever. It had just seemed like some fun and nothing long-term, and I'd been realistic that we wanted different things and hadn't really envisioned a future for us.

Suddenly I needed to confess my love. Not to Ewan. There was no way I was going to bring up something as deep and meaningful and full of future intent to my carefree lover, but I needed to tell someone. Amber was sitting on her bed, typing on her laptop. I peeped through the crack in her not quite closed door.

With long red hair and big curls, Amber always has a good hair day. She can be out drinking all night, get in at 3am, fall into bed, and when she wakes up the next day her hair is still as lovely and glossy and hanging perfectly around her face just as it was when she went out the night before. Unlike me who struggles to ever get my hair to look anything other than a frizzy mess.

I nudged the door open and stood in the doorway for a few moments, not wanting to interrupt her. She looked up, her hair falling around her face.

"You okay?" she asked.

"I love Ewan," I told her.

She smiled at me.

"I know."

"You do?"

"We can all tell. You're obsessed with him."

"Does he know?"

"I doubt it. Men rarely do."

I wasn't entirely satisfied, but went back to my room and mooched around for a while.

I looked for a definition of 'obsessed' and decided that I most definitely wasn't. Obsessed is when you're continuously troubled by something. I wasn't troubled by Ewan. Only by the fact that he didn't seem to be the type who was going to settle down and be what I wanted. And I knew I couldn't change him and shouldn't really try to, even if I could.

How was I going to deal with this? I couldn't imagine Ewan staying put for much longer. He had this urge to travel and when he left, who knew how long he'd want to be away. He might like me to come with him, but he'd never mentioned it, and I wasn't sure I even wanted to go. I had plans, after all. The whole relationship was doomed.

As I lay in bed that night, cold in my little room and listening to the wind rattling my window pane, I thought about calling him and talking it all through, but I wasn't sure I wanted to hear his response. I picked up the phone a few times but put it down again. I needed to concentrate on something different.

So I started to think about a game Helen and I used to play in bed when we were little. It was called 'Ring, ring'. My teddy, called Cinderella, would make a phone call to Helen's stuffed rabbit, called Bunny, in the next room or vice versa. We'd both get into bed first and let our parents go downstairs. It'd be quiet for a few minutes and then:

"Ring, ring! Ring, ring!" Helen, or rather Bunny, would call.

"Hello?" I answered as Cinderella.

"Hi Cindy. It's Bunny. How're you? Good day?"

"Oh hi, Bunny. I had a great day, and you?"

And it'd go on like that, with us calling between rooms until my mother called up.

"You two had better go to sleep. Don't make me come up there!"

I shifted in bed, smiling, wondering what ever happened to Cinderella and Bunny. They were probably in amongst the boxes in the attic back home. I decided I'd go visit the next day and look for them. If anything, it'd stop me from calling Ewan and showing him how needy I was.

So the following morning I got up early and took the train home. Dad picked me up at the station and when we arrived at the house Mum came out to greet me with a hug. She had aged twenty years the day Helen disappeared and had never been quite the same again. She left her job and spent most of her days reading true-life stories and watching daytime television. She never spoke of Helen. Once, my grandmother had suggested we have a memorial service. She said it'd help us all move on. Dad had been interested but Mum had yelled and screamed and said that Helen wasn't dead and no one should give up hope. We've not really talked about it much since then. Dad and I went to see a counsellor for a few months, years ago. Mum wouldn't come with us and didn't want to hear about it when we got home.

Now, at 45, she looked more like 60. She was too thin, her skin was tight and lined, her hair was faded. She'd kind of given up on life and I sometimes felt that whoever took Helen had taken my mum, too. He (or she) had taken my sister and my mother. Mum never bought new clothes or cared much about anything really, except for cleaning and finding new books to read. And me, of course. She worried about me constantly.

"You look thin," she said, following me into the house. I was tempted to say she was the one who looked too thin, but I kept my mouth shut. I'd been down that road before and it only ended in unpleasantness.

"I'm fine, Mum."

"I'll give you extra roast potatoes at dinner."

I turned to my dad. "Can I look through the old stuff in the attic?"

"Sure, why?"

"Just wanted to find some old books, that's all."

He helped me find a ladder and, after telling me to be careful, went off to help Mum.

I loved being up in the attic. Dad had boarded it all out so you could walk around most of it fairly safely. There were Christmas decorations and dusty boxes of photos and then in the far corner, were boxes marked with 'Helen'. Her clothes and belongings had been packed in there by Dad and me when we moved to this house. Mum had made us promise not to throw any of it away, but the boxes had remained untouched ever since.

I went over to them, hoping neither of my parents would come up and find me looking at Helen's stuff. The packaging tape had come unstuck over time, so it was easy to open each one. There were moth-eaten clothes in the first two and a bunch of objects from her room in the third: plastic jewellery; a photo frame with a photo of Helen and her best friend; a rusty mirror and a hair brush. It all seemed so foreign and yet familiar at the same time.

The fourth box had a bunch of old toys, including a Barbie I remembered playing with. And then there she was at the bottom: Bunny. I lifted her out carefully. She smelled a bit musty but she looked in pretty good condition, considering how long she'd been up there.

Next I went to my boxes and rifled through, looking at old

toys, games, books and mementoes from school and holidays. I found Cinderella and reunited her with Bunny. Then I took them both downstairs, passing the kitchen quickly and quietly, and tucked them into my bag before my parents could see. I wasn't sure they'd remember which toy belonged to which daughter but I didn't want Mum getting upset that I'd taken something of Helen's, just in case.

"Found what you wanted?" Mum asked as I joined her in the kitchen. Dinner smelt good.

"Yes, just an old book I read years ago. I wanted to read it again."

She smiled and turned back to her gravy.

I was glad I came. The rest of the afternoon passed by with conversations about books, Ewan and what was on TV. Then we moved on to what I might do after university and I told them about the personal assistant thing, without mentioning that I wanted to work with someone famous. I didn't want them to think I was being unrealistic.

Dinner was delicious. There's nothing quite like your Mum's roast beef and crispy potatoes on a Sunday afternoon. While Dad was mowing the lawn I told her about Ewan's travel plans and she reassured me that if we loved each other we'd figure it out.

When I got back I put Cinderella and Bunny on a shelf in my room next to each other.

Chapter Six

"It's so nice to see you," Jade said as we sat in the same pub that Ewan and I had had our first date in. We'd both been busy lately and hadn't seen each other for months.

Jade was more than my cousin; she was a surrogate sister. I'd spent a lot of time at Aunt Ruth's house while my parents had been trying to figure out how to put our lives back together.

We both ordered a glass of wine and sat chatting about the family and how everything else was going in our lives. Jade's enthusiasm for life was infectious. She was bubbly; always saw the glass as half-full; was always laughing and usually had a funny tale to tell. Today she was telling me about a hideous date she'd been on with a man who, as he later confessed to her, liked to dress as a woman at weekends.

"I've got an open mind," she said, "but when he suggested we go dress shopping together, I decided he wasn't the one for me."

We giggled and I looked around the pub, scanning for Ewan. We were due to meet him and his brother, Alex, who was also visiting. I'd never met any of Ewan's family, or even any of his friends (he didn't seem to have any, or not in London anyway), and I wasn't sure what to expect. All I knew about his brother was that Ewan suspected he was gay and had been waiting for him to admit this for years. I didn't understand why Ewan didn't just ask him, but they weren't particularly close. And Ewan wasn't one for talking about anything, really, only superficial stuff. Much to my frustration.

Still, I couldn't help but grin as he walked into the pub, his hair messy and a few days worth of stubble. Those bright blue eyes darted around, seeking me out.

"Wow, is that him? He's not what I expected!" Jade whispered as Ewan spotted us, grinned, waved and went over to the bar. Alex looked like a miniature, skinnier version of Ewan with shorter, tidier hair.

"What did you expect?"

"Someone neater. He's kind of scruffy. Gorgeous, though. You get to shag that? Ha! Good for you, Izz."

I smiled at her smugly, quite proud of myself. We watched them get their drinks and then come over to us.

"Alex, this is my Izzy," Ewan introduced us.

"And this is Jade," I said, glowing happily at his use of the word 'my' and what it implied. We all smiled politely and sat down. Ewan kissed me on the forehead and I sat back, glad that Jade thought he was good-looking.

Alex didn't look how I'd imagined. Ewan had painted a picture of a slightly effeminate pretty-boy with a passion for shopping. It was pretty clear by the end of the night that he wasn't gay; either that or he was doing a pretty good impression of a straight guy. He'd been flirting with Jade like she was the last woman on Earth. Ewan and I left them to chat about something he'd read in the news. After a while, Jade and Alex went off to play pool.

"I don't think he's gay," I said, laughing.

"No, guess I was wrong!"

"Don't you talk about stuff like that?"

"Not really."

"Has he met any of your other girlfriends?"

"Only Taylor. My ex. Took her to my parents once for dinner."

Huh. Taylor. I felt jealous. Of course he'd had another serious girlfriend; he was three years older than me.

"Why haven't you told me about her before? We've been

35

together almost two years."

"It just never came up. And why do people always do that anyway? Share their little sob stories about past girlfriends or boyfriends? It's in the past - it doesn't matter now."

"I guess so."

"Having said that, what about you? Past relationships?"

So I told him about Stephen, my boyfriend when I was seventeen. He was cute but not the most intelligent boy I knew. He'd asked me to our high school Christmas disco and I'd gone along mostly because I liked his brother, Louis, more than I liked him. But he was sweet enough and when he tried to kiss me I let him. We spent the next six months going to the cinema and eating in McDonalds, and I lost my virginity in Stephen's bedroom while his parents were downstairs playing Trivial Pursuit with his aunt and uncle. After that we went at it like rabbits for about three weeks until Stephen told me he wasn't sure it would work out once we started university as he was going to Bangor and I was headed for London.

I wasn't upset and we parted on good terms. It was more friendship than anything. I never felt much for him but spent most of the time wishing I was with his brother Louis instead. If only he'd looked my way ... but he never did.

"So you've never been in love?" Ewan asked me as I told him this story.

"Not until now," I said, before realising straight away that I'd admitted something I hadn't meant to.

I'd managed to go for almost two years, holding it in. It wasn't that I didn't think he loved me. He showed he cared in many ways: the way he kissed me, took care of me and spent time with me. But he never said it. He didn't ever talk of anything serious. So I'd avoided saying it too - scared to be the first one to declare it.

I looked down at the floor, then up at his face. He was smiling, and then he leaned in slowly and kissed me. It was a lingering, meaningful kiss. He wrapped his arms around me and we sat quietly for a while afterwards. It felt like a special moment.

"Men!" Amber shouted at me when I repeated this conversation later. It was easy for her to say. She'd had a string of boyfriends and they'd all said the three words we girls are usually desperate to hear. Although in all fairness, they more often than not took it back a few months after that. At least Ewan had been my boyfriend for this long, even if his 'I love you' hadn't been forthcoming.

Chapter Seven

I stood on my parents' doorstep and waved at Ewan who had come to have lunch with us while I stayed with them for the weekend. He put his helmet on and straddled his scooter, leaving me to admire his bum as he started it up. He really was the best looking man I knew. I sighed as my eyes flitted to his hands, remembering how they felt when they touched me. His scruffy blonde hair was sticking out from under the helmet. He waved and off he went. I turned to go indoors and hear the verdict.

"He's very nice," Mum said, clearing away the lunch things as I returned to the house.

"Yes, I liked him." Dad winked at me. "He passes."

"Good," I said, beaming.

"Not what I expected though. I imagined you going for a really academic type, someone with a big career ahead of them."

So he didn't like him, after all.

"That's what I like most about him," I explained ... well, besides his blue eyes and sexy, firm behind and muscular torso, but I didn't want to mention that. "All my life I've been so organised. I've studied hard and wanted to plan out my future. Ewan is just fun and upbeat. He lives in the moment. It's refreshing and he makes me happy."

I saw Mum give Dad a look warning him to be nice.

"I can see that," he said, smiling, "and it's not like you're about to marry him. It's nice to see you happy."

I thought about this while I sat in my old bedroom, gazing

out of the window instead of studying like I had intended. No, I wasn't about to marry him but I would one day, surely? The thought of not being with him was unbearable. This was it. He was the one. Then one day we'd settle and marry and see about that cottage by the sea. Chimney. Blue front door. Golden Retriever. The whole package. Just like Helen had wanted.

It was more than just fun.

"How're you getting on?" Mum asked, peeping around my door with a cup of tea.

"Not great," I admitted. "Thank you for lunch, it was lovely."

"Your dad didn't mean to be unsupportive about Ewan, you know. He liked him. I did too. And you're young and you should be having fun."

"I love him, though," I told her. I felt defensive; like I needed to justify things.

"I can tell that too. But he'll be one of many, Izzy. I'm sure of that."

"I'm not," I said, a little too fast. "I'm not sixteen anymore. This is it. He's the one."

"We'll see," she said smiling and closing the door. I shook my head in disbelief at their attitude and flopped back on my bed to stare at the ceiling. I'm an adult now, I thought to myself. I know this is what I want and it's Ewan - forever. I could never fall in love with anyone else. It'll always be him.

I told Amber about the conversation a few days later and she said I needed to chill out and not allow myself to become obsessed with him. After all, he was just one man on a very big planet full of men. Even if he was the sexiest man of our acquaintance. I laughed and wondered if she was right. But I still only wanted him. I knew I'd never love anyone like I loved Ewan.

Chapter Eight

My hen night. One week before my wedding day.

"Ewan!"

It was like someone had thrown me up in the air; all the blood rushed to my heart and it started pounding faster. Seeing Jason was one thing. Bumping into him at some point had been not entirely unexpected. But Ewan. Here. Right here in front of me. I thought I'd never see him again and now here he was; real, alive, breathing, looking as sexy as ever and almost immediately I wanted to touch him.

That wish was quickly fulfilled when he grabbed me and hugged me hard. His torso felt as strong and muscular against mine as it always had. Wow, he still had it; he was still the sexiest man I'd ever met.

"I've missed you so much, Izz."

I squeezed him tight, happy to have my arms around him again; not really wanting to let go but disappointed as I felt his arms relax.

"Your hair's shorter," I said as he released me. "It suits you." It really did. He looked ... grown up.

"Thanks. You look great."

"Thank you." I gave him my best beaming smile.

Why did I still care so much what he thought of me? I took in his clothes: a black shirt and blue jeans. Much smarter than the casual t-shirts and baggy cargo trousers he'd always worn when we were a couple.

"What's this?"

He pointed to the plastic willy, and the sash, which was twisted. I pulled it straight.

"It's my hen night," I told him.

"You're getting married." It was a statement, not a question. He looked disappointed which made me feel happy in a sickening, guilty kind of way.

"Yep," I said, mimicking his disappointed tone like this was bad news. I felt guilty for a moment but the feeling soon passed as I looked once more into those blue eyes and his gorgeous face, which hadn't changed much. More defined maybe. He looked a little older, but it suited him.

"Well, I guess I thought you might be married by now anyway."

"Really?"

"Yes. I think of you often, actually."

"Really?" I felt a little dizzy. I willed myself to stop swooning and grinning like a teenager but I couldn't help it. It was Ewan! My Ewan. Here, in the flesh.

"Do you want to meet up for a drink one day this week, maybe? We could catch up properly?"

Of course I did! But what about Greg? What about Amber and Jade? What would they say? What about the fact that I had never been more sure that I loved him than while I stood there, tipsy on wine and nervous I might see Jason again when I left the bathroom. Oh God, did I still love Jason too? Yes. Yes, of course I did. How could I love them both and yet they both feel so alien to me? Almost like strangers?

"Izzy?"

"Yes," I said, focussing back on our conversation, "I'd love to meet up."

I went back to my friends and didn't mention Jason or Ewan. We drank champagne cocktails and laughed and giggled while they all told me how wonderful Greg was and how lucky I was to be marrying him. Jade snogged some Italian guy she met at the bar as Amber and a few friends got up for a little dance. It was a fun evening and I played my part of the excited bride, hiding the fact that I was conflicted ... that I was in turmoil. That I was screaming inside, desperate for escape. I needed time to think about all this and time was running out. But I carried on acting like the happy bride-to-be. What else could I do?

Chapter Nine

It was one of those really hot summer days when every Brit declares that "Summer is here at last", before rushing out to bask in it - while it lasted. Ewan and I were renting a little cottage in Pembrokeshire for a short holiday to celebrate my graduation. We still hadn't spoken about the future and I only had a few weeks left on the lease of my house-share. I hadn't done anything about finding a job; I just figured I'd stay with Ewan until I sorted something out. But I hadn't asked if he'd mind. Conversations rarely took a serious turn. The future was tomorrow and we were living for today.

A big conversation was hanging there in the air between us. I just didn't want to be the one to initiate it and part of me was actually quite annoyed that he hadn't asked me what my plans were. Did he think I was going to just bum around now I'd graduated? But I was too stubborn to bring it up. And I didn't want to risk saying or presuming the wrong thing only to lose him.

Ewan had mentioned he was a drifter on so many occasions that I felt he was always preparing to break up with me. So being invited on a little holiday gave me a sort of relief. It meant he probably wasn't going to dump me in the next few weeks at least.

We'd set off early for the beach. It was almost empty when we arrived so we set up our blankets, stripped down to our bathing costumes and put on our sun cream. However, by midday there was no square metre of sand uncovered. Hordes of locals and tourists alike were soaking up the sun; children were running in and out of the sea and making sandcastles; dogs were bounding along the sand, and the ice cream van was doing a roaring trade. Ewan, asleep next to me, had built a mini-castle out of sand and shells before lying down on his stomach, revealing the tiniest fuzz of hair on his back.

I love days like this. I like watching the crowds; from those who turn a bright lobster colour to those who cover up and sit beneath an umbrella, remaining milky white. I like the lollipop sticks dotted around the sand. The sound of the waves is soothing, despite the shouts and cries of the children. And I enjoy watching the sea gulls circling above, hunting discarded picnic food. I nudged Ewan to check if he was still asleep, but got no response. I got up and walked slowly down to the shore, dodging the families and seaweed. The water was cold but felt refreshing against my hot feet. I looked out at the horizon and tried to play out a conversation in my head where I asked Ewan if he wanted to live together, but my thoughts were quickly interrupted by a voice.

"Hi."

I turned and locked eyes with a tall, quite frankly, *beautiful* man with short dark hair, grey eyes and a cheeky grin. I felt instantly attracted to him and became aware of myself blushing.

"Hello," I replied.

"Are you here alone?"

"No," I said, laughing. Who came to the beach alone? "My boyfriend is back there." I gestured with my thumb over my shoulder in Ewan's direction. The grey eyes didn't move from mine.

"Look at this," he said, showing me an unusual shell in his hand. It was pretty.

"Nice," I said. "Do you collect them?"

"No, my niece does. That's her splashing in the water with my sister."

I looked behind him and caught the eye of a woman with

long blonde hair who nodded at me and smiled. A little girl was playing with her.

"How old is she?"

"My sister? She's twenty nine."

I laughed. There was something sexy about his voice.

"I meant your niece."

"Annabelle is three."

Even though he was just standing there in a pair of swimming trunks, he seemed somehow sophisticated with an air of confidence. A different kind of confidence to what Ewan had. Whilst Ewan didn't care too much about other people or what they thought of him, this guy was confident and aware of things around him. I felt drawn to him and suddenly giddy. Was this love at first sight? Don't be ridiculous, I told myself. It's just lust. Pure hormones and chemistry.

He bent down to pick up another shell and moved closer to me. We locked eyes and I realised I was holding my breath. Later, when I told Amber about this, he almost sounded creepy. But at the time it felt natural. I liked it. I liked him.

"Shame," he said, smiling and still not looking away.

"What's a shame?"

"That you've got a boyfriend."

Then, from out the blue he leaned forward and kissed me. And I kissed him back, without giving any thought to it - like a reflex action. I'm not sure why, or how, but it was the most passionate, lustful moment of my life. I closed my eyes and felt his tongue devour me. I threw my arms around his neck as he put his around my waist and I just gave in, without any thought for Ewan or who this stranger was. I was completely lost in the moment; my heart raced and my head swam with lustful thoughts. His hands moved up and were in my hair and then they slid down my back and pulled me closer to him. We stood like that, kissing, with the waves flowing backwards and forwards over our feet for at least a minute or so. Yet not for long enough.

"I'm sorry," he said, eventually pulling away.

I stood there astonished and weak at the knees. I wanted to do it again. I wanted to push him to the ground and pull his shorts off and climb on top of him, right there in front of everyone. I wanted, no ... I needed, to feel this man all over me. I'd never felt so turned on in my entire life. The thought of never seeing him again was painful. We locked eyes again and I was tempted to grab him and kiss some more.

Instead I looked guiltily back towards Ewan. He was too far away to see me properly and it looked like he was still lying down.

"Sorry," the mystery man said again, smiling and looking at me intently as if trying to gauge my reaction.

"Not at all, I liked it." My voice sounded breathless. I took a large intake of air to try and calm myself. I was suddenly very aware of being in a bikini and wished I had something to hold on to, to steady myself. I looked over his shoulder wondering if his sister and niece had seen, but they had moved further down the beach.

"I couldn't resist. You're just so beautiful." He started to walk away. "Have a nice day!"

I didn't reply. I just stood there smiling, watching him go. He kept glancing back and smiling at me. I was afraid if I opened my mouth I'd only beg him to kiss me like that again. I glanced back towards Ewan and then when my mystery man was a fair way off I reluctantly turned and walked back, avoiding the sea weed and picnic blankets again, hoping that Ewan wouldn't be angry when I got back to him. I glanced back a few more times but my mystery kisser had moved out of my sight.

Ewan hadn't seen anything, of course. When I got back I was quickly swept up into a conversation about his travel plans. He often talked about packing everything up and just 'drifting' as he always put it, which involved moving from place to place, working in bars. He talked about it more and more lately but this time I could hardly listen. I kept glancing towards the shoreline, trying to spot where my mystery man was. I kept wondering what he was thinking and feeling. Did he do this all the time? Probably. He seemed pretty confident. And yet it'd been so intense, like he couldn't help himself.

I knew I must focus and try to listen to what Ewan was saying, so I watched him talking but felt guilty. For the umpteenth time, I wondered when he was actually going to leave me and go off on these travels that he'd been talking about ever since we met. Amber and the girls had been telling me for months I should just ask the question, but I'd never wanted to know the answer and so I had just avoided talking of the future.

Later on, sitting in the cottage and watching him heat up pizza for dinner, I couldn't help but think again about the guy on the beach and that incredible kiss. It was more than just a kiss; it was a moment. A perfect, wonderful moment. If it wasn't for Ewan I wouldn't have let him walk away. The thought that I'd never see him again and never be kissed that way again made me ache inside.

I forced myself to focus on Ewan and smiled as I watched him slice the pizza with his hair falling in his face. His bright blue eyes looked up and winked at me and suddenly I needed to know that we had a future. I needed to know for sure if he loved me.

"What stops you from going?" I asked as he put my plate down in front of me. He stopped for a moment, smiled and said:

"You, of course."

Yes! My heart leapt. I felt guilty again about the guy on the beach and told myself it was just a kiss. A silly kiss. Nothing that special really. It was just new and exciting. That's all. Ewan went and got his plate and sat down opposite me.

Was I really the only thing stopping him from living his dream?

"I don't want to hold you back," I said; although I did. I wanted him to stay here with me and never leave.

"You're not. I've just been waiting for you to graduate. You've got that party next week and then a few more weeks' lease on your house. Then I was going to say that we'll go together."

It wasn't a question. Just a statement. I was so thrilled that he'd wait for me; so happy that he'd want me to come, that I didn't actually consider whether I wanted to or not. I didn't mind his presumption. I was just relieved.

"Great," I said, smiling.

We went for a romantic walk after dinner, and found a little bench that looked out to sea. And as the sun set on the horizon, Ewan leant his forehead against mine and for the first time, he said: "I love you."

It wasn't until we were lying in bed that night that I touched my lips and thought again of the mystery guy who'd had enough confidence to just kiss a girl when her boyfriend was within throwing distance. Half of me was furious. How could he tell I'd wanted to kiss him back? But the other half could still remember the feel of his lips, the warmth of his body, his hands on my hips holding me to him. Like a magnet, I almost felt him pulling me back to the shoreline for more.

***

The rest of the holiday was spent on the beach taking cliff-top walks, having sex in the cottage and reading books. I was on a high - finally happy to know that Ewan loved me; that he didn't want to be without me; that he was waiting for me. I was excited about travelling with him; eager about the future and all the possibilities, and relieved that he had taken control of what would happen next. I had avoided making plans. I hadn't thought about jobs or where to live because I'd been waiting for him. And now he was leading me and that was fine. I could be a drifter too.

I kept an eye out for my mystery man with the grey eyes, but didn't see him again. When we got home he was the first topic of conversation when I de-briefed Amber on the week's events. I explained how he'd approached me, how he'd spoken, how beautiful his eyes were, how he'd kissed me and ... how magical the whole thing felt, but then how hard it had been to watch him walk away.

"Wow," she said as I finished. She'd been silent throughout, which was unusual for her. She normally interrupted my story-telling with little quips and questions, but for this she'd seemed as mesmerized by my mystery man as I was.

"It was certainly wow ... Yes."

"But why the hell didn't you slap him? I can't believe you just kissed him back with Ewan not far away!"

"I have no idea what came over me. It was just this crazy, wild moment. No one's ever kissed me like that. Not even Ewan."

I wished he would kiss me like that, I added mentally. Not that Ewan was a bad kisser. I just didn't feel that magnetic pull towards him in the same electric way as Mr Grey Eyes.

"So Ewan has no idea?"

"No, of course not. It was just a kiss."

"Sounds like one hell of a kiss."

From then on The Guy From The Beach, as we always referred to him, was only ever brought up when I was drunk. Whenever I had a drink, I'd think about that moment and wonder what if...? What if I'd been single? Would he have asked me for my number? Would I have pursued him or let him walk away? Where was he now? And did he remember me? Did he have a girlfriend?

On the odd occasion I'd dream the whole scene over again, or I'd glance at someone who looked like him and do a double-take. But mostly I tried to forget it happened because it only made me feel guilty. I figured I'd never see him again.

After the week in the cottage, Ewan's parents invited us to stay with them in their sleepy little village in Kent. We took the train and I chatted nervously the whole way there.

"Why did it take you so long to introduce me?" I asked just before we arrived.

"I don't see them that often."

He'd not really ever talked much about his family life or what it was like growing up. I was immensely curious to see where he'd come from. We got a taxi from the station and pulled up outside a semi-detached house with roses growing in the front garden and a Volvo in the driveway.

"This is my mum, Penny, and my dad, Richard," said Ewan, pointing them out as if I might not know who was who.

"Nice to meet you," I said, offering my hand.

"Oh, give me a hug," said Penny, pulling me into her. She had shoulder-length, permed hair; a plastic apron on, and she smelt of cigarettes and Lily of the Valley. I turned to Richard, a short, round man with a beard and kind eyes, who obviously felt uncomfortable with the hugging but planted a quick peck on my cheek. Richard said something to Ewan about a project in the garage and they disappeared pretty quickly, leaving me to the excitement of his mum.

"Let me show you around dear," said Penny, gesturing to the first door off the hallway. I walked in to the living room. There was flowery wallpaper in shades of pink and pale green, a large fireplace and an old TV on a stand. There were china ornaments everywhere: on shelves, in cabinets, on table tops. Plates hung on the walls, including one to celebrate the marriage of Charles and Diana. I listened to Penny telling me how she came to own each one.

My parents' house seemed so modern in comparison. It reminded me of my great-grandmother's house. She'd died when I was small, while Helen was still around, and I barely remembered her - just her house. This was almost a replica. In fact, I'm sure I'd seen Penny's exact silver tea service before. I studied a few framed photos above the fireplace; one in particular of Ewan aged about fifteen.

"He was as handsome then, as he is now, huh?" said Penny, lighting up a cigarette.

"Yes," I smiled at her, although the acne and greasy floppy hair wasn't quite as attractive as his now smooth skin and wild locks.

"This is the dining room," she said, leading me to the next room, which contained a large oval table with a white tablecloth and a flower pattern she told me she'd embroidered herself. There were more glass cabinets with yet more china; plates and cups. I could see Ewan in the back garden with his dad, who appeared to be pointing out something he'd planted.

"Ah, look at the two of them," Penny said, watching me watching them.

"My Richard grows roses. Beautiful roses. All different colours."

"How lovely."

We moved on to the kitchen, which had similar old-fashioned wallpaper but surprisingly modern appliances. Something which smelled nice was bubbling on the stove.

"Sit down, I'll make us a cuppa." Penny pointed to a stool at the breakfast bar and put the kettle on.

"Thank you."

"You're so polite."

"I'm honoured to be here."

Penny stopped making the tea, placed her hand on her hip, and looked at me very seriously.

"I know that God sent you. To make him happy."

I didn't know how I could answer that, so I just smiled.

She turned back to the cups and then passed me some tea. It was sweet, even though I'd not asked for sugar. I drank it anyway and she told me about a crossword she'd been working on then asked me if I knew how to sew. I told her that I did, suspecting it was what she wanted to hear.

"His trousers look too long, dear," she said, watching him outside. "You ought to take them up for him."

The rest of the afternoon and evening passed by pleasantly enough. Penny and I made a steak and kidney pie. I felt like it was a cookery lesson and on more than one occasion she hinted that I'd be able to make it for Ewan when we got home. She talked non-stop; the opposite to Richard who barely said a word all evening. I wasn't sure if he was just shy or if he couldn't get a word in edgeways because of his wife and had just given up trying. We all watched a film on television while drinking more sugary tea and eating chocolate digestives until eventually, to my relief, Ewan suggested we call it a night.

I got into Ewan's old bed and pulled the duvet around me. He was on the floor on an airbed. Apparently he'd been given strict instructions prior to our visit that no "hanky-panky" would be permitted in his mother's house. The thought of doing it with them next door was horrifying to me, anyhow.

"I'm glad you brought me here," I said, although I wasn't too keen on his mother at all. I got the feeling she wanted me to be a housewife. "You should have brought me sooner."

"Well, you see what my mother's like. Doesn't stop chatting, always nagging about something. Going on about God all the time. Living in the dark ages."

"So, why bring me now?"

"I don't know. We're more … serious. Well, more serious than anyone I've ever been with before."

"Me too," I said, propping myself up on my elbow to look down at him.

"Where do you think we might go first?" I said, a few minutes after he'd turned the light off.

"I'm thinking about Switzerland, actually."

"Wow. Can we get work there?"

"Well, just a week in Switzerland, hiking, taking in the scenery, and then maybe down to Italy."

"Sounds amazing."

"Where would you like to go?"

"Anywhere you want to."

"Okay. I'll get us organised."

"You want to snuggle?"

He got up and climbed under the covers, wrapping his arms around me. I always felt safe like that; he was so muscular and strong. I felt protected.

It didn't occur to me until much, much, later that I let Ewan lead me from that day. He made the choices, the decisions. He told me where he'd like to go and I followed. It didn't concern me that I wasn't giving any thought to where I'd like to go or what I'd like to do. It was all about him. About keeping him happy and taming that spirit of his so that I might, one day, be enough to satisfy him without the need to continuously travel and drift from place to place. I was wrong. Ewan couldn't be tamed, just as I wasn't the drifting type. But it was sure one fun ride, while it lasted.

Chapter Ten

It was my friend Zoe's twenty first birthday and Amber and I were baking a variety of cakes to take along to a celebratory picnic party in the park. Amber was preparing fuchsia pink and electric blue icing while I inspected our selection of sparkly toppings.

"Tanya's bringing sausage rolls," Amber told me, "and Dan and Neil are on Scotch egg and crisp detail. I think Eve's bringing some sandwiches."

I was distracted, staring at the label of a tub of chocolate sprinkles.

"You okay?" she asked, without looking up from her icing. "You're quiet today."

"I'm contemplating something," I told her, snapping out of it as the buzzer on the oven pinged. "Ewan asked me to travel with him." I wasn't sure why I hadn't told her before. We'd both been quite busy but really I wasn't sure how she'd react.

I took the cakes out. They were a little burnt.

"Really? I kinda thought he'd just put all that on hold."

"Well, he did. He was waiting for me to graduate. He invited me to go with him."

Did he invite me or did he just assume I'd come?

Amber looked up and put her hand on my shoulders.

"Izzy, you're so lucky!" she said, smiling. "You're crazy about him and he wants to take you on an adventure!"

Despite my initial excitement, I'd been wondering about this for a few days. I didn't like not knowing where I'd be in three months or a year's time. I didn't like not having a defined plan of where we'd go and, most importantly, when we'd come home again.

"But it's just not part of the plan is it? What about my career?"

"What career? It's not even begun. Go see the world, come back in a year and start your career then. People will still need personal assistants in a year's time, I can assure you."

She turned back to the cakes and began spreading the icing.

"I think you're supposed to wait for them to cool," I told her, picking up the tiny sugary flowers we'd found in the cake shop and trying one.

"No time for that. Seriously, Izzy, if you don't go with Ewan, I will!"

Half an hour later I was laughing with my friends as we tucked into our picnic. Zoe, who had pointed out that this was probably the last time we'd be together for a long time, got a little tipsy on the champagne provided by a friend of hers I'd never met. Amber told us all about someone in her Art class who wanted to paint her nude. I laughed; I smiled; I responded. But something inside of me realised all I wanted was Ewan. I didn't really care where, but I just had to be with him. When I was with him I felt safe. My friends would be going off soon, scattering about the country to various jobs or back to their families, and yet Ewan would be my constant. He would remain by my side, so long as I followed him wherever he wanted to go. I just had to put all my organisation and planning tendencies to one side and stop concerning myself with where this trip might lead, or for how long.

After the picnic I went home to my parents and I told them about the travel plans over dinner.

Mum said it sounded wonderful. Dad said I must be careful.

Then there was an awkward silence and I saw them glance at each other.

"You don't like Ewan, do you?"

How anyone could not like him was beyond me. So he was a little aloof, but he was funny. And those blue eyes ... and how sexy he was. But then, I don't suppose my parents cared about that. Especially not my dad.

"I do like him," Dad said, putting his fork down. "It's just, I sometimes think you maybe go along with what he wants to do, rather than making your own decisions."

Well, that was partly true, but how else could I keep hold of him?

"I *want* to go with him."

"And you're very young, to be so serious."

"Well, we're not getting married," I said, wishing that we were. "We're just going to travel and see how it goes."

"How exciting and romantic!" Mum said.

"Just be careful, okay?" Dad said, wiping some sauce from his chin.

After dinner we sat outside, enjoying a little more warm British summertime. Nana came over for the evening to join us for desert.

"So, Nana," I said, feeling full to the brim. "Ewan and I are going to travel for a while after I graduate."

"Oh how wonderful. Where to?"

"Not sure yet. Going to go to lots of places, work in bars and restaurants, you know?'

"Oh, well that's where I can help," she said, reaching for her bag. She handed me a crisp, white envelope with my name on it.

"Wow. Thank you Nana - you shouldn't have!"

"Yes, I should. It's my gift to give and I will do as I please," she said, smiling.

Inside was a card to congratulate me on my degree with a cheque for five thousand pounds.

"Nana, oh my goodness, this is too much! Where did you get that money?" I said, feeling faint and throwing my arms around her.

"Well, it's from some savings. I want to see you enjoy it before I go. So, no working in bars and such on this trip. You just go and have a nice time."

"Really, Nana, this is just too generous."

"I insist. No arguments."

I hugged her tight. I couldn't wait to call Ewan.

***

"So Switzerland first, yes?" I asked him on the phone that evening.

"I'm thinking Paris."

I didn't care. I was just happy to go wherever he wanted. I told him about the cheque and he insisted I only spend that money on myself. He said he wanted to work as it was always part of the plan; that the money was mine and if I really really had to share then I could, on occasion, treat him to a decent meal.

"I've got a surprise to show you, later," he said, just before we hung up. I spent the rest of the evening wondering what it could be. I kept thinking it was something to do with the travel plans but a small part of me hoped it might be an engagement ring. The next day I discovered it was a tattoo.

Ewan had two tattoos when I met him. He had a small panther on his right shoulder. He'd got it done when he was a teen and wasn't too keen on it now. The other was a barcode on the base of his foot, and the thought of him holding still while they did it always made me squirm; my feet are too ticklish. I occasionally wondered with amusement whether it'd scan if put through a till but I never said this to him. I figured he'd think I was making fun.

His new tattoo was a tiny lizard on his upper left arm. It was kind of cute but I'd been hoping for something more personal. Maybe something to do with me. I told him I liked it, anyhow.

Then we started packing up our stuff and preparing for our trip. The day after my lease ran out on the house, Ewan and I went to Kent and spent the weekend with his parents. His mum cried and wished us well as we left. Then we went home. I hugged my friends and parents goodbye and we got on the train to Paris.

My dad paid for the first five hotel nights and during that time we did all the usual sights; including a romantic night time walk looking at the city all lit up at night. We went to the Louvre and looked at the *Mona Lisa* (much smaller than we expected); and we climbed the steep hill up to admire Sacré Coeur. We strolled hand in hand along the Seine and Ewan whispered "I love you" to me for the second time as we watched the sun setting from the top of the Eiffel Tower. I wondered if he was only able to say it at sunset but then decided we'd just have to see many more if I wanted to hear it time and again.

Despite the fact that he didn't say it often, at the time I didn't think anyone could be more in love than we were, or that I could love anyone more than I loved him. I thought we'd be together forever. Once we'd got this out of his system, we'd go home, maybe in a year to eighteen months, settle down and live a normal life. Perhaps we could get that golden retriever and a little house by the sea. We'd live happily ever after.

Chapter Eleven

It was our second week away. I opened my eyes. Ewan was nudging me and I grumbled. My neck ached from being in the same position for too long. I lifted my head and glanced out of the window, but all I could see was another train and a platform.

"Izz, we're here."

I glanced at my watch. Dead on time. I liked Switzerland already. We gathered our bags and stepped out onto the platform

Ewan looked up at the signs. "We need to head this way."

Another short train ride - again precisely on time - took us to Lauterbrunnen. We climbed a steep slope out of the station and it was just how I'd imagined it. Alpine buildings with triangular roofs, flower boxes and shutters at every window; grey mountains with snowy peaks; the sound of a waterfall in the distance; and a clear, pure air in my lungs.

"Mmm ... breathe in that fresh, alpine air," Ewan said, pulling out a map he'd printed from the internet. We headed through the small village, past a beautiful church and out to the campsite we were staying at. We'd arranged to sleep in a ready-made tent.

"And that," said Ewan as it came into view, "must be the Staubbach Falls. Seven hundred metres high."

We both stood still a moment, taking in a huge waterfall, cascading water from the top of a mountain into the valley we were in. I took in my surroundings in awe and glanced back at Ewan who was grinning at me. As it turns out, they were one of seventy two waterfalls in the same valley.

"This is the most beautiful place I've ever seen," I said, so happy we were there. My bag was heavy and I was tired but it didn't matter anymore. It was worth it to see the beauty of this place. We settled into the campsite and noted we could hear the falls from our tent and then we were delighted when we discovered that they were lit up after dark. I slept the best night's sleep I've ever had that first night in Lauterbrunnen.

The next day, we bought a pass to allow us to travel on the mountain railways and cable cars for the duration of our stay, and we made sure we made the most of it. We travelled all over the area, hopping on and off the trains and cable cars; hiking in different places and taking in the beautiful lush green hills and stony grey mountains. We remained warm in the sunshine and yet watched the mountain snow above us sparkle in the sunlight as if someone had sprinkled glitter or fairy dust over everything.

We walked everywhere hand in hand; taking in the views, the people, the mountains, the snow, the food. We sipped hot chocolate at the top of Jungfraujoch, the highest railway station in Europe, while looking out at the glacier. Another day we went to Schilthorn, and ate in the revolving restaurant which was used in the Bond film, *On Her Majesty's Secret Service*. It felt very glamorous and romantic, and the panoramic views were spectacular. Afterwards we went for a short walk and peered over the sharp drops in awe.

I thought I could stay there forever; walking in those mountains, chatting with the friendly locals, admiring the sloped roof tops and flower boxes at each window. I'd happily have found a job and set up home for a while. There's something serene, calm and wondrous about a natural beauty spot that no city can substitute. But a week was enough for Ewan; he liked the views but he wanted the noise and life of a city, and I loved him enough to go along with whatever he wanted to do.

So, after our week in the glorious Bernese Alps we moved on to Verona in Italy, planning to stay for several months renting a tiny studio apartment. I was disappointed to leave the mountains behind. We found a little flat to rent with a small living and kitchen area in-one; a bedroom with a large double bed and a single wardrobe, and a tiny bathroom. It was enough space for the two of us and we settled in there quite happily. Ewan found work as a waiter, surprising me with his ability to pick up the Italian language pretty fast. I struggled to remember more than a few words. While he was working I spent the time reading the entire works of Shakespeare, wandering around the city alone, taking in the romantic atmosphere. I made friends with our neighbour - a bubbly Italian called Sabina who spoke perfect English. Ewan and I ate a lot of delicious food and Italian ice cream. We visited the arena which was second only to the Colosseum in Rome, we drank a lot of wine and life seemed simple, easy and carefree.

We got a train to Venice one day and walked around the little piazzas and shops. I was disappointed somehow; I'd expected to find it romantic and magical and instead felt it was overcrowded and touristy. I saw Ewan's jaw drop a little at the price of a gondola ride and insisted I didn't want to go on one anyway. We got coffee in a little cafe not far from St. Mark's Square and paid four times the amount we would for a larger cup in Verona.

"Verona's nicer," Ewan said, sipping his drink, "don't you think?"

"Definitely."

I personally preferred the mountains to either city, but I kept quiet. I was thrilled when we made a trip to Lake Garda which was big enough that we couldn't see to the other side. We went for a walk along the shoreline; the water was clear and turquoise and the mountains just took my breath away. We had a delicious meal by the waterfront where the lights from the restaurant reflected on the water.

We sat there eating, and I noticed other couples were talking. When had we stopped talking, I wondered? Did we ever talk that much? I realised we didn't. Ewan shared his opinions or talked about whatever we were looking at, but it was always brief and to the point and then we'd slip back into our comfortable silence. I decided I was quite content with this. I didn't need to talk all the time; I just needed to be with Ewan. He took care of me and loved me and that was all I needed.

To: Amber Carpenter
From: Izzy Swan
Subject: Hello Stranger

Hey Amber,

I can't believe I haven't seen you for three months! I'm writing this email from an internet café in Verona. It's pouring with rain outside, but up until now I've seen a lot of sunshine for the time of year. We are having such a great time. Most days, Ewan goes out to work in a restaurant as a waiter. I walk along the river, take in the sites, wander around little boutiques and book shops, read, and sip coffee. I paid the rent upfront on a tiny studio apartment we're staying in for a few months and Ewan gets cash in hand, which we spend mostly on alcohol and cheap meals out. Ewan buys me flowers and we spend quite a bit of time in bed ;-) Sometimes it feels like we are the only two people in the world.

I do feel a little lonely on occasion when he's working, but have no inclination to look for work myself (I'm on holiday!) and I've made friends with our neighbour, Sabina, who is giving me cooking lessons (she is an amazing chef). Her English is perfect.

Paris was amazing, then spent a week in the Alps surrounded by beautiful mountains before coming here. It's all been so lovely.

How are you? Tell me what's new… I miss you.
Love, Izzy x

To: Izzy Swan
From: Amber Carpenter
Subject: RE: Hello Stranger

Izzy!

Great to hear from you. Missing you too hon. What a glamorous life you are living, not working, a lady of leisure, chilling in Verona! Good for you. It all sounds fab!

I'm doing fine thanks chick. All is much the same, but my new job is rather dull. I've started work in an insurance office as an administrator. Dogsbody would be just as appropriate a job title. I spend a good proportion of time filing letters and documents and listening to a girl called Rhea bitch about everyone else in the office. She turns up every day with three tonne of make up on and talks a lot with her hands. I just stare at her manicured fingernails and smile, and nod, and wonder if I'm going to be this bored and unfulfilled for another forty years. Maybe I should have been a zoo keeper or a farmer or something. I like animals and would rather be outdoors. Still, the money is nice and I'm looking at renting a flat. I won't be able to afford to eat much, but at least that'll keep the weight off.

Be safe, have fun and don't do anything I wouldn't!
Much love, Amber x

I smiled at Amber's email and pictured her in smart office suits filing away paperwork and dreaming of escaping to work at a zoo instead. I also pictured her moving into a flat, setting up her own little home and felt a little envious.

December in Verona was filled with festivities. My new friend Sabina and I spent a day at a Christmas market beside the Roman Arena, wandering around the stalls buying toys for her nieces and nephews and eating lots of yummy goodies. We went into the arena to see a nativity scene and Sabina told me what delight she'd taken in coming here as a child with her two sisters.

She invited Ewan and me to a party for the said sister. Then another evening we went to a party hosted by the owner of Ewan's restaurant, and another to a party of a friend he'd made who owned a book shop. I felt so carefree and somehow managed not to think of Helen. Every Christmas leading up to this point had been full of thoughts of her, missing her, noticing my parents' sadness that she wasn't with us. We used to have certain traditions at Christmas that were lost after Helen left. Helen loved to bake and on Christmas Eve we'd always make shortbread and decorate a cake. When I was very young she'd help me to write a letter to Santa and wrap presents for our parents.

The last year, before we lost her, she'd asked for a hairdryer and makeup for Christmas. We'd woken up that morning and gone downstairs to sit around the tree with Mum and Dad, and we'd unwrapped the various goodies they'd no doubt spent a lot of time and money obtaining for us. Helen had been delighted with her bright purple hairdryer and a bag full of makeup. She went up and washed her hair and then dried it all neatly around her face. I watched her putting her makeup on and she rubbed a little eye shadow on me too. She did a better job than when we were little.

Another tradition was to go to Aunt Ruth's for dinner. There'd be a large family group and we'd all help out, chopping vegetables and preparing desserts until it was time to gather around for a delicious dinner. Then Helen, our cousins and I would play board games while the adults snoozed in the living room, relaxing after dinner.

We stopped most of that after Helen had gone. Mum said she wanted to stay home, keep things simple. We didn't bake shortbread and we didn't see our relatives. We'd just have a simple turkey dinner, the three of us. This year, being in Italy, I wouldn't have spent Christmas with Helen anyway so it somehow made me less sad than usual. I didn't think about the past, just the present. Me and Ewan and our Italian

Christmas.

Sabina helped me erect a small tree in our apartment which we decorated with twinkling lights and a few hanging decorations. Ewan and I spent Christmas day alone, eating turkey with pasta in a sauce Sabina helped me prepare, followed by warm panettone for dessert. We watched DVDs and read. I tried to start a conversation about the Christmases of our childhoods but Ewan seemed reluctant. He wasn't a big conversationalist. Sometimes I wanted to ask him to let me in, to open up and share what was on his mind and what he was thinking or what his memories were. I resisted the urge to ask, thinking he'd tell me eventually in his own time. But the more time that passed the less I felt I knew him. I knew all of his opinions but not really how he came to have those opinions in the first place.

I was happy though during that time, albeit a little homesick. January came and we carried on with our routine: Ewan working; me reading and mooching around with Sabina. She taught me how to make my own bread and pasta and I began to love cooking and presented Ewan with a different feast every evening.

The time passed so quickly, I was shocked when Ewan said we'd been in Verona for almost four months and asked if I was ready to move on. I said yes ... yes of course we could move on. But what I really wanted was to go home.

I liked Verona far more than I had expected; I'd only come because Ewan wanted to after all. But I was ready to go home. I had spent the majority of the money Nana had given me and I couldn't see myself working in a bar in Australia, like Ewan could. I could see myself becoming the best personal assistant that anyone had ever had. I could see myself buying a little place and making it home. I could even see myself going on holiday to Australia one day. But I didn't want to continue this journey. I missed my parents and Amber and Jade.

And when I thought about it, wasn't it my turn to make a

decision? Wasn't it time I led the way? Wasn't it time to compromise? I just had to figure out how to tell him.

"You know what," said Ewan as we sat down for breakfast. "I'm so glad we did this. So, where to next? It's time, don't you think?"

"To move on?" I asked, unsure how I might explain how I was feeling.

"Yes. I wanted to see more of Europe, but right now I am really keen to get to Australia. We could stop in Singapore a few days, first. I think we've got enough money to do that."

I didn't want to go to Australia or Singapore, but I just smiled and nodded. He talked about it for a while longer and I blanked him out. After returning from the bathroom he changed the subject.

"I met a British couple in the restaurant who are getting married here tomorrow. I told them it's a great place to get married, you know. It's romantic with the *Romeo and Juliet* history and all that. I see why so many people marry abroad. You know, ditch all the fluff and the fancy expensive stuff and just come away, tie the knot. Done. Just like that."

"Is that a proposal?" I asked, grinning and stuffing a pancake into my mouth. It tasted good. Sabina had taught me well.

"Well..." he laughed awkwardly and then he said: "Yes, why don't we?"

I laughed out loud, mostly from excitement at the thought and fear that then I'd never be able to stop following him.

"Ewan, I need to tell you something."

He nodded and continued with his pancake.

"I don't want to go to Australia."

His head flew up and he stared at me, surprised.

"Why not?"

"I just don't. We've been away for a long time now, all these different places—" I tried to continue but he interrupted me.

"Okay, so where else? Maybe California? Or somewhere in

Asia? Or we could move around here for longer. Go to Florence maybe? Or up to Munich?"

"Nowhere else. I want to go home. Start a career. Live … *normally*, you know?"

"But we don't care about normal."

"I do!" I said, a little too loudly. He frowned, surprised.

"Why didn't you tell me this before?"

"I didn't know how. I want to be with you so much, but this life has to end sometime, doesn't it?"

"Not yet. You're talking like we're approaching middle-age. I don't want a mortgage and two point four kids right now, and not for a very long time. Maybe not ever. That's not me. You know that."

"I do know that. I'm not proposing all those things. I just want to go home and get some … continuity. I never had it normal, you know, as a child. With my sister and everything nothing was ordinary for a long time. I just want to be normal. To feel normal. I guess I need to stay in one place to get that sense of balance in my life. Holidays will be great. But I need to be close to home. To nest somewhere."

I only realised that's what I needed when I said it. Home. I wanted home. I wanted to be around my mum and dad - and Amber and Jade. I wanted to go to work every day. I wanted a routine. And most of all I wanted to live the life that Helen dreamed of: a house by the sea, a husband, a dog. I tried to explain these things.

"I'm not sure I ever want those things," he said quietly.

"Well, I'm not going to Australia."

I was sure this would work. He couldn't stand to be without me; he'd have to come home.

"Well, I'm not going back to London."

I let this sink in.

We sat in silence for a few moments. I kept looking at him - trying to smile, catch his eye, work out if it was all going to be okay - but he just stared out of the window. Then without a word Ewan got up, went into the bedroom, grabbed his suitcase and started throwing clothes into it.

"What are you doing?"

"Packing. I think it's best I move into a hotel or I'll stay with one of the guys from work or something for a few days."

"Come on Ewan," I said, sitting down on the bed. "This is ridiculous."

"Are you coming to Australia?"

"No. I'm going home."

"Then this is it, surely?" He finally looked me the eyes, and for the first time I saw all the emotion in him.

"Don't do this," I said. "I need you. I can't be without you. We can go to Australia one day on holiday."

I hated my pleading voice but I couldn't stop myself.

"Please Ewan. Please. I love you."

"I love you too, Izzy. But I can't come home with you."

He continued to pack.

"Won't you even consider it?"

"I'm not that guy," he said, going into the bathroom for his razor.

"What guy?"

"The guy you want. The guy who settles down. You can't change me and you knew this was me. I wasn't going to get that corporate job or want to buy a house. I want adventure. I'm a drifter!" He shouted this last part and I suddenly wondered how rich I'd be if I had a pound for every time he'd told me this. And yet I'd never really believed it was true.

"I waited for you, delayed the whole travel thing until you'd graduated, and for what? Not even six months of travel and you want to go home."

I didn't know what to say so I just sat there, watching him pack, convinced that our feelings for each other would overcome this.

"You could at least stay tonight," I said eventually. I was pretty sure this was just an initial reaction. He'd come around.

"No, let's not delay the inevitable pain of separation tomorrow."

He'd realise he didn't want to do this without me, soon enough. Perhaps a night apart might be a good thing. I pulled the armchair around to face the window and looked out at the street.

"I guess this is goodbye," he said, and I turned to see him standing by the door, suitcase zipped up, rucksack over his shoulder. I stood up. Panic rose up in my chest and I realised this might actually be it. I might never see him again.

He came and hugged me then kissed me on the cheek. I started crying and we held each other for a long time.

"This is so hard," he said.

"I know," I whispered. I was surprised as we pulled apart to see that he'd shed a few tears too.

"If you change your mind," he said, "you can still come meet me. You can email me or whatever and I'll be waiting for you."

I nodded but I was still sure he'd change his mind. Maybe I'd see him in the morning. He walked out of the door, closing it quietly behind him. I took a deep breath. He wouldn't leave me here, not like this. Our relationship couldn't end like this. So I slept well that night, alone for the first time in almost three years of being with Ewan, relieved that I'd finally told him and stupidly confident that his feelings for me would overrule his desire to go to Australia.

I woke up the following morning feeling calm and serene, just for a few seconds. Then I remembered. Ewan was gone. I sat up, my head aching, and took this in. We should have talked, I told myself. This was all too ... hasty. As it was only seven, I went in the shower, tidied up the stuff Ewan had left lying around when he'd rooted through my stuff to find his own. Then I made French toast and ate it with some raspberries. I was half way through when the panic set in again.

I found my mobile and dialled his, but it was switched off just as I'd expected. He had only turned it on a couple of times since we'd left London.

I sighed. Where was he? Would he come back here? I decided it was the best place to wait.

I busied myself with more tidying: packing up my things; curling my hair; painting my toenails. I tried to read my book but couldn't concentrate on the words. Finally, trying to calm the panic in my chest, I decided to go for walk. I wrote a note:

Ewan,
I knew you'd come back. Going stir-crazy waiting though so I'm going for walk. Please wait for me. We need to talk.
Izzy x

I got out of the apartment building and walked down the street, past the cafes and restaurants and ended up at Juliet's house (of *Romeo and Juliet* fame). It was a mild day, not a cloud in the sky. I sat down for a while and then figured I may as well head home. I wandered back slowly, hungry for some lunch, hoping Ewan had returned.

As I opened the door I immediately saw the note on the bed. A whole page. I rushed to it, leaving the door to slam shut behind me.

Hello Izzy,
You are right, we do need to talk. But I've waited here for you for almost an hour and I have no time left. I booked a flight, it was the last seat available and non-refundable, and I'm going to miss it if I don't leave now. I'm sorry it has to be this way.
I'm also sorry about yesterday. I thought you were asking me to be someone I'm not; you know me. I told you when we met that I wanted to travel the world; and we've hardly touched it yet. I understand and respect that you want to go home, but I can't. Not yet. I just wish you'd told me your feelings earlier.

I want you to know that I love you and I always will. Maybe one day, when my travelling bug has died down, I'll be back. But don't wait for me. You have so much to give, and you deserve to be happy.

If somehow you change your mind, then drop me an email. I am leaving today on a flight to Singapore, and then I'm planning to be in Sydney for a while. Otherwise, I think it's best we don't keep in touch. It'll be too hard. I hope you understand that.

I miss you already,
Ewan x

I was crying pretty hysterically as I stuffed everything I could into my case and struggled to zip it up. I scribbled a note for Sabina including my email address, shoved it under her door, ran down to the street and wheeled my case until I found a taxi.

"Airport, as fast as you can," I told the driver in dramatic fashion. I pictured myself running to the gate and catching him at the last minute, like some scene from a corny romantic film.

I had no idea what I'd do when I got there. It was busy and there were no flights to Singapore on the board. I was pretty sure he'd said something about having to fly to Rome or Paris first - I couldn't remember. I'd never find him.

Admitting defeat, I sat down and did the only thing I could think of. I called Amber.

"Do you really want to go to Australia today?"

"No. But I can't—"

"There's your answer. You're scared and lost because you're in a foreign city, all alone, and you've just lost the love of your life. I know it feels like he's your whole world and he has been for the past few years, but there are others here who love you too. I'm not saying you shouldn't go. I'm saying that you don't have to go if you don't want to. You're okay on your own. You can cope. We're all here for you. He wasn't willing to come

71

back to the UK for you. Are you willing to fly to the other side of the world for him?"

She was right of course. I went to the desk and booked myself on the next flight to London.

I managed to go the whole flight without crying and I really felt that maybe I could cope. Maybe I could move on. Maybe Ewan wasn't essential to my happiness. I had Amber and my other friends and family. I'd find an awesome job and a lovely flat of my own and, one day, maybe Ewan would come and find me. Maybe. I had to hold on to that hope. In the meantime, I sat back and put my earphones in and listened to nineties pop music with my eyes closed. The music bought back memories of happier days.

Helen was a huge Take That fan. She had posters of them on her bedroom wall and could talk about Mark Owen all day long, if you let her. Once, Mum took us to Wembley Arena to see them live. We counted down the days for months beforehand and listened to them every day. When the time came Helen was about ready to burst with excitement.

We had seats close to the stage at the side, quite high up. Helen and I screamed and cheered, danced and sang until we were hoarse. Occasionally we'd look at each other and grin, then we'd shout together: 'We love you Take That!' as loud as we could. On the way home Helen said it was the best night of her life. As I sat on the plane, I tried to decide what the best night of my life had been. I couldn't decide but it had to be one of the nights I'd spent with Ewan. I couldn't imagine how I'd have any happiness in my life without him.

The plane landed and I stood staring at the baggage carousel, wondering how it'd come to this. I hadn't expected to return home alone. I found a cab and went straight to Amber's flat where I collapsed on her sofa in floods of tears.

Chapter Twelve

Saturday. One week before my wedding day.

"Jason and Ewan were *both* there?" Jade repeated as we sat in the taxi, heading home.

"Yes," I said, trying not to grin because I was so happy I thought I might burst. I hiccupped.

"What are the chances?"

"Very slim," I said quietly.

"Jason's got a really nice girlfriend," Amber told her. I shuddered again at the thought. Of course he did. I'd split up with him so I certainly had no right to be jealous. Yet it still bugged me. For some reason whenever I thought of him, I imagined him single.

"I'm meeting Ewan for a drink on Thursday night," I told them, realising I may need them both right after I'd seen him.

Amber just looked at me and shook her head with disapproval.

"Izzy, do you really think that's a good idea?" asked Jade.

"Just to catch up. As friends. I'm fine with it. Things were left a little unfinished between us. There's so much to catch up on. Really, all is fine."

My mobile started to buzz.

"My darling husband to be," I said, answering.

"Hi love bug," he said. "Oh, sorry," he added quickly, remembering how I'd explained his affection was a little suffocating at times.

"It's okay. How're you?"

"Great." He sounded drunk.

"Having fun?"

"Yes. How's the hen do?"

"Lovely, we had a really fun time. How's Amsterdam?"

"Fun. I'm in my hotel room. Just thought I'd say good night."

"I'm just in the taxi with Amber and Jade."

"Okay, good, well have fun."

"I will."

"I can't wait to see you on Monday."

"Me too."

"Love you."

"Love you too."

I ended the call and wondered if I'd just lied to the man I was supposed to be married to this time next week. After settling Amber and Jade into the spare rooms, I lay in bed remembering the way I felt when I'd seen Jason again. And now Ewan too. Who had I loved most out of the two? I couldn't be sure. Maybe Jason. But seeing Ewan ... well, I hadn't expected to feel like that. Who did I love most out of the four, Greg included? That was the problem. I wasn't sure I loved Greg as much as I'd loved either of them and surely that meant I didn't love him enough to get married ... or did it?

Was I just repeating a cycle? Were all relationships eventually doomed anyway? And if so, what did that mean? That I'd either drift from one relationship to the next, or be alone for the rest of my life? Neither sounded like a fun prospect and yet I couldn't see myself growing old with Greg.

Exhausted, both physically and emotionally, I drifted off to sleep. I dreamt of Ewan and Jason standing in a room smiling at me. If only I could merge all the men into one and somehow create my perfect mate.

Chapter Thirteen

Two days after returning from Verona I was back at my parents' house.

Dad collected me from the station and we chatted about Paris, Switzerland and Italy without any mention of Ewan, for which I was immensely grateful. As we pulled up on the driveway I spotted our cat, Sherlock, sunning himself on the grass and went straight over to stroke him. He purred and licked my fingers. Jade had come over to welcome me home and was standing in the front doorway grinning at me. After long, hard hugs they all threw hundreds of questions at me, skirting around the fact that I'd not mentioned Ewan.

The first few days were tough. I kept wondering where he was exactly and more importantly who with. Surely he'd meet some hot sexy Australian surfer girl the minute the plane landed and the two of them were having the best sex any two human beings had ever had. I kept staring out of the window imagining myself flying all over the world searching for him until one day, as a poor old lady, I'd find him somewhere romantic like the Taj Mahal or a remote island in the Seychelles, and we'd embrace and he'd tell me he'd loved none but me.

I spent hours wondering whether any of it had been worth it. If the fun of being with Ewan made up for the pain I was feeling now. I decided it didn't. But none of this would last long.

My Aunt Ruth had a friend, Sian Matthews, who was looking for a live-in personal assistant. All I knew was that she was an entrepreneur, worth millions according to Jade, buying small businesses and selling them on.

"She's like one of those Dragons," Jade told me, "from the den." I looked up *Dragon's Den* online. The thought of living with or working for one of them terrified me, but I had no work experience and the idea of living in her apparently very nice Notting Hill house was too tempting to ignore. Ruth set up a meeting and I went to Sian's house to find out what the job would entail.

"Welcome," said a tall, thin, blonde woman with a pointy nose and long gold earrings. She was wearing a beautiful tailored grey suit, and her wide smile made me like her almost at once. I followed her through a pale yellow hallway, glancing at a large oil painting of sunflowers on my way through.

"I bought that at an auction in Milan," Sian told me, seeing me glance at it. "Stunning isn't it?"

I didn't have much of an eye for art. It just looked like sunflowers to me.

"Yes," I said, hoping I didn't look or sound as nervous as I felt. Don't blow it, I told myself as we entered the living room. Cream leather sofas, plump chocolate-brown cushions, the largest television I've ever seen, plus enough books, DVDs and music to keep me entertained until I was at least twice the age I was now.

"Quite a young, new artist, I can't even remember his name." She laughed. "But I should, the amount of money I paid for it."

"You have a lovely home," I said, because it was true as well as polite.

She smiled, showing me dazzling white teeth. I wondered if they were natural.

"Please, sit." She gestured to a seat and I almost sighed as I felt how comfortable the sofa was. Yes, living here would be no hardship at all.

Sian had already poured out two glasses of lime cordial. I

took a sip, willing myself not to spill any on the cream rug which felt so soft under my feet that I thought I could probably sleep on it. The cordial was sharp and I swallowed hard, fighting a shudder.

"So, I'm not sure what Ruth has told you," Sian began, "but I have an urgent need for a live-in PA and I'd like to offer you the position."

"To offer me?" I asked, surprised. I'd been expecting an interview.

"Well, yes. I don't have the time to advertise the post and I trust Ruth beyond belief. We've been friends over twenty years. She's mentioned you to me many times; I know you're smart, ethical, honest, and highly organised. I also think you'll work pretty hard. Am I right?"

"Yes."

"Right. So what I need is this," she took a deep breath. "I need someone to live here, in this house. I have a cat, Fred; a fluffy, gorgeous ginger thing who's about somewhere. I'm away a lot, so I want someone who will live here, look after Fred and the house for me while I'm gone. No cleaning is needed; I have a lady come to do that every week. Then the second part of the job is a personal assistant role. I need someone to literally book my hotels, flights, meetings and venues, restaurants, manage my diary and always be at the end of a telephone when I need them for all sorts of admin and general help. I simply don't have time to book medical appointments or even, to be honest, arrange to see my family and friends, buy Mother's Day gifts for my mother or ... well, you get the picture."

She took another breath. Her eyes were darting around the room as she said all this, quickly summarising the duties which I'd soon be responsible for.

"It might all sound easy, but I can be demanding, I warn you."

"It all sounds great. Really," I said, sounding just as

enthusiastic as I felt. "I just—"

"Don't worry, I know you don't have any experience, but I like that. I want someone I can mould, who comes with no expectations other than to work hard."

"Okay," I said, wondering if this was too good to be true.

"Fabulous. Right, well, shall we start with a three month trial?"

"That would be great, thank you."

"Wonderful. Let me show you around the house then."

The kitchen looked like it'd hardly ever been used. There was a double oven and the largest spice rack I've ever seen. Various utensils and gadgets were dotted around. The dining table could sit ten people, easily. There was a wrought iron candelabra in the middle with short white candles melted down to almost nothing.

"Such a waste, really," muttered Sian, "as I'm rarely here, but please make use of everything. Invite friends over, whatever. So long as you leave it clean and tidy."

"Thank you."

"Please, no need to thank me anymore. It'll be nice to think someone's using the place."

"It's a beautiful house," I told her again.

She ran her hand along the counter top and led me to French doors at the back of the room.

"The garden," she said, opening the doors to a small but pretty little patio with wooden furniture and a reasonable patch of grass, some flower beds and a few small trees. "I have a gardener who comes every couple of weeks, so you don't need to worry about maintaining it."

Next she led me upstairs, pointing towards her own bedroom.

"The only room I ask you not to go in."

"Of course," I said. "I wouldn't dream of it.'

"And this is your office," she said, opening the door to a small room with a desk, a laptop and a cork board on the wall.

"Do whatever you want with it; paint it however you like, get any furniture or stationery you need. I'll sort you out your own credit card. This is a place for you to work, write letters and emails, look up information for me and so on."

"Great," I said, wondering what colour I might paint it.

My bedroom was on the third floor. Sian opened the door and led me in. It was a good size with olive-green walls, a king-sized bed, fitted wardrobes and two windows that cast lots of light. There was expensive-looking bedding, just a few shades darker than the walls, scatter cushions and lamps on bedside units.

"The furniture is all new but if you don't like anything..."

"I love it," I told her, delighted.

"Great. Right, well," Sian continued, "let's talk money."

The salary wasn't huge, but Sian said as I got more experienced and did well she'd review it again and she'd also pay for any courses I wanted to do. Perhaps some Excel and PowerPoint, she suggested, but anything from Spanish to Biology would be considered if I could give her justification for my job. With free board and no need for a car, I estimated that I'd be quite comfortable. My outgoings would be few.

"I want you to be happy here," she said, "because if you're happy then the house and the work will be looked after well, if you see what I mean."

"I think I do," I said, although I wasn't actually sure. How could anyone not be happy living here? I looked at her eyes as I thought this and wondered if she was happy jetting off all over the world, never in one place for long. She'd suit Ewan, I thought for a second, and then shuddered at the thought. She was too old for him and he'd never like her posh furniture, or her workaholic attitude.

"Just be honest with me, even if you think I've behaved like a bitch, which sometimes I will, just let me know. We have to be open and trust each other."

I nodded, smiling. I liked her already.

"Come over with your things next Saturday," she'd said. "I'll be leaving for New York on Tuesday, so you'll have the house to yourself almost right away."

***

"How on earth did you get so lucky?" Amber nudged me as I told her all this over cocktails the Friday before I moved in with Sian.

"No idea," I said, "but it does sound like it'll be hard work. Ruth said Sian told her to expect I'll be run off my feet straight away. But I don't mind that."

"I'm so happy for you. I was worried you'd be a manic wreck over Ewan."

"Well, maybe I was for the first few days, but I accept that we want different things."

I bit my lip, wondering if I could say the words out loud. Would the pain lessen or become worse if I talked about it?

"What?"

"When Helen ... went missing," I began, realising it was too late to stop now, "I felt this huge empty hole open up inside me."

"Something had been taken from you, that's natural," Amber said, squeezing my hand.

"Well, when I was with Ewan the hole healed a little. I thought of her less, and it's like he filled the gap she'd left."

"I can understand that. You were obsessed with him, after all. No time to think about much else."

"Well, now he's not in my life and it feels the hole is opening up again. I just feel so ... hollow."

Amber frowned, not quite understanding. I didn't know how to explain it; I just had this empty place inside me. Ewan didn't fit the gap but he made it seem numb somehow by allowing me to ignore the hole. Now he was gone, I felt lost.

But moving in with Sian soon gave me plenty to take my

mind off Helen and Ewan, and the emptiness my life had without them in it.

I arrived on the Saturday as planned, lugging all my clothes and other bits and pieces up the stairs to my new bedroom. I lay down on my new bed to feel the expensive bedding envelop me. After I'd unpacked Sian ordered pizza and we made a little social conversation. She told me she'd bought the house a few years earlier as a London base, but it was too big really and she was there very rarely.

"I hope you don't mind living alone," she said, "this isn't a co-habiting situation. I'm here about one night a month, to be honest. But I don't want to sell and there's Fred to consider. So..."

I insisted that it was fine and I was quite happy, which was the truth. Ruth had already told me Sian was rarely home; I'm not sure I'd have wanted to move in with her otherwise. I watched her eat her pizza slowly, carefully avoiding getting anything on her expensive clothes or her tanned chin. She told me a little about her business empire, although I didn't really understand how much of it worked.

Before leaving on Tuesday morning she left me a list of numbers and instructions on how everything worked, which had been prepared by her last PA. "I'll call you later," she said, grabbing her coat and suitcase.

After she left I skipped around the house; all this, just for me!

It wasn't quite as easy as it sounded though. Fred was delightful company and would sit on my lap purring all evening. I enjoyed the house and I loved living in Notting Hill. There was something quite glamorous about telling people where I lived. I expected to bump into Hugh Grant and Julia Roberts every time I ventured out.

But Sian was right; she was demanding. She'd ring anytime from 7am to about 11pm at night, asking me to book a restaurant or to find a hotel at a moment's notice in Tokyo,

Cape Town or Madrid. She wanted me to find an emergency dentist in New York, then to find, buy, and send her six year old niece a birthday present. But I loved it and I worked hard. I liked having a purpose. I enjoyed organising her schedule and booking flights and providing all the support she needed. Even when she came home she was rarely there, as she rushed about to meetings and social engagements.

Mostly it was just me and Fred, and I spent most of my time working when I wasn't with Amber, Jade, or visiting my parents. I didn't look through the photos of the trip with Ewan; I didn't consider where or what he may be doing and I resisted the urge to send him an email.

I did email Sabina in Verona though. I told her what happened and apologised for not giving her a proper goodbye. She sent me photos of her nieces and nephews and complained about the tourists, promising to come and visit me someday.

I spent a lot of time with Jade. She'd come and stay over, sleeping on a futon in my office. We'd go shopping or to the theatre and talk about work, life and the men she dated. I felt closer to her than ever before. Her lust for life, her cheerfulness and sense of humour kept my spirits high, which just reinforced in my mind that home was where I wanted to be.

Four months after returning, I bumped into Alex, Ewan's brother, when coming out of Gucci with a new handbag that Sian had asked me to get for her.

"Izzy!" he said, giving me a quick hug.

"Hi Alex," I said, taking a deep breath. "How are you?"

He looked older, more mature than when I'd last seen him at a little tea party his parents had given before Ewan and I set off for Paris. He had filled out and was wearing a blue shirt with a grey jacket and his hair was swept back from his face. He looked like Ewan did when I met him; only smarter and better dressed.

"I'm good, really good. I just moved to London a few months ago."

"That's great." I smiled and then added, mostly for Ewan's benefit: "I'm living in Notting Hill."

"It's too bad about you and Ewan. I thought you made a great couple."

"Yes, well..." I didn't know what to say but felt the familiar lump in my throat and swallowed hard. I wasn't going to let Ewan find out I was still upset. Not one email: no call - nothing. Come to think of it, how did he even know I'd got home safely?

"Ewan's a mess without you. Seriously. Mum's been so worried. He won't come home though."

A mess? Well, good.

"He's been in touch, then?"

He had only called home once while we were travelling together, and even then I'd had to persuade him to do it.

"Yes, well he called her a couple of times. First to say that you weren't together anymore, and another time just to check in, I think. She said he sounded pretty depressed."

I didn't want to think of him in pain or suffering, but I was also glad he wasn't doing so well. That I wasn't that easy to get over. And maybe he might come back for me and ... *Stop*, I told myself. *Stop that thought right there.*

"Yes, well, I wanted him to come home and he wouldn't, so..."

"I don't think he's ready. You look fantastic Izzy, really. And Gucci, nice!"

"Thank you. The Gucci is for my boss, actually."

"Still, you look beautiful. Really. Stunning."

He was looking me up and down. Was he seriously flirting with me? I was wearing a suit Sian had given me because she rarely wore something more than a couple of times. In fact, most of my wardrobe now consisted of Sian hand-me-downs. I was secretly hoping the Gucci bag might become mine, eventually.

"Thank you," I said politely, feeling myself blush.

"So, do you want to get a drink?"

"No, thank you Alex. I've got to get going."

I had a little fantasy as I walked back to the tube station. About getting drunk with Alex. Maybe seducing him, closing my eyes and imagining it was Ewan. Some sort of revenge perhaps for all the hurt and pain and rejection. Then I shuddered at the thought and got on the train feeling calm and, I realised with surprise, happy. Everything was going well and for the first time since coming home, I recognised that I didn't need Ewan. I'd gone and created a life for myself. I'd worked hard and Sian had seemed impressed with me. Amber and Jade had persuaded me to get out and about, and I'd forced myself out of the depression which had been looming when I flew out of Verona.

I can live without him, I thought as I arrived in Notting Hill and carried Sian's Gucci bag home.

Chapter Fourteen

Sunday. Six days before my wedding day.

I sat up in bed and wondered for a moment if seeing Jason and Ewan at my hen night had been a dream. The sunlight was coming in through the windows and I squinted, realising I was a little hung-over despite the litre of water I'd downed before bed. I rubbed my head.

Now that I was sober, I couldn't believe how thrilled I'd felt when I saw them. I pictured each of them again. Jason had been with that beautiful woman whose name I couldn't remember. They didn't seem like they were a good match. She was too fashionable for him, too well dressed. I wondered, with sadness, if he cooked for her. Of course he did. He did all the lovely things for her that he'd done for me. And she was probably a grateful, happy little thing, less selfish than me, which was why he was happy and I was miserable.

Or was I? How could I be miserable when my Ewan - my lovely, yummy, sexy hero - had come back into my life? I couldn't wait until I met him for that drink. Just as friends, of course.

Then I thought about Greg. If anything, I was even more uncertain now. Could I really marry him while I had these feelings about Jason and Ewan? Would that be fair to him? Or to me?

I know. I'm a horrible, selfish person. Ugh. But I'll give myself credit for at least realising and admitting it.

Amber and Jade were in the living room when I went

downstairs. I made us coffee and toasted some cinnamon and raisin bagels, which we ate on the sofa in our pyjamas.

"Thanks for a great evening, girls," I said.

"It was so much fun," Jade said, tucking into her bagel. "Still can't believe you saw two ex-boyfriends. That's just weird. That's worse than having a stripper turn up."

"You're not really going to meet Ewan on Thursday are you?" Amber asked.

"Of course I am. It'll be nice to catch up. And anyway, I haven't got his number. I can't stand him up."

"You sure it's a good idea? You know, with your cold feet?" Jade pointed to my slippers as she spoke.

"It's just lunch. Really. I'll be fine."

They left soon afterwards but only after I'd promised to keep my feet firmly on the ground, repeated the reasons why Greg would be a great husband and agreed to call them if I had any more doubts.

I sat and read a book for while but gave up because I couldn't stop wondering what Jason was doing. How did he feel about seeing me again?

Then I kept thinking about what Ewan would have to say when I met him. I pictured him again from the previous night with his hair cut shorter and a bit of a beard. And his brilliant blue eyes, as gorgeous as ever.

It was just a lunch. I mean, so I'd loved him once ... so he'd had some sort of power over me. That was all in the past.

Honestly. It was just a lunch.

Chapter Fifteen

Jason was very different to Ewan. And our relationship was completely different, too. I don't think I've ever talked so much with a man as I did with him. He was my best friend, right from the beginning. I'd been living with Sian for six months when I met him.

Amber and I were sitting in Hyde Park, near the lake. The sun was sparkling on the water like golden glitter. I squinted up at the sky and glanced back to Amber.

"I can't believe how long it's been since we did this," said Amber, picking up her book.

Amber and I used to do this regularly when we were students. I'd bring the old, worn, red tartan blanket and some junk food, Amber would bring a handful of magazines and some diet coke and we'd sit in the park watching people go by, snacking, chatting, and reading.

Amber often commented on the variety of different faces: tourists from other countries speaking different languages; the regulars walking their dogs or jogging; the occasional day-tripper; an old man who fed the squirrels and birds. I loved the colourful flower beds and the hum of traffic in the distance. Some days we'd walk down to Buckingham Palace, others we'd just sit and try to catch the sun. Amber would tan and I'd stay a nice shade of pasty white tinged with bright red.

As Amber read, I sat and thought about Ewan. I missed him. Or rather, I missed having a boyfriend. Fred usually slept on my bed but it wasn't quite the same as having a man wrap his arms around you, or snuggling up when you felt chilly. I'd gone on a few dates. One with a guy I knew as a student who was as boring as a person can be, and another with a lovely man Jade had introduced me to, who I thought was a potential to become something more but after date three he told me he had some personal issues to deal with and I never heard from him again.

"Welcome to my world," Jade had said. "It's hard to find the decent ones. They're all either married already or hiding someplace I'm yet to find."

What I didn't understand was that before Ewan I'd never even wanted a boyfriend, and now I was on my own I couldn't stand to be without one. I kept thinking about emailing him, but the only thing I was sure of was that I didn't want to travel. I liked being home. I loved being able to see my parents and friends whenever I wanted, and I enjoyed my job. I missed him and I still loved him, but I couldn't run after him.

"It's been six whole months since I saw Ewan," I told Amber as we chilled in Hyde Park.

She didn't respond as she was engrossed in her book. I realised then how much I'd missed her. I told her all about Ewan and how we'd parted; about some of the places we'd seen and the people we'd met, the food we'd eaten and then she'd told me about the rat race, how annoying her colleagues were, how her veterinary nurse training was going, how she loved living in London, and how she had been flirting with a guy she liked at work.

She was now renting a studio flat and she'd painted each room a different vibrant colour and filled the small space with big cushions and furniture from IKEA. She seemed ... mature. I felt like I'd been in some sort of fantasy land travelling with Ewan. Now real life was underway and although I missed him and felt lonely sometimes, I loved it. The pain was still there and yet I knew this had been the right thing to do.

"Did you say something?" Amber asked, putting her book down.

"Nothing important."

"Amber?" We both looked up, squinting in the sun. A man in a bright orange shirt was looking down at us, with another guy hovering in the background.

"Tristan!" she said, putting her book down and standing up. Tristan had been mentioned in our emails to each other during my absence. He was someone Amber liked a lot, I'd gathered, and from the way he was looking at her he liked her too. His friend stepped forward and gave an awkward wave and a nod. He had very dark brown hair and eyes and wore black rimmed glasses. He wasn't conventionally handsome, but when he smiled nervously at me I realised he was very cute in a geeky sort of way. I smiled back and felt myself blush a little.

"This is Jason," Tristan said, gesturing towards him. "This is Amber, a colleague of mine, and…"

"Izzy," Amber told them, "my good friend."

We all smiled and nodded politely and Tristan invited us to join them on a walk and to get some lunch, so Amber threw her book and the rest of our stuff into her enormous bag and we began walking. Tristan and Amber paired off a few paces ahead almost immediately.

"So, Izzy, what do you do?" asked Jason. He had a well-spoken accent and a nervous discomfort that just made him seem all the cuter.

"Well, I'm a personal assistant," I began, picking up on his nervous energy and feeling anxious myself. "My boss, Sian, is the busiest woman I've ever known and I organise her life for her. I even take care of her cat."

I told him a bit about Sian, then I told him how I'd been travelling and how she'd helped me out as I needed a job and somewhere to live when I got back. I was talking too quickly, feeling self-conscious. I wanted to appear confident, intellectual and well spoken, but was aware I seemed nothing of the sort.

"What do you do?" I asked, glancing sideways at him. His eyes were so dark I could hardly make out his pupils. He looked at me intently for a second and I felt blood rush to my chest.

"I'm a chef." He said it very casually, but glancing at him again, he looked embarrassed.

We stopped to cross the road.

"He's famous," said Amber, turning back to us. "Izzy has been away, she doesn't recognise you," she said, grinning. "I've seen you on TV."

Jason smiled and looked even more embarrassed. I couldn't quite picture him on the TV. He seemed too unsure of himself.

"So you're a celebrity chef?" I asked, liking him all the more for being so down-to-earth and humble about it.

"Not really. I'm head chef at my own restaurant. That's my calling. I've done a few series for the BBC. I'm not that well-known. I'm not Jamie Oliver." He was blushing again.

Jamie Oliver made me think of Sainsbury's and then of Ewan. I quickly pushed the thought out of my head.

"He's got a book out," Tristan told me. "My mum loves it."

"Wow. I'm sorry I haven't heard of you until now."

"Well, you haven't missed out on much," said Jason, smiling again. "It's nothing too exciting."

I decided to look him up on the internet as soon as I got home. We'd reached a little Italian restaurant and went inside. It was very busy, with customers squashed close together.

"I can only give you two tables of two and not together I'm afraid," said the waiter, "or, you can wait for half an hour."

"Two tables of two will be fine," said Tristan, guiding Amber to a vacant one near the back. I turned and smiled awkwardly yet again to Jason, who gestured that we sit at the other free table near the window.

"Some friends we've got," he said, sitting down opposite me.

"My thoughts exactly." I wasn't disappointed though. We studied our menus in silence and then ordered the exact same thing; linguine with king prawns and chilli.

"Excuse me, could I have your autograph?" asked a lady at the next table, just as our waiter left.

"Sure." Jason looked embarrassed again. She rooted around in her bag for a pen and some paper and he signed his name. It didn't have the glamorous feel I'd expected, mostly because he continued to seem nervous, awkward and embarrassed ... which I found completely adorable.

"So, where have you been travelling?"

I told him about the different places; how we'd loved the Alps and about Christmas in Verona.

"We?"

"Me and Ewan. He was my boyfriend. We split up."

The waiter bought our food.

"I'm sorry."

"Don't be," I said. And for the first time I realised I wasn't sorry. Here was an intelligent, cute, kind of famous man who obviously could cook well, and I was sitting here having lunch with him, hoping he liked me as much as I liked him. Maybe life without Ewan wasn't going to be so bad after all.

"Why did you become a chef?" I asked, wondering if he'd cook something for me, sometime.

"I always loved cooking; I helped my mother out when I was young." His eyes lit up as he spoke and for the first time, he didn't seem so nervous. "I liked to experiment, make up recipes. I never intended to become a TV chef. I was just happy running a kitchen, but someone thought I'd be good at it and it's gone okay. My passion is the food. The TV stuff has made the restaurant more popular, though."

"What cuisine does your restaurant offer?" I asked. He was very easy to talk to, despite his anxious exterior.

"British with some French twists."

I nodded my head. "This linguine is good."

"Yes, delicious."

"Well, you're the expert."

"Do you mind..." he said suddenly and seriously, putting his fork down, "I mean would you like to see me again?"

I almost laughed. It seemed so formal, so gentlemanly compared to what I was used to. He really was rather posh.

"I'd love to," I told him.

We continued our lunch, talking about the places I'd been and the work he did, and I found out he lived in a house which was small but 'perfectly adequate' in Hammersmith. He asked whereabouts I lived and said he often walked past my house on his way to Portobello Market. He talked about buying fresh fruit and vegetables and a little about cooking and his enthusiasm for the food was quite infectious. I wanted to eat something he'd made and test it for myself.

Then he told me that today he was heading to the BBC studios for a rehearsal of a charity comedy event, and he was going to be cooking something with Jimmy Carr. I tried not to seem star-struck, but I was impressed.

He insisted on paying for lunch and I put my number directly into his phone while he paid. Amber and Tristan were waiting for us at the door when we got up to leave. We said our goodbyes and Jason walked off down the street with just one backwards glance and a smile.

"Well, look at you," said Amber as we walked back to the tube station.

"What?"

"Swapping numbers with Jason Edwards! He's not exactly the hottest thing on TV, but he's very popular."

"Really?"

"Yes. Google him. Seriously."

So I did. I got home and I went straight to my laptop and I read all I could about him. First, I read all about his restaurant, which had a Michelin star. The fact he'd failed to mention this just made me like him all the more. I admired his modesty.

Then I read about him on various other websites, which as well as repeating the information on the website, taught me that he was thirty years old and currently single.

Next I clicked on the images and found hundreds of photos of Jason, usually wearing chef's whites, and even a few photos with celebrities including Jonathan Ross and Prince Charles. I gasped a few times, looking at them all. It all looked pretty glamorous and yet somehow I couldn't imagine this shy, awkward man mixing it up with showbiz personalities.

But that night I had a dream that Ewan turned up on my doorstep. I invited him in and we had fast, exciting sex on Sian's massive dining room table. The next day all I could think of was him. I imagined him chatting to girls in bars, 'drifting' as he loved to do, all over Australia. Drinking beer and having barbeques on the beach. Did he miss me? Should I email him?

"He won't change," Amber told me when I called her to suggest this.

"I know."

"Jason liked you, according to Tristan."

Jason was nice. Nice, and sweet, and cute. But was there any chance Ewan would ever come back to settle down? If there was a chance then shouldn't I wait for him? Jason texted me a few days later, asking if I'd like to meet for a few drinks. I replied to say I was really busy but I'd be in touch.

"You're crazy," Amber told me. "What's wrong? Are you afraid of getting involved with someone else?"

"No, I just don't know if I'm really ready, now that it comes to it."

Even though he'd seemed keen, I couldn't imagine kissing him or having sex with him without feeling guilty about Ewan. On top of this, I had built up a bit of a fear of rejection. What if I got hurt again?

"Jason's mature and sweet and funny ... and you know

what? Lots of girls would love to go out with him."

"How does Tristan know him?"

"They used to be neighbours. Tristan says Jason is the nicest guy he knows."

"He was very nice. And cute, too."

Amber had started seeing Tristan regularly and talked about him for a while. She seemed happy and I knew she thought it'd be fun if I got together with his friend. I wasn't sure what was holding me back, but when I looked back on our lunch I felt that maybe he liked me more than I liked him. Then I thought about his cute, nervous smile and confused myself by thinking the opposite. I *had* really liked him, at the time.

"Stop making it so complicated with Jason," Amber said.

"I guess seeing him again would be nice."

"Just call him. I dare you. It's time to move on, Izzy."

Chapter Sixteen

I texted Jason exactly two weeks after we'd met.

Hi Jason. Izzy here. So sorry I haven't been in touch. Would you still like to get together?

He called me straight away.

"Izzy, hi. I didn't expect to hear from you." He sounded enthusiastic and less nervous than when we'd met.

"Sorry, I just had some things to sort out."

"No worries. So, how are you?" He was also better-spoken than I remembered.

"I'm alright, and you?" I said, glancing at the clock. It was 7pm. I'd just put a homemade pizza in the oven.

"I'm very well, thank you. So Izzy is short for Isabella? Isabelle?"

"Isabelle. I prefer Izzy."

"I'm glad you text me. You see, I was wondering if you'd like to go out, sometime? If you're not too busy, I mean. It's just that, well, I had a nice time, last time, and I was wondering if you'd like to, you know, do it again. Have lunch I mean. Or something. Just a drink even, if you'd rather."

I smiled as he fumbled over his words; he sounded nervous again. He told me later he was sure he'd blown it, that this little speech would send me running, but it had the opposite effect. I fell for his cute vulnerability and charm and it was clear he really liked me, which gave me a much-needed confidence boost.

"I love your voice," I said, without responding to the date invitation. I wanted to give him a boost too. "You should do voice-over work."

"I have done, actually, for a supermarket food ad, and to be honest it probably would suit better than the TV stuff. People don't have to look at my face then." He chuckled.

"I'd like to see your face. I can't remember it if I'm honest."

"Google me. Plenty of hideous images, I assure you."

"I have a confession to make," I said, taking the pizza out of the oven.

"Oh dear. I suppose you found lots of false information, saw photos of me three stone heavier, and ... oh God, I guess you saw that hideous photo of me coming out of that pub drunk?"

"So you've googled yourself, then?" I interrupted. "By the sounds of it?"

"Yes, about once a week, sometimes less often. I try not to, but I can't help it. So what did you discover?"

"Well," I said, trying to remember. "You've got a Michelin star."

"Ah, yes, I do indeed."

"Well done." I took a bite of pizza. I'd used Sabina's recipe which was pretty good.

"Thank you. Undeserved, I assure you."

"You were voted second cutest TV chef by readers of a cooking magazine."

He laughed. "Even more undeserved."

"You're single and have been for some time."

"Yes, well ... what else?"

"You're thirty and you have two thousand friends on Facebook."

"Well, that's all true. Or so they tell me."

"I also watched some clips online."

"And you're still talking to me? Shocking. I think we need to question your judgement."

96

I laughed. "No, it was excellent. Michelin star-award stuff."

"This isn't very fair, now you know all this about me and I know so little about you."

"Well, whatever you'd like to know, just ask."

"Do you want to do something?"

"What, now?" I looked at Sian's fancy clock - it was getting on for 8pm.

"Well, it is Saturday night, we could be wild and go out late."

I laughed. "Come here, if you like," I told him, "but I warn you, I'm in my pyjamas."

"Oh I don't want to intrude. Tomorrow, maybe?"

"No, really," I said, feeling lonely and in desperate need of some company. "Come over. Please." I cursed the pleading tone my voice.

"Are you sure?"

"Yes. Really."

I gave him Sian's address.

"Okay that's smashing, you're just around the corner, I'll be there in ten minutes."

I rushed around tidying things up and putting a little makeup on, and had just changed into my best pyjamas when the door bell rang.

"Hi," he said, holding a bottle of red wine up. That same nervous smile. He was better looking than I'd remembered and, I realised, he'd lost a lot of weight since the video I'd watched.

"Hi," I said, resisting the urge to kiss him and drag him to my bedroom as I closed the door behind us. I grabbed some glasses from the kitchen and we went through to the living room where he poured us some wine.

"Help yourself to pizza," I said, gesturing to the now cold ham and pineapple sitting on the coffee table.

"Thanks. This place is amazing."

"Comes with the job. Nice, huh?" I sipped some of the

wine.

"So, where were we on the phone?" he said, looking nervous again. He'd sat down at the other end of the sofa to me. Something was different and I realised he wasn't wearing his glasses. I wondered if he'd put contacts in for me, just as I'd put make up on for him. I tucked my feet under me and looked at him again, wondering if he might be the next big love of my life.

"I said you could ask me anything you wanted," I said feeling strangely confident in the presence of his nervous energy. I just hoped he wouldn't question me about Ewan and lead me into a mess of tears, runny mascara and confessions about the pain I was still suffering.

"Okay, life story. Spare me no detail. We have all night," he said, grinning his cute grin. We locked eyes for a moment longer than necessary and I thought he might move closer and kiss me but he didn't. We just looked at each other and then he smiled, looked down and took a bite of his pizza.

"This is good, did you make it?"

"Yes. I love to cook. Nothing like your standards, I'm sure."

"It's really very nice."

"My friend Sabina gave me the recipe. She's Italian."

"Okay, so tell me more. Tell me about you."

"Life story. Right. Okay. Well. I was born," I said, smiling, "and my parents are pretty normal."

"Brothers, sisters?" he asked.

"I - well, yes. A sister."

"Me too."

"Really? The internet said you had a brother."

He laughed. "Contrary to popular belief, the internet is not the source of all knowledge."

"You have a little something," I said, leaning forward, "just there." I took a piece of cheese from his shirt and put it on the plate. I hesitated for a second, just a few inches from his face.

"Thank you," he said. His breath smelt of the wine. I

looked into his eyes, barely able to make out his pupils they were so dark. He swallowed, looking panicked.

"Relax. Don't move," I said, taking the plate from him and putting it on the floor.

I leant in slowly and kissed him gently at first. His lips were soft and he put his arms around my back and pulled me in closer. It was slow and heavenly, but then his lips became firmer and suddenly we both lost all control and it was all lips and tongues and pulling off of clothes, but then I remembered where we were and whose couch we were on.

"Can we, just," I said, trying to pull away from the kissing, "go upstairs?"

He nodded, grabbed his glass and the half empty bottle, whilst I grabbed my glass and he followed me up the stairs to my room, making a comment about my "cute bum" as we walked up the stairs which made me giggle. I switched my bedside lamp on and pulled the curtains shut. I turned to look at him, his shirt undone, and behind him I could see my reflection in the mirror; the strap had come down on my pyjama top and half my breast was showing.

I giggled. So did he.

"Do you just want to sit down a minute?" he said, gesturing to the bed.

I nodded and pulled my pyjama top straight, covering myself up. The moment had passed. I cursed myself for worrying about Sian's sofa and wished we were having wonderful, passionate, urgent sex right now on top of all those lovely cushions. Or even on the cream rug.

I sat down on the bed, my back against the head board, my feet out in front of me and he sat beside me in the same position. I moved a little closer so our thighs were almost touching and picked up my wine. We both took a sip.

"My sister. She's ... she's missing." I blurted out.

Way to kill the moment, Izzy. Well done. I don't know why I said it. It just popped out. It was partly because I'd

99

mentioned I had a sister and it felt deceitful, somehow, not to have told the whole story. I'd never spoken about it in detail with Ewan and somehow I wanted Jason to know from the off.

"What?" Jason looked horrified. He put his wine down straight away and turned towards me.

"She went missing," I said, "when she was fourteen."

"How old were you?"

"Twelve," I said, cursing myself. The mood would be dead now. As dead as Helen, probably.

"Izzy, that's just awful! I'm so sorry. What happened?"

"I don't know ... we can only assume she's dead."

"Izzy," he shook his head, put his arm around me gently and pulled me closer. He planted soft, gentle kisses all over my head and then moved down to my neck. Slowly, he pulled my top over my head and I pulled his shirt off. It was much slower, less intense than before, but more romantic somehow.

Now, sex with Ewan had been ... just that: sex. It was passionate, but also, I realised now, it was all about him. With Jason ... we *made love*. He was all about me. I felt like I was the centre of the universe; a goddess he wished to serve and please. And oh my God, his tongue. It was like he'd read a guidebook or something on perfect oral pleasure. Maybe he had.

Afterwards, I almost cried as he held me there. We lay in silence for a long time with my head on his chest. I could hear his heart beating, fast at first, and then slowing down.

"Sorry if that was insensitive of me," he said, out of the blue.

"It wasn't," I said, smiling. "It was perfect."

"I'm so sorry about your sister," he said quietly.

"Me too."

We lay there for a little longer. I was almost drifting off to sleep when he spoke again.

"Izzy, I really enjoyed this evening."

I leaned up and kissed him again, and then fell asleep on his chest.

I woke up the following morning in an empty bed and smiled at the memory of the previous night. Jason had been so gentle, so romantic. Everything about his presence made me smile. I sat up, pulling the duvet around me as I realised I was naked and cold. His socks were still on my bedroom floor, as was his shirt. So he was still here. I grinned.

"Good morning," he said, pushing my door open a second later with his foot. I watched him, wearing only his trousers, bring me breakfast in bed. He'd prepared poached eggs on toast and put a single rose from the garden into a tumbler of water.

He climbed into bed beside me and we shared the eggs.

"This is delicious," I told him.

"Thank you. I like cooking," he said, dipping a bit of toast into the yoke.

"Well, you're good at it. You should be a chef."

"Now there's an idea."

"I saw you've met Prince Charles. Impressive," I said, nudging him in the ribs with my elbow.

"Yes, albeit briefly. It really isn't as glamorous as it looks. Most of the time, I'm just in the kitchen. Sweating in my whites."

"You're very down-to-earth."

"Thank you. And I'm flattered. About the googling."

I blushed and ate some more eggs.

"Do you mind if I ask you about your sister?" he said as I sipped orange juice. "If you don't want to talk about her, that's fine."

"Sure," I said, a little nervous.

"Do you think about her a lot?"

"On and off," I admitted. "Sometimes I can't think of anything but her, and I think I'll go crazy if I don't find out what happened."

He nodded, taking another mouthful of egg.

"Otherwise, I just accept and get on with my life. But it's like there's this constant, empty hole inside me."

"I get it," he said. "It's like she's a part of you and that part is missing. You can't get closure because you don't know what happened."

"That's exactly it."

Somehow, he'd got me already; more than Ewan had. We had already talked about Helen more than I had with Ewan. This is going to be something serious, I realised. He was going to give me what I'd needed from Ewan, right from the start. He was going to be committed and open and talkative. Don't mess it up, I told myself.

The morning continued much the same way. We got to know each other. We shared stories, anecdotes, likes and dislikes, ideas and plans. He told me about his restaurant and I told him about my love of the Swiss Alps. I quizzed him about the celebrities he'd met and he asked me about what'd gone wrong with Ewan. And it didn't even hurt too much when I told him. It was refreshing, to talk so much and to really get to know a person, when Ewan had always been a slight mystery to me; I could never tell what he was thinking. Somehow, I felt I knew Jason better than Ewan already.

My stomach grumbled. We'd been talking for hours and I realised it was lunch time already.

"I guess I'm hungry," I said, blushing.

"Let's get showered and go out someplace. My treat."

His nervousness suddenly gone, he pulled me out of bed and into the shower, where he made me feel like the centre of the universe again. Seriously, he would get a Michelin star for sex; in fact he'd get several. Then, after a string of calls I had to receive and make on behalf of Sian, who was having a mini-crisis in Berlin, he took me for lunch and we talked even more, until, eventually, it was time to say goodbye.

"I'll call you," he said, looking nervous again. "If that's

okay?"

"Of course it is," I said, kissing him firmly on the lips.

"Wow," said Amber on the phone after he'd walked off. "It all sounds so ... romantic."

"We could just talk all day long," I told her dreamily. "He wants to know my opinions and he gives me choices. It's quite refreshing."

"Much healthier."

"What do you mean?"

"You let Ewan lead. Now you're in control and making your own decisions. Jason sounds much, much better for you. The Ewan thing, it wasn't healthy, Izzy. I worried about you, always liking the same things, always doing what he wanted. I think Jason will be more ... normal."

I laughed.

"I'm serious," she said. I realised she might just be right.

Chapter Seventeen

Monday. Five days before my wedding day.

I wasn't sure I'd be able to get through a working day with any level of concentration, but somehow I did. Sian was in New York at some sort of important conference and the managing director of one of her companies kept calling me and leaving urgent messages for her to get in touch. I spent most of the day trying to track her down until eventually she answered her mobile.

"Hi Izzy."

"Hi, I've been trying to get hold of you for hours."

"Sorry, I met an old friend last night. Didn't go back to my own room. Don't tell a soul."

She knew I wouldn't, anyway. After all this time she'd come to trust me, or at least I hoped she did. She'd admitted before that she didn't have time for a boyfriend but had a few men in a few different cities which she met regularly to 'satisfy her needs', which sounded like booty calls to me. She wasn't the type to be in a relationship, being too independent and head-strong. In all the years I'd worked for her I'd organised hundreds of dinner dates with men she knew, liked and respected, but none of them had ever lasted more than a few weeks.

"Of course not. Edmund needs you to call him in the office urgently."

"Yes I've got some missed calls. I'll get in touch."

"Great."

"How was your hen night?"

"Fun. Lots of fun. I saw Ewan and Jason, weird huh?"

"Who's Ewan?"

"The one I went travelling with."

"Oh, yes. Well, and Jason, how's he?"

"He's good. He seemed happy. He was with a thin, blonde supermodel."

"Bitch."

This is why I loved Sian, she always said what I needed to hear.

"Yeah, well."

"Did you book my flight for Friday?"

She was flying in for my wedding. I was quite honoured. She'd cancelled her plans just to be there.

"Yes. All booked. I've emailed the information."

"Thanks. And how are you feeling? Nervous? Excited?"

"Yes, both."

"Well, I've been to lots of weddings and seen lots of friends get nervous and excited leading up to the day, then when it arrives you have some champagne and it's just excitement and then it's all over in a flash. You'll be fine."

"Thanks Sian."

"Honestly. Divorce him if it doesn't work out. It's no big deal."

We hung up a few minutes later and I spent the rest of the day shopping online for her mother's birthday. I decided to go for a voucher for a spa weekend and sorted it all out.

The previous year I'd sent her flowers, chocolates, some goodies from Lush, with a voucher to dine at Gordon Ramsey's restaurant. Sian's mother had called me and said "Thank you, dear, I know you organised this." I'd protested, but it was true and she knew it.

Just as I finished work, I heard the front door open and I came out of my office to see all six foot of handsome lovely Greg. As I looked at the beaming smile on his face I hoped I'd realise how much I wanted to marry him because I couldn't break his heart.

"God, I've missed you," he said, wrapping me in his arms.

"I missed you too," I lied. I was the worst fiancée in the world.

Chapter Eighteen

My time with Jason was wonderful. He was sweet and romantic and cute and we had plenty in common; he'd show me how to cook extravagant and delicious meals and we both liked going for long walks, where we'd talk and bond and get to know each other, perhaps better than I knew anyone else.

"Wow, Jason Edwards," Jade said when I told her over the phone that I was seeing someone.

"I'd never heard of him," I told her. She laughed.

"Maybe that's better," she said. Fred was on my lap and he stretched before closing his eyes, putting his head down to sleep.

"I've eaten in his restaurant. The food was amazing."

"He's cooking for me tonight."

"Wow, lucky you."

"So how's Rupert?"

Now, Jade, my longest friend, my loving cousin, the closest thing I had to a sister, was the most kind, caring, friendly person you could ever meet. But she was terrible when it came to men. She was a school teacher and this suited her perfectly. She was a natural with children, and yearned for one of her own, one day. But I didn't know how that'd ever happen because she always fell for the wrong men. You know the types: the commitment-phobes who sleep with you a few times and then move on. She loves those guys. It's like they have a beacon calling out for naive, easy women and she was always first in the line to pull her panties down and submit. She was always first to be crying bitterly two weeks later, too.

"Rupert is lovely. But I haven't heard from him in three days. I don't want to crowd him."

I'd given her a lecture about crowding a month earlier. She was always texting her latest flame. She was too clingy.

We chatted some more and arranged to meet up soon. I promised to introduce her to Jason, if it continued to go well. After the call was over I made myself some lunch but it wasn't until I looked at my phone and saw the text from my Mum that I realised.

Thirteen years today. Love you honey x

Had thirteen years really passed already? I've had more years without Helen than I'd had with her? I closed my eyes and pictured her face. I wondered how similar we would have been now, as adults. What would she think of Jason?

By the time I'd run through Sian's 'to do' list for the day, it was gone five and I only had an hour until I was supposed to be at Jason's house for dinner. I dithered over what to wear for a long time before calling Amber who told me to keep it casual. "Save your best outfits for dates out, not dates in," she told me.

So I settled for my best pair of blue jeans and a black low-cut top Sian had bought me for my birthday; she'd laughed when she gave it to me and said I was the only person in the world she had to buy gifts for now; I was her personal shopper when it came to everyone else. It seemed harsh somehow, that she'd pick out a gift for me but not her own mother. But I was grateful. I loved the top and it seemed to fit me perfectly.

"Hello," Jason said as he opened his front door. He looked nervous, and again I found it adorable.

He kissed me lightly on the cheek, as a woman with gorgeous wavy blonde hair came into the hall. I felt a surge of jealousy and wondered who she was and what she was doing here.

"I'll be getting off then, Chef," she said, nodding at Jason and pulling her coat on.

"This is Chloe," he explained, "my sous chef. Chloe, this is Izzy."

"I've heard a lot about you," said Chloe smiling at me with lovely blue eyes. "We were just having a meeting about a frustrating member of staff. Have fun." She stepped out into the cold night, leaving us standing in the hall. I felt myself relax.

"I've not said that much about you," Jason said, blushing. "May I take your coat?"

He hung it up on a hook next to his and I followed him into his living room. It was simple: cream-coloured walls; no pictures or paintings; an old, faded green sofa; an ancient television; a large, old book case; and a worn coffee table.

"I haven't redecorated or refurbished in years," he said, apologetically.

"It's nice," I told him. It didn't feel like much of a home, somehow. Just a room with some old furniture.

"A lot of this stuff is from my parents. They gave me odd bits and pieces when I first moved in."

"It's nice," I said again. Not what I was expecting, though. It was smaller than I'd pictured, and just so ... old fashioned. Surely he earned enough to fancy it all up a bit?

"This is the kitchen," he said, leading me into a small room at the back of the house. "I've done this up, since moving in. It was a state when I bought it." The kitchen was much better; black marble worktops; grey tiles; an oak dining table. There were two empty, used mugs next to the sink and a pan simmering on the stove.

"Something smells good," I said, sitting down at the table.

"You look lovely," Jason said suddenly. I looked at him again. He looked panicked.

"What's wrong?" I asked. "You seem ... wired."

"To be honest I'm just nervous. I haven't ... well, you're the first girl, well, woman, I've dated in a long time."

"I see," I said, standing and wrapping my arms around his waist. "Lucky me."

I kissed him and he almost resisted at first, but kissed me back and I felt his shoulders relax.

As I pulled away he grinned and went to stir the dinner.

"I really like you, Jason," I said, suddenly wanting to declare myself; to reassure him somehow.

"Good," he said, smiling and looking down at the tiled floor. "I really like you, too."

"Then what's to worry about?" I asked. He shrugged and starting making small talk, asking me about my day.

After a delicious dinner consisting of chicken and herbs, a red wine jus, fondant potatoes and perfectly cut carrots followed by a white chocolate cheesecake with a raspberry sauce, we moved into the living room. We sat together on the sofa, a glass of wine each, and I congratulated Jason on his cooking.

"Really, it's no big deal," he said.

"It was wonderful."

"Well, thank you."

"Do you mind if I ask another question about your sister?"

"Sure."

"What do you really, honestly think happened to her?"

I swallowed. No one had ever asked me this before. How could that be? Were they avoiding the subject? Did they think it'd make me upset?

"I think she's dead. I think someone took her, for whatever twisted reason, and she's dead. She has to be dead. I just hope she didn't suffer. I hope she wasn't raped or anything like that." I shuddered.

He nodded. "I'm sorry."

"No, it's fine. It sounds strange but I like to talk about it, now and then."

"You're very ... inspiring. I admire your bravery."

110

I shrugged. "I owe it to Helen, to live life to the fullest."

"You're amazing, Izzy," he said, smiling. I swallowed hard to keep from shedding tears.

"Well, I want to enjoy all the things that Helen never got to. Like the simple things, you know? Having a job and having fun and all this ... you know, the dating and just having a boyfriend, falling for someone..."

I stopped myself and looked at Jason. His face was slightly alarmed, but then he relaxed, grinned, kissed me on the head and stood up.

"Coffee?" he offered.

"Yes, please," I said, feeling my face turn hot with embarrassment. He went out to the kitchen and I pulled my phone from my pocket to text Amber.

Hey I think I am falling in love with Jason! x

She replied just as he was coming back with our drinks.

Of course you are! So dinner was yummy I take it? Ha ha x

I woke up the next morning and blinked a few times, trying to remember where I was, and then realised I could hear Jason breathing gently beside me. I glanced around his room; there was a small pile of books in the corner. The wardrobe doors looked like they needed replacing and the walls were just bare and white.

"Sounds like the whole place is crying out for a woman's touch," Amber would tell me later.

I slowly got out of bed, found his shirt from the night before and put it on over my underwear. It came down to my knees. I'd always wanted to do this: wear a boyfriend's shirt. I snuck out to make tea and heard a gentle knock at the front door. I opened it a cracked and peered out. Chloe was standing there in her coat. She raised her eyebrows when she saw me. She smiled and held up an envelope and I noticed she had a wedding ring on, which made me feel less paranoid.

"Oh hi, Izzy! I am so sorry," she said. "Just needed to drop this off for Jason on my way to work and I saw a shadow behind the door so thought I'd say good morning."

"Good morning," I said, self-conscious about my bare legs and messy hair. "Jason is still asleep."

"Would you mind giving him this?" she handed me the envelope. "It's just a summary of some new ideas we talked about."

"Of course."

"That'd be great, thank you." Chloe didn't move. "So you and Jason, huh? Seems to be going pretty well?"

"Yes," I said, unsure where this was leading.

"I've never seen him so ... cheerful," she said, smiling. I realised that, now I wasn't being paranoid and jealous, I quite liked her.

"Well, that's good, right?" I said, trying to smooth down my hair with my hands.

"Yes." She grinned, and I couldn't help but grin back. "Well I'd better be off. Have a lovely day." She turned and started off down the street.

"You too, bye," I called after her.

I went to the kitchen and searched for mugs and tea bags and made us each a cup to take upstairs. Jason opened his eyes as I came in.

"Good morning," I said, smiling. I made him cheerful. Something about that made me feel happy.

"Morning," he grinned, sitting up. "How can you look so beautiful in my shirt?"

I handed him his tea and got into bed beside him.

"Chloe just dropped off an envelope - it's on the table downstairs. She says I make you cheerful."

"You do."

Chapter Nineteen

Meeting Jason's parents was quite different to meeting Ewan's. First of all, I didn't wait for quite so long; we'd only been seeing each other for about a month. Second of all, I didn't get lectured about sewing or cooking, or have to look at quite so much porcelain.

That I was invited to even meet his parents seemed amazing to me. Ewan had taken a year to do this; but then everything about Jason was more open, serious, and fast moving than it had been with Ewan. We were already in a serious relationship, when I'd never really felt that Ewan was very serious about me. I sometimes wondered why; what it was about them or about their makeup or their history that made them behave so differently. Sometimes I wondered if it was me; if I was just older and wiser and more mature and had therefore picked a boyfriend who was more the settling-down type this time.

Jeremy and Magda lived in a beautiful house in a village near Cambridge and they were, as I expected, a little posh but very welcoming. They had a vast collection of garden gnomes, which made me laugh, but that was it on the ornament front. They also had a little brown spaniel called Winston who took to me straight away and spent the majority of our visit perched on my lap.

"Well, that went well," Jason told me on our way home.

"You really think so?"

"Definitely. They liked you. Especially Winston."

"I liked them too."

Jason squeezed my thigh. Now was the time, I decided. I'd

been thinking about it a lot lately and finally wanted to tell someone else; someone who might understand.

"I've always wanted," I began, "a house by the sea. With a blue front door."

"Sounds quaint," he said, looking over his shoulder as he overtook a slower car.

"It was Helen, actually, who gave me the idea."

"How so?"

"A few weeks before she ... disappeared she told me she was going to get married one day, and have a cottage by the sea with a blue front door and a golden retriever. A fourteen year old's dream, and chances are by now she'd have had many more plans for the future, but I just figured ... as she'll never get that then I should do it for her. One day I'll find a house by the sea. Paint the door blue. Adopt a dog. Maybe that sounds stupid..."

"No, not at all. I think you should do it. I think it'd bring you some sort of inner peace."

"One day, then." I almost carried on. I almost said, one day let's do that together. But I didn't, because I didn't want to get carried away.

After meeting Jason's parents I began to meet his friends. And he had lots of them. Ewan had never kept in touch with old friends and hadn't seemed to be bothered about making new ones. Jason had tonnes.

There were his old school friends who I met at a wedding. Some of them I liked, others not so much. He'd gone to a private school and a couple of them were a bit flash with their cash. Others were more down-to-earth.

Then there was his best friend James, who he'd met at college. James seemed to be the eternal bachelor; different date every week, no intention of settling down. He was funny and nice to me from the off. He'd come round on a night Jason wasn't working with DVDs and a freshly made dessert which was always amazing, and tell us about the women he saw and the joys of working as a pastry chef for some French chef/God-wannabe.

Most of all I liked Chloe, Jason's sous chef. Jason told me he hired her straight out of college and she was the most creative chef he'd ever had working for him. She worked hard and was now his deputy - his number two - and he trusted her completely. Sometimes I'd go to the restaurant and chat with her on her breaks while I waited for Jason. Her passion for food was obvious. She talked about herbs and spices in a way that made me want to experiment too. Occasionally she'd treat me to a taste of a recipe she was working on; it was always delicious.

Now and then, usually on a Monday when the restaurant was closed, we'd go out for a meal with Chloe and her husband Harry. Chloe and Jason would make lots of comments about the food and Harry and I would roll our eyes at each other. Then the men would talk about cars or sport so Chloe and I would talk fashion, books and so on.

Jason got on well with Amber, too. She and Tristan would come over for food and wine and we'd talk about that fateful day in Hyde Park that had set us all up together.

Over the course of several months, we merged our lives together easily and seamlessly. It was effortless. One day I realised I hardly ever thought of Ewan anymore. I no longer worried or cared particularly where he was, or what he was doing. My life was here, in London, organising Sian's life, being a part of Jason's life, and making my own choices rather than blindly following someone.

Chapter Twenty

It took me a while to introduce Jason to my parents. Partly because my mum kept asking me to. I wasn't trying to be mean, but I knew she loved him on TV. When I told her who he was, she'd gone all star-struck and giddy and asked a bunch of questions about what he was like and when they could meet, and did I think he'd sign her cook book? I had a feeling the first meeting would be embarrassing and so avoided it for a while.

Then one weekend I decided it was time. I texted my mum beforehand and told her to 'be cool' but she didn't reply which made me nervous, although she didn't always have her phone turned on, or charged, so who knew if she had even seen the message. Jason drove us to their house. We knocked on the door and I took a deep breath. Then my father appeared and there was no going back.

My dad shook hands with Jason, who was as nervous as ever, and then my mother appeared behind him.

"Wow, you're that chef. From TV!" said Mum. "Izzy, you didn't tell us! I love your show!"

I had told her, of course, but she obviously thought I wouldn't want him to know that. I smiled anyway, proud of him and he smiled at my mum and told her "Hello." Jade came bounding along the corridor and introduced herself. Turned out she'd invited herself over so she could meet him, too.

"So, you're a chef?" asked my dad, leading him into the living room and gesturing for him to sit down on the sofa. I sat beside him.

"He owns a restaurant," chimed in Jade, sitting down opposite us with a big smile, "and he has a Michelin star, don't you?" she giggled and blushed.

"Ah yes, yes I do," said Jason, also reddening.

Mum took an order for cups of tea. I was surprised to find my dad and Jason fall into easy conversation. My dad had a book on the side about the war and Jason obviously wanted to latch onto something he felt comfortable talking about. Half an hour later they were still discussing something to do with the evacuation of Dunkirk whilst I was listening to Jade and Mum's raptures about Jason's work. I was grateful that my dad was keeping Jason occupied while they got over the excitement of meeting him. It was nice to see my mum so elated and cheerful.

We moved into the dining room where Mum served a glorious roast dinner with all the trimmings, and we all fell into easy, idle chatter. As I helped clear away the plates, Jade took Jason back into the living room and started asking for cookery tips. I helped with the washing up and then went to join them.

"He signed my cookbook," Jade beamed, holding up a book with Jason's photo on the front. I had bought it myself a few weeks before, then hidden it in my office drawer so he wouldn't know.

Jason smiled as he turned to my mother, holding her own book and pen out for him. I felt myself swell with pride again. Here was my boyfriend signing autographs for my family. He might not be A-list famous but it was still pretty cool. And who wanted an A-lister as a boyfriend anyway? Too much attention and publicity. But this - this was pretty cool.

"I really liked your dad," said Jason, as we drove home.

"Thank you. He's great isn't he?"

"Yes. And Jade's a pretty big fan of the show," he laughed. "She said something interesting when we were alone."

I cringed. Jade loved to embarrass me. Mum had told me she'd invited herself over as soon as she'd heard Jason was coming over.

"Oh yes?"

"She was pointing out various faces in some photo frames on the wall."

"Did you see Helen?"

"Yes. She was pretty."

"Yes," I sighed, "she was. So what did Jade say?"

"She said that there was still hope for Helen."

"Hope?" I said, surprised that Jade still held out. We never spoke of Helen anymore.

"Yes. She said she still believes she might be out there somewhere."

I sighed. "I didn't know she still felt that. So does my mother, I think."

We were silent for a while. I couldn't comprehend it; couldn't understand why anyone thought Helen could be alive. They were sensible, educated people, how could they come to that frame of mind? My only answer was that they were in denial. I wasn't sure if I'd rather be that way myself: blissfully ignorant and holding out hope for something that would never be; or be in this reality, where I knew she was dead and never coming back.

We got home and sat down for a cup of tea.

"Now", said Jason, "I have something to invite you to."

"Okay."

"It's a television award thing. A television producer friend of mine gave me a couple of tickets. Lots of minor celebrities. Champagne. I thought you might find it fun. A chance to dress up."

"Oh wow. Yes. Of course I'll come!"

Chapter Twenty-One

Two days before the award ceremony Jason had invited me to, I received an email:

To: Izzy Swan
From: Ewan Harris
Subject: I miss you...

> *...I'm sorry it's taken me this long to get in touch. Are you back in London? Can I call you? I should have told you more often that I love you. I regret that, now. I'm sorry. Please get in touch.*
> *E xx*

I stared at the screen feeling conflicted. Why had he waited so long? How I'd yearned for him to tell me he loved me, over and over. How I'd yearned for this email when I'd first got back to England. How I'd missed the way he made me feel. He had been my whole world.

"Bit bloody late!" said Amber when I read the email out to her.

"I know. Do you think I should reply? Speak to him?"

"No! What about Jason?"

"I know, I just feel mean not replying at all. Maybe we could be friends."

"Izzy, seriously? It's not going to happen. He said he regrets not saying 'I love you'. How can you be friends?"

"I don't know—"

"Listen, you love Jason. Right?"

"I think so."

"It's too late for Ewan, right?"

"You're right. It is."

"Then why would you even consider replying?"

I deleted the email without responding, closed my laptop and went out to meet Jade for lunch and shopping. We had to find me an outfit.

"Now," she said, squinting her bright blue eyes at the menu as we sat in the restaurant. "Jason is wonderful. Don't screw this one up. Even if he wants to move to Australia."

I laughed.

"Right, okay," I said, watching her newly dyed blonde hair fall into her face. She swept it away and tucked it behind her ear. "He told me what you said about Helen."

Her eyes shot up and looked at me in alarm. The waiter appeared. We both ordered crab salad and white wine. As soon as he walked away, I continued.

"Do you really think that?"

"My mum does. She's kind of convinced me over the years."

Aunt Ruth? Really? She seemed so sensible.

"Does my mum, too, do you think?"

"Yes, they talk about it all the time, apparently."

Mum had always been close to her sister-in-law, but I somehow couldn't imagine them sitting there, talking about Helen. Mum never spoke about Helen, or not to me anyway.

"Your dad," Jade said, "told your mum a long time ago to let it go. So she doesn't speak of it in front of him. But she still hopes. How could she not? There's no evidence to suggest she's dead."

I took this in for a second. Surely they couldn't believe that she was alive?

"But where is she then?"

"Abducted. Brain-washed. In another country, perhaps. Your mum hopes somehow she'll remember and come back."

"She was fourteen, not four! Of course she'd remember."

"Well, I don't think your mum will think she's dead until there's evidence to prove it."

I wasn't sure what I wanted to do first. Talk to my mum, or my dad. I wanted her to explain why or how she could think that but I wasn't sure I could handle hearing what she said. And I wanted to tell my dad, to find out what he thought of all this. Yet the topic somehow remained closed, trapped in that old house, in that old life that we had moved on from.

Most of all, I realised, I wanted to be with Jason and tell him how I felt.

"Now," Jade said, as we stood up to go, "let's find you an amazing dress for this shindig. Jason called me and asked me to surprise you. He gave me some cash."

"Oh my God. Really?"

Jason had never mentioned how much he earned, and I never wanted to ask him. He owned his own home but he didn't seem to go on many holidays or spend much money at all, apart from a few fancy meals out. I'd wondered a few times if he was just saving his earnings, maybe for a rainy day ... or to buy his new girlfriend a posh frock.

"He said it'd be a surprise and he figured I'd want to come with you."

Jade had always been into fashion. She always looked good, always found clothes that suited her and always wore a lot of colour, as opposed to my daily black and grey. No, actually I did have one dark green jumper. And some bright stripy socks, but they were both gifts from Jade, anyway. She startled me when she pointed out a dress that was my month's salary.

"Really, that's too generous," I began.

"Jason's orders," she told me.

I tried about a dozen dresses on before Jade said: "This is it. This is the one."

It was a purple dress with thin straps, very simple, which showed off my curves, had a plunging neckline and apparently was created by a very important designer, according to Jade.

She picked me out a bag, shoes and jewellery while I got dressed and told me she'd come round to help with my hair and makeup.

By the time she was through with me I felt like a minor celebrity myself.

"Beautiful. Stunning!" Jason said as Jade led me into Sian's living room.

"Very handsome," I told him, admiring his tuxedo. "And thank you for paying for the dress, it was very thoughtful."

"You're very welcome."

"You both look gorgeous. Are you nervous?" Jade asked.

"Yes," we both said. We all laughed as the door bell rang.

The rest of the night passed by in a blur. The car took us to the venue where we walked down a red carpet, feeling very important. A few members of the press called to Jason but he ignored them, guiding me into the building with his hand on the small of my back. We entered a room and I started looking all around, catching the faces of a few people I recognised. I turned back to Jason and saw him shaking hands with David Mitchell, who leaned in and said something into his ear. They both laughed and David moved on, while I stood there starstruck, thinking of all the episodes of *Peep Show* I'd enjoyed: and now, here I was, in the same room as one of the stars.

"You could've introduced me. I love that guy," I said. Jason winked and we found our seats on a table with some other television chefs I recognised. I managed to calm myself as he introduced me to a handful of minor celebrities, mostly comedians, actors and a few television presenters.

The awards were a little boring after that, to be honest. They seemed to have an award for everything you could think of. Jason whispered jokes to me now and then and held my hand throughout.

I suddenly realised that Jason knew people. He knew famous people. It hadn't really occurred to me before. The images I'd seen on the internet looked more like chance encounters, rather than people he knew. It felt glamorous for a while, especially when a soap actor came up and said they'd seen him on an episode of *Masterchef*, and appeared to be really impressed. I didn't even know he'd been on *Masterchef*. But the glamour wore off as the night wore on, and by the end I was quite happy to leave.

"I hope you enjoyed that," he said as we travelled back to his house in the back of the limo.

"I did," I said, squeezing his hand, "but it's not real is it? None of that is real. This is real." I leant in and kissed him.

"You're incredibly wise," he said, putting his arm around me.

Chapter Twenty-Two

Not long after that, Sabina came to stay with me for a week. I took some time off and we did all the touristy stuff. I dragged her all over London, showing her the sights, and we had a traditional British afternoon tea at a posh hotel near Buckingham Palace one afternoon. She loved it, and she loved Jason too. Whenever we were alone she'd repeatedly tell me how Ewan was fun and she liked him, but that Jason was the one who suited me best. I'd just laugh, but I knew she was right. I just didn't want to think or talk about Ewan. One evening we went to Jason's restaurant and Sabina said it was the best food she'd ever eaten. I agreed, but then I was biased, of course. At the end of the week I was sad to see her go and promised to come and visit her in Verona at some point.

A few days after she left, it was Jason and my six month anniversary. Somehow, in that half a year we'd been more intimate than Ewan and I had ever been, and I felt more sure of his feelings for me than I ever had been of Ewan's.

To celebrate our six months together, Jason pulled out all the stops. He closed the restaurant to the public and when I arrived, thinking we were just meeting there before going out someplace else, every table but one was filled with fresh flowers and candles. We sat at the empty table and a waiter appeared with a bottle of champagne.

"Thank you," I said as my glass was filled.

"Thanks, David," Jason said.

"No problem, Chef," came the reply.

"This is amazing. How romantic," I said, taking it all in.

"I'm glad you like it."

"I love that your team call you Chef."

I also loved the food. Chloe cooked us a superb meal and a live pianist arrived and played just for us.

It'd been incredibly romantic, and we'd returned home for champagne-induced love-making and fallen asleep in each other's arms. This was quite a novelty, having him home. More often than not he was at the restaurant in the evenings, so we spent time together during the day time, or at weekends when he pulled himself away to leave Chloe to run things.

The following morning, I looked at Jason's concerned face and felt nervous.

"What is it?" I asked him, watching him carefully as he came into his bedroom. His phone had rung and he said he needed to pop out for a minute. I busied myself getting dressed and didn't think much of it but by the time he came back it'd been almost half an hour. I was confused and now the look in his eyes was worrying me.

It'd been a wonderful morning up until this point. I'd woken up to see the sun pouring in through the blinds and Jason had held me there, telling me how beautiful I looked and I thought maybe we were about to partake in some delicious early-morning sex, until we were interrupted by his mobile.

"It's just a story in the paper," Jason said, pulling out one of the tabloids from behind his back. "I've never exactly attracted much attention before, but it seems someone saw us last night."

"What?" I asked, sitting up in bed and holding out my arms for the paper.

"Just … it's just media talk, okay? Try not to get upset."

"Just show me." I couldn't possibly imagine what could be so bad. Were they slating my dress, my haircut, what?

He turned to a page inside and held it out for me to see, and I realised immediately. There, right in front of me, was a photo of me and Helen, taken not long before she went missing. Next to that was a photo of Jason and me leaving the restaurant last night. He was looking at me intently and I was laughing. It would have been a great photo of us, in any other circumstances. I read the headline with horror.

'TV Chef Jason falls for missing girl's sister."

I continued reading the story, the first paragraph of which detailed how my sister had gone missing; how there had been a big search, but no trace had been found. I glanced up at Jason and back to the page.

"Take a deep breath," Jason told me. I ignored him.

The article then talked about the media speculation. Why didn't I know of any of this at the time? I didn't even consider that we'd been in the newspapers or that anyone knew who I was. My parents must have hidden the newspapers from me.

"I'm so sorry, Izzy," Jason said almost in a whisper. I read on.

And then the story was about me. About the tragedy of my life and how sad it all was. They had no idea about sadness. I looked at the journalist's name; Natalie Wright. I wanted to yell at her picture. What did she know about sadness, loss, pain, grief? Nothing - obviously. The article turned quite poetic towards the end. It was all about how I'd obviously found happiness with Jason and how an 'inside source' had revealed that Jason loved to cook for me.

"This is just outside!" I said, shocked. "They followed us here?"

Jason nodded sadly. I could feel the anger boiling up inside me.

'At least the smile on her face may bring her parents some consolation; one of their daughters did grow up.
Do you know anything about Izzy or Helen Swan? Email us.'

I stared at the images again for a few minutes. Helen's smiling face looking out at me; Jason and I looking like the perfect happy couple.

"Are you angry? Upset? Can I get you a cup of tea?" Jason asked quietly in a calm voice, sitting down next to me on the bed as I let the paper fall to my lap.

"I'm not sure, I'm just ... confused. Why is this of interest to anyone?"

"You know what these papers are like, Izzy."

"How did they know? How did they make this link?"

"It's not that hard. I guess they found out who you were easily enough."

My mobile started ringing in my bag. Jason went to reach for it.

"No," I said, throwing the paper on the floor, "I don't want to answer it."

He came and sat beside me on the bed and I leaned on his shoulder for a while, still bewildered that Helen, Jason, and I could make the news. The doorbell rang a couple of times but we ignored it. I couldn't understand this sudden interest. I felt for my parents; what must my mother be thinking? I was fairly sure that they didn't read the tabloids but surely one of their friends, or someone they knew, would spot it and tell them.

Jason rubbed my shoulder.

"You okay?"

"Yes."

We sat there for a while longer, with me wondering whether this would be good for Jason or not. All publicity was good publicity, right?

"Let's carry on with our day," I said after a while.

"Don't you want to talk about this?" Jason asked, looking concerned.

"Nothing to say is there really?" I said, deciding not to think about it.

So, we got showered and dressed. Jason made me eggs and

French toast which we ate in front of the TV. I had just about managed to push the whole thing to the back of my mind when the doorbell rang again. Jason got up and I heard him open the door, but he didn't appear to say anything. He came back in with an envelope in his hand.

"No one there?" I asked.

"No, just this," he said, holding up the envelope. "It's addressed to you."

I swallowed hard. Couldn't they leave me alone?

"Do you think they want to interview me or something? Because I'm not interested. I just want to be left alone."

"Do you want me to open it?"

"Sure," I said waving my hand. I picked up the remote and scrolled through the channels. I looked up again at Jason as I heard him take a piece of paper out of the envelope. His face went pale and he gulped.

"What?" I said, worried.

He shook his head lightly.

"Sick bastards," he said, walking quickly out of the living room and to the front door.

"What?" I asked, coming after him. He was in the street, looking up and down the road. I came out after him and reached out for the letter. He held it away.

"It doesn't matter," he said, walking back in and closing the door. He started to crumple the paper into a ball, heading straight for the kitchen to throw it in the bin.

"Don't, Jason," I said, "it's addressed to me. Show me."

"It's just some sicko, really, you don't need to see it," he said, but I held out my hand impatiently.

"Show me."

"Just don't let it get to you, because that's what they want."

"Jason!" I raised my voice. I'd never been angry with him before.

He held out the crumpled sheet.

I spread it out again and stared in disbelief. There, in the middle of the page in typed font it said:

'I know where your sister is.'

Chapter Twenty-Three

"I think this is probably from a fan of Jason's," said the police officer, "but we'll check it for prints and follow up what we can, just to be sure, okay?" She had a patronising tone which I didn't care much for. I wiped a tear from my cheek and nodded.

"I doubt I have any psycho fans," Jason said quietly. "And even if I did, how could anyone do this? It's just horrible."

After I'd seen the note I completely freaked out and started ranting about the fact that maybe Helen was alive. Then Jason called my parents and I started rambling in hysterics until my voice reached the pitch of some sort of demented cat. Dad had agreed it was some 'sick bastard' wanting to freak me out and I should just ignore it, but Mum suggested I call the police. I was frightened she'd latch on to some form of hope, but I was pretty sure there wasn't any. If someone knew where she was, why would they tell me about it?

"You do have fans," I told Jason. "I've seen them on Facebook talking about you."

"Perhaps there's someone with a bit of an obsession," the police officer continued, "and she just wants to scare Miss Swan."

Jason told me later he found this idea ridiculous. I didn't know what to think.

The rest of the day went by in a bit of a daze. Jason suggested we watch a DVD, so we curled up on the sofa together, forgetting the newspaper story and the note for a few hours. I didn't want to go home. I felt safe here with Jason, and the thought of returning home to Sian's empty house made me nervous. I said as much when we were clearing away our dinner plates.

"You can stay here as long as you want," Jason told me, "or I'll come stay with you. Really, you've no need to be frightened."

I nodded, smiling, hoping my face didn't give away the horrific images in my mind of his crazed, obsessed fans coming to lynch me. Or Helen's murderer coming to finish me off, too.

The next day we went back to my place and I called Sian to tell her what had been going on.

"This is just awful," she said, but she sounded distracted.

"Well, it's no big deal. I just feel a little vulnerable, so I was wondering if it was alright if Jason stayed with me a few days," I said, biting my bottom lip.

"Of course, no problem. You didn't have to ask."

"Thanks, Sian."

I enjoyed Jason staying with me. He brought home meals from the restaurant for me most nights. He spoke to the police a couple of times, but they hadn't found anything and no more notes were delivered. We never did find out who sent it. Things seemed pretty normal again. That is, until Sian returned home.

Jason had gone back to his place, not wanting to intrude when Sian arrived. I'd stocked the fridge and planned various meetings, a dentist appointment and even scheduled time for Sian to visit her parents during her three week stay in the UK. I was looking forward to seeing her. We spoke nearly every day anyway, and I felt we'd become friends. She usually turned up with a bunch of 'old' clothes for me to inherit, a bottle of perfume or, the last time, a Tiffany bracelet. She treated me more like her best friend than her PA.

"So, darling," Sian said, sipping coffee and tucking her legs underneath her, "you're still enjoying the job?"

"Very much," I answered truthfully, smiling and taking a sip of my own coffee.

"Great. I think we work well together." She smiled but it seemed fake, like she was apprehensive.

"Is something wrong?" I asked.

"Not as such. It's just the living arrangement. I've decided to sell the house. You see I'm hardly ever here and it seems pointless, really. I'm going to buy a place in New York, and maybe just keep an apartment here. I want to free up some capital for other projects."

"Right," I said, not sure if I was homeless and jobless, or just the former.

"I'm sorry; I know it's worked out well, like this. But what I propose is this: I'll double your salary. Which means you'll have plenty more income to fund your own place, and I don't have to feel guilty about throwing you out."

"Double? Really, Sian!"

"I insist. After all, I expect it to sell fast, which leaves you homeless. Now, do you think you could you arrange for estate agents to view the place, and what not?"

"Of course," I said, thrilled at the salary increase but saddened that I'd no longer be living in this beautiful place.

"Fabulous. Now, I'd better get ready to go visit my parents. What time did you tell them I'd arrive?"

"Two o'clock."

I remembered the conversation I'd had with Sian's mother. It seemed as ludicrous to her as it did to me; to be arranging to see your daughter through her personal assistant. Still, she was polite enough. "We'll be here waiting, my dear," she'd said.

I felt edgy for a while, after she'd gone. My first thought was: why don't Jason and I move in together? But I didn't want to approach it; I didn't know how to even start the conversation. Somehow, Ewan had made me afraid of rushing anything with a man, even one who was as attentive as Jason and had made it clear he was crazy about me. I went to the

132

restaurant that evening with Amber, and after she'd got a cab home, I waited for him and sat chatting with Harry, who'd turned up to collect Chloe.

"You seem nervous," Harry said after a little while.

"No, I'm fine," I told him, hoping Jason wouldn't notice as well. I wasn't sure how he'd react. Harry continued making small talk, telling me about his job and making a joke about the long hours the restaurant demanded of Chloe and Jason and then, finally, they both appeared and we left just after midnight. After hugging our friends goodbye, we drove back to Sian's house.

"Goodnight, babe," Jason said as we reached the front door.

"Aren't you going to come in?"

"I'm so tired, do you mind if I don't?"

"Oh, okay," I said, trying to hide my disappointment. "I'll speak to you tomorrow."

I kissed him goodnight and went into the house. Fred was hungry so I gave him some tuna, made myself a hot chocolate and went to sip it in bed with my book.

My phone beeped. A text message Jason:

Everything alright? x

I replied. *Yes.*

I knew that putting one word would only highlight that no, it was not alright. He took the bait.

Jason: What is it?
Me: Just wanted to talk to you about something tonight. It's fine, we can do it tomorrow.
Jason: It is good or bad?
Me: Good.
Jason: You want me to come over?
I hesitated. He had said he was tired.
Me: Yes. Please.

Ten minutes later I was blurting out that Sian wanted to

133

sell the house and that I didn't want to live alone, and how we were so happy together that I thought maybe he might like to move in together?

"You want to move into my house?" he said awkwardly, shifting about in his seat.

"Well, yes, or we could look for a new place. Whatever you think."

He looked away, frowning. I wanted the ground to swallow me up.

"Don't you think it's a bit soon?"

"Well..."

You obviously do, I almost said.

"Just forget it," I said, pulling at my pyjama sleeve and attempting to keep a straight face. I really wanted to stick my bottom lip out and sulk like a child.

"It's just a bit ... out of the blue," he said.

"Okay. Well, why don't you just go home? Think about it."

"You don't want me to stay over?"

"No."

"Look, Izzy, this is a big step and I can't be pressured into this. We should live together when we're ready, not just because you're homeless and don't want to live alone. I'll help you find a nice new place."

"Sure," I said, nodding, "it was just a suggestion." I felt the tears bubbling up and was determined not to show how upset I was. How rejected I felt.

"Come on, Izzy, don't take it personally," he said in his nervous voice.

"How can I not take it personally? You don't want to live with me."

"I do, someday. Just not quite yet."

"Just go, please," I said, sounding angry rather than upset. I felt childish, and emotional and just wanted to be on my own so he didn't have to see me this way. How had I got it so wrong? He seemed so different to Ewan, so much more ready to make it serious - to take the next step. Maybe Jade was right; all men were commitment-phobes.

"Come on, Izzy."

"Just go home!" I shouted. He shot me a look of disdain, grabbed his things and left.

Chapter Twenty-Four

Jade was telling me about yet another one of her messed up relationships, chatting about how men can be useless and unreliable; something I was keen to agree with her on. She only realised I was upset when she asked, "How's Jason?" and I let a few tears fall. I told her about the whole stupid fight.

"This was your first argument?" she asked.

"Yes."

"That sucks. But you'll work it out."

"I guess."

"You know what they're like. Men don't like commitment, they get scared."

"I know. But Jason's so ... mature and sensible. I really thought we were ready. It's so much more serious than I ever was with Ewan. I wish I hadn't said anything. I should've waited for him to ask me. If he ever wants to ask me. Oh God, maybe he doesn't care about me as much as I thought he did?"

"He was just surprised, that's all. And he's right; you shouldn't move in because you're homeless. You should move in because you're ready."

I nodded but inside I knew I was ready. I just hadn't given it a lot of consideration until I was going to be homeless, that's all. I checked my phone for the umpteenth time - still no call or message. I knew I should be the bigger person. I should apologise and make it up to him, but I felt hurt and rejected and was hoping he'd get in touch first. Yes, I know, I can be stubborn. And silly.

I bought Jade dinner, and we spoke a little about the family and work, and yet all I could think of was what Jason was thinking and feeling. I resisted the urge to text him all day, but as soon as Jade said good bye I raced home, planning to call him as soon as I got there.

No answer. For two hours. I went to bed, feeling hurt and confused. Then Jason texted me a few minutes later. I glanced at the clock. It was gone 11pm.

I've just been mufged. No battery.

I stared at the text for a few minutes. Did 'mufged' mean mugged? A sudden panic rose in my chest and I called Jason, but his phone was already switched off. I pulled my long black coat out of the wardrobe and put it on over my pyjamas, forgetting the chocolate chip ice cream stain which I'd managed to dribble over myself earlier.

It was cold and dark out, but I just wanted to get to him as soon as I could and didn't want to wait for a cab. I walked as quickly as I could, arriving at his house a little breathless, pressing his doorbell over and over.

"Hello?" he called through the door.

"Jason, it's me."

He opened the door without a word and I went in. He left the front door open and returned to sit on the sofa.

"Hi," he said, as I came through. "I was mugged." He looked as if he might cry.

"Oh my God, are you okay?" I rushed over to him.

"Yes. It was all very civilised. Two thugs with lots of piercing and tattoos and a big knife asked for my wallet and phone. My phone was at home. I turned out my pockets to prove it, so they just took the wallet and ran off." He had a look of shock and disbelief in his eyes.

"We need to call the police."

"I already did. They said they'll stop by tomorrow. But it was dark so I don't have a very good description to give them."

"Fucking hell, Jason."

"I know."

"At least you're not hurt."

"I'm going to have to cancel all my cards."

"Yep."

"Bloody hell."

"Why was your phone here?"

"Does that matter now? I just forgot it." He leant forward and put his head in his hands.

"Are you drunk?"

"I'm sobering up pretty fast."

I went to the kitchen and got him some water.

"Thanks," he said, taking a sip.

"I'm just glad you're okay. I'm sorry about yesterday."

"Me too. I'm an arsehole, and for the record I am completely in love with you and of course I want to live with you. You just put me on the spot."

He took another sip of his water.

"I love you too," I said, putting my arm around him and breathing a sigh of relief. He leant back and I put my head on his chest.

We sat like that for a long time, before eventually going to bed. I clung on to him as if he'd been hurt, trying to protect him from the shitty evening and then made him bacon sandwiches for breakfast while he called the bank, the credit card company, and even cancelled and re-ordered a Nectar card.

"What's that on your top?" he asked as we both munched on our bacon.

"Ice cream. I was drowning my sorrows in calories."

"While I drowned mine in alcohol. How pathetic."

We both laughed and I looked down, feeling awkward. It was the first time I really felt uncomfortable in his presence.

"I've got to go home in these clothes."

"Why don't you bring some clothes here?"

"Are you sure?"

"Yes. I want you in my life. I admit I'm scared and this is a huge step for me, and I really hope you can cope with my mood swings and OCD ... but I love you and of course I want to live with you."

"How about a two month trial run? See how we feel about it?"

He smiled. I felt myself relax back into the seat, relieved.

"Great idea."

I went home to get some stuff, feeling a mixture of emotions. Did he want me there or did he just feel bad? I packed up enough clothes and toiletries to last me a few weeks and went back. As I sat down with a cup of tea, Jason handed me a tiny gift bag.

"What's this?"

"Open it."

It was a shiny, brand new key.

"Thank you," I said, throwing my arms around him.

Chapter Twenty-Five

"The last time I flew anywhere was to New York," Jason told me as we sat in Departures eating chicken salad sandwiches which had too much mayonnaise in them. "Chloe and Harry got married there." I could picture them getting married in New York. Harry had to travel a lot for his job and Chloe was always eager to go with him when she could get time off.

"I love airports," I said, glancing around. "You see so many different people milling around. I wonder what their stories are. Where they are heading to and why? Who they are leaving behind, or who they are travelling towards? When will they come back and will they be happy about it?"

"Seeing all these people also reminds me of my own insignificance. Which I find strangely comforting." Jason put down his sandwich. "Yuck. That really is horrid."

"You're right. There's so many people, going to hundreds of different places, all for different reasons. It just highlights that you're one in six billion," I said, feeling kind of flat.

"But I'm the only one of those six billion who gets to wake up with you every day," Jason said, kissing me on the cheek. He was so different to Ewan. More romantic, more open with his feelings. We chatted more, we got on better, and I had my own opinions now. I wasn't just following him; we were making decisions together. It felt healthier, somehow.

"When was your last holiday - other than Chloe's wedding?" I asked him.

"Let me think..."

"That long huh?"

"I went to Tenerife with my family about five years ago."

"Five years! I don't get it. You can afford to holiday at least once a year surely?"

"Well, I had no one to go with."

"Fair enough, well ... now you've got me." I squeezed his knee.

He winked and nodded his head. "I sure do. This sandwich has too much mayo," he said, pushing the remains away from him. We chatted for a while about how hard it was to find a decent pre-packed sandwich these days.

Living together had gone well so far. We had a little bit of an issue when Jason realised I would be bringing Fred with me. It was either that or the RSPCA and I couldn't give him away when we'd become so attached. Sian didn't seem to want him anymore. She'd inherited him from an Aunt who was a "crazy cat lady" and had mostly kept him out of obligation. Her house had sold fast, as she predicted, and I'd moved the remainder of my stuff into Jason's. I regularly asked him how he felt about me being there and he was always enthusiastic and positive. We'd fallen into our own little routines, me making breakfasts, him preparing lunches and dinners. I'd clean while he was out working and he'd leave me alone when I fielded calls for, or from, Sian.

Our flight was called at last and we made our way to the gate, me a bundle of excitement, Jason just smiling and looking more calm and relaxed than I'd ever seen him. Holidays were good for him, I realised.

I watched two parents trying to control their excited children, and figured they were going on a beach holiday; another couple were kissing each other frequently and wore new shiny wedding rings - honeymooners. Several people looked anxious; were they escaping something or flying into trouble?

I said as much to Jason. "You're so interesting," he told me. "The way you perceive things ... you're a people watcher."

"You mean I'm nosy!"

"No, you're just curious. You're interested in people, and that's not a bad thing. Too many people are only wrapped up in themselves. And, maybe those anxious people are just nervous about flying, had you thought of that? It may be simpler than you imagine."

"Hmm..." I said, looking around again to find the nervous folk.

"Do you do this every time you fly?" he asked.

"Well," I told him, "it was a game Ewan and I used to play to kill time in the airport or train station, or whatever. We'd both have to guess what each passenger's story was."

"Do you ever think about him?"

"Yes, quite often," I said too quickly, distracted by my people watching. I turned to face him, horrified, but he was smiling.

"At least you're honest," he said. The smile was fake, I realised. He was hurt.

"Not in that way," I said, rushing the words, "I just wonder where he is, you know? I don't have feelings for him anymore. I just feel like I didn't get closure sometimes. There was no proper goodbye, he just left, just like that, and I guess I'm a little angry and haven't quite let it all go yet. I like to think he misses me, but I'd never consider being with him again. I'm so glad I met you and you are what I want now. I love you."

He kissed me in the forehead. "Good," he said. "I don't mind you thinking about Ewan. Honestly." I was pretty sure that wasn't true but appreciated him saying it. I leant my head on his shoulder.

"Excuse me, very sorry to bother you, but are you Jason Edwards?" I quickly lifted my head up again. Really? When he was obviously at the start of his holiday?

Jason was polite and signed the woman's receipt from her own, no doubt mayo-loaded, sandwich, and she told him how much she liked his style of cooking and he blushed and muttered thank you like he always did.

"You're very kind," I said when she'd moved back to her friends. "I think I'd have told her to leave me alone. We're on holiday now."

"I know, but being polite doesn't harm anyone, and now she may go buy my book."

I laughed. "I sometimes forget you're a celebrity, but then someone comes along and stares at you for a few minutes and I realise they recognise you."

"I'm not a celebrity," he told me. "I'm just me."

The rest of the journey was non-eventful. I tried not to think about my last flight; alone and weeping over Ewan a year earlier. We both read quietly and after a couple of hours I realised something; this was perhaps the longest Jason and I had been together and not said a word. This seemed significant somehow. Ewan and I were often silent, even at the beginning. He didn't have much to say. Jason and I were always talking; he'd ask me how my day was, and we'd talk about everything from the people I'd spoken to, to the various recipes he was working on, about our childhoods and youths. We'd talk about weekend trips we'd like to plan, books we'd read, films we wanted to see.

For the first time, I was happy that Ewan had left me in Verona. Because I'd rather be in cold, rainy London with Jason, than sunny Melbourne with Ewan. There was no competition.

There was no need to think about wet and cold London right now though, as we were landing in Dubrovnik, Croatia. Jason had surprised me on my birthday, over Spanish tapas which he'd cooked at home and served up on rectangular white plates. He'd passed me an envelope across the table and at first I was a little confused; he'd given me a card and present that morning, the former with a slushy pink heart and poem inside it, and the latter a green velvet box containing a silver watch which I loved and had worn all day, even though it was a little big and needed several links removing.

Inside the envelope had been a post-it note that said 'I love you!' and printed confirmation that Jason had booked us two weeks at a private villa with our own pool. I'd gasped, leant across the table to kiss Jason and then sat back again, wondering out loud if Sian would be happy at the short notice; but Jason had already spoken to her and apparently she'd said it was about time I had a break. I was impressed with his forward planning and thoughtfulness, and admitted a holiday would be wonderful.

The villa was beautiful. White stone walls, modern interior and set on a hillside with stunning views; we could see tree tops, more villas and the sea in the distance. I sat out on the warm terrace with my feet in the pool while Jason made us cocktails.

That's pretty much how we spent the next two weeks. We both sat on the terrace most days, reading and talking, playing cards or scrabble, then dipping into the pool when it got too hot. Jason prepared us breakfast each morning, usually poached eggs or fresh fruit, and then we'd snack on cheese, olives and bread for lunch. Each evening we'd walk to a cluster of restaurants in the centre of the village, where most days we'd both eat fish and sip wine until we were tipsy enough to race each other home to the bedroom. Or, sometimes, the terrace.

I'd never felt so comfortable with another person. I could just lie, naked in his arms, talking about the food we'd eaten or the view, or the book I was reading. We were in our own little bubble, just us two, in love and happy. It was bliss.

"This has been the most relaxing two weeks of my life," I said to Jason on the second to last day. We were on the terrace, having just eaten our breakfast: melon and mango neatly arranged by me, as I'd felt guilty that Jason was doing everything for me.

"Me too," Jason said, licking his fingers.

Chapter Twenty-Six

Time passed, and before I knew it I'd been living with Jason for three years. We didn't even comment or notice when the two month trial ended.

We got on brilliantly. I set up an office in the spare bedroom and continued to organise Sian's life for her from there. We spent time decorating and buying new furniture, and after a while it felt just as much mine as his; I'd put my stamp on it. I'd spend hours browsing online for the perfect bedding to match the new teal coloured walls. We debated which plates we wanted in John Lewis and I bought candles and photo frames and big plump cushions. We turned his barren house into our home and it was a fun, rewarding, lovely time. I felt settled and content.

Jason worked long hours. I'd wait up late for him and he'd get home and tell me about his day, his food experiments and his staff and satisfied customers. I always watched every TV show he made an appearance on, but he hated watching himself so he'd sit in the bedroom and then ask me what I thought afterwards. I was so proud of him; he seemed to have gained confidence and appeared more relaxed on screen than previously. He wrote another book, and I had a lot of fun trying out the recipes and helping him to lay it all out.

When we weren't working, Jason gave me relaxed cooking lessons, encouraging me to try new techniques and ingredients. He taught me to trust my instincts and experiment. We went for long walks and spent time with our friends. We talked a lot, whenever we had time together. He really did become my best friend and I shared everything with him.

We went on holidays. We went to see bands play and to comedy gigs. We attended the Good Food Show each year, and I watched with pride as Jason was treated like a rock star by all the foodie-types. We were happy. I was content. I enjoyed my job, and I enjoyed my relationship. Of course we occasionally argued, but overall life was good.

Amber and Tristan had moved in together soon after us, and Tristan proposed soon after that. The past year had been a whirl of bridal magazines and dress fittings, shopping for favours and viewing venues. Amber had wanted my opinion on every detail and I'd cried when she asked me to be her only bridesmaid. On their wedding day I watched her in her veil, with her manicured fingernails and her bright red hair up with a few wavy sections falling around her face. She looked stunning and Tristan looked at her adoringly. He watched her dancing and their love was clear for all to see. I swallowed hard to remove a lump forming in my throat.

Amber never had any doubts about marrying Tristan.

"You look so beautiful!" I told her on the dance floor, as she spun around in her gorgeous white dress.

"You really think so?"

"I know so."

She squeezed my arm and drifted off as a slower song came on, looking for her father. I returned to my seat beside Jason who'd just got us two glasses of champagne.

"Amber and Tristan look so happy," he said. I nodded. They really did.

"I don't deserve you," Jason said, in my ear.

"I think it's the other way around," I said back, smiling and sipping my bubbles.

"Why do you love me?" he asked.

"Because you're the best person I know. You're my best friend."

He grinned. "Do you want to dance?"

I laughed. Jason never danced. He must be pretty drunk. "Sure."

He led me to the floor and spun me around the rest of the night, laughing and swinging our hips. At the end of the evening we went up to our hotel room and talked for an hour about the day. As I fell asleep I thought of Ewan for the first time in months. I wondered where he was, what he was doing and who with. I still missed him … in a way. Then I forgot about him and thought about my own wedding day and what it might be like.

I knew Jason was going to propose soon. Amber told me he'd asked Tristan where he'd bought her ring. I couldn't wait to tell him yes.

Chapter Twenty-Seven

Tuesday. Four days until my wedding day.

"Hello?"

"Hi, Izzy."

"Jason?"

I admit I was happy to hear his voice. I couldn't imagine what he wanted, and my heart started beating faster. I thought about the way he looked on Saturday night, how his dark eyes had looked at me the same way they had when we were together. Then I remembered that beautiful girl who was with him and felt a little sick.

"Yes, it's me," he said, sounding nervous as ever.

"Hello."

What did he want? My head whirled into a spin.

I'd done a lot of thinking, as you might imagine. I kept thinking about seeing Jason and Ewan the other night, and with Ewan I felt passionate and ... if I was honest, turned on. He gave me a thrill and I was tempted by that.

When I thought of seeing Jason, I felt nervous. I wanted him to like me. I wanted him to forgive me for all the hurt I caused. I wanted to see him smile, be happy. And yet when I thought of him with that shockingly beautiful woman I felt a surge of jealousy. To summarise, he just made me confused and slightly emotional. I thought of his dark eyes. Remembering how it felt to lie in his arms. Stop it, I told myself. Think only of Greg. Difficult when Jason's voice was on the other end of the phone.

"I just wanted to ask you something."

"Okay."

"Can we meet? For a drink or something?"

I thought about Amber and Jade's reactions when I'd told them I was meeting Ewan. What would they say if I told them I was meeting Jason too? They'd advise against it, I knew. But I wanted to see him and I didn't want them to talk me out of it, so I said:

"Sure. How about right now?"

We met in a bar not far from his restaurant. It brought back memories. He was already there when I arrived with two glasses of red wine in front of him. He looked up with that same nervous smile he'd had when we first met and gently pushed a glass towards me as I sat down opposite him.

"Hey," I said, smiling.

"Hey. How are you?"

I took a deep breath.

I'm scared I'm making a mistake. I'm missing you. I've messed up over Ewan. I'm terrified, actually. You're the greatest friend I've ever had and what I really want is to talk about all my mixed feelings with you and ask for your help to figure out what I want.

That's what I wanted to say. But instead I lied.

"I'm good."

"Are you happy?" he asked, taking his eyes away from mine and looking down at the table. Goodness, even now he knew me so well. He knew. But I lied again.

"Yes."

"I'm glad."

"Are you happy?"

He didn't answer. Instead he said:

"Is it Dexter? Is that who you're marrying?"

Realisation dawned.

"No!" I said, alarmed at the sound of his name. "No, it's

someone else. Greg. You don't know him."

He looked relieved.

"Thank you. I just wanted to know. I hope you'll be very happy."

"Thank you."

"You haven't known him long, then?"

"No," I said, embarrassed.

He smiled at me and I wanted to kiss him, to somehow find a way to make up for all the hurt I caused. Suddenly I knew. I didn't want to marry Greg. I wanted Jason back. He gulped down the last of his wine and I realised he was probably going to leave, so I tried to think of something to say, fast.

"How are Chloe and Harry?"

"They're great, thank you. You should stop by the restaurant and say hi to Chloe. She'd love to see you, I'm sure."

"Good idea." I would be so happy to see her again, plus it meant more time with Jason. "Shall we go there after our drinks?"

"I've got to go home, but Chloe's working today so feel free."

"Oh, okay."

He picked up his coat, smiled sadly and got up to go, but I put my hand on his arm and pushed him back in his seat.

"I'm so sorry Jason, for everything. When I think about how I treated you, I'm pretty ashamed of myself."

I saw the pain flicker across his face.

"It's okay. It all worked out in the end. I mean you're happy with Greg, I'm happy with Anna."

Anna. The supermodel. I had almost forgotten about her again. And Greg. Lovely, dependable Greg.

"I guess so."

"Look, Izzy, you deserve to be happy, so stop feeling guilty. Really. It's fine, and we've both moved on."

"Okay. Thank you, Jason."

He gave me a kiss on the cheek - a quick peck - and then he walked out of my life again. He'd been so quiet, so reluctant to chat; so different from the Jason I knew. I missed the openness. It had been so easy yet today it felt so awkward. Despite his reassurances, he obviously hadn't forgiven me, otherwise he'd have stayed and we would have chatted for longer. He was either angry and bitter or he was still in love with me ... surely?

I took several deep breaths and swallowed hard, to stop the tears from coming. Then I got up and went to the restaurant. It looked exactly the same: oak tables with white linen napkins; each place setting perfectly set up. A few later lunchers were still eating but it was almost empty. I went to the back and explained to a waiter I'd never seen before that I knew Chloe, and how Jason had told me to come by. He let me through the staff door and there, in her whites, with her gorgeous wavy blonde hair, was my friend. She hugged me and I almost cried again.

"You should have kept in touch," she said, releasing me and looking at my face. "I've missed you."

"I didn't know how it'd be, after Jason and I broke up."

"It was hard at first, and he was so ... distraught. But these things happen."

She organised some coffee for us and we sat and chatted, caught up in each other's news. She congratulated me on my forthcoming wedding and I acted the part of happy bride again. I asked about Harry and she filled me in on their past year or so.

For a few minutes it was like I was back there, back in Jason's world, back when things were simple, when I knew what I wanted, when I was certain about the man I wanted to marry. How had I got to this point?

After an hour or so I went home and Greg was there, happy to see me and, somehow, I pushed the thoughts out of my head for a few hours while we had dinner. But my mind was soon drifting back, thinking about Jason again and how I'd messed it all up.

Chapter Twenty-Eight

On our fourth anniversary of being a couple, Jason and I were sitting in the exact spot where we met. He had suggested we take a short stroll through Hyde Park and packed up a picnic of salmon sandwiches, gorgeous bubbly white wine and strawberries with cream. It seemed quite a momentous occasion, reaching four years together. But, as I'd told Amber only the day before, he'd been completely right for me from the beginning. He'd swept me up, given me confidence and inspiration, and pushed me into adulthood - something that Ewan had carefully been avoiding.

With Jason's encouragement, I'd become the person I'd always wanted to be; calm, patient, thoughtful, responsible and successful. He guided me to the path I felt I was meant to be on. In return, I brought a female presence to his home which I'd now filled with modern furniture, bright paint on the walls and ... what else had I given him? Love and companionship, Amber told me. I smiled when she said that.

So we were having this wonderfully indulgent picnic. It was a perfect day. We could hear birds singing and the faint hum of traffic in the distance. We nibbled on the food and squinted at each other in the bright sun.

"To us," I said, raising my glass.

"Yes. To another amazing year," Jason clinked my glass and looked nervous. I then started to feel nervous myself, realising this must be it.

"It has been amazing," I said, putting my glass down and smiling at him.

"The thing is," he said, reaching into his pocket, "well, you make me so happy and what I'd really like to know is ... would you do the honour of becoming my wife?" He produced a beautiful ring with a solitaire diamond, dazzling in the sun.

"Jason! Oh it's beautiful! Of course, yes!"

He slipped the ring on my finger and I tried to hug and kiss him but I knocked his glass over and we both had to jump up as Prosecco ran all over the blanket. We both looked down at our wet legs and laughed. I shrugged, giggled, and kissed him.

We sat on the grass after that, having discarded the alcohol-soaked blanket to one side. Jason sat behind me and I sat between his legs, as we dipped our strawberries in the cream and talked about what our wedding might be like. We agreed: something simple, small, romantic. Fabulous food, of course, and a beautiful location. Maybe even a beach somewhere warm.

If my future self had come back and told me then, that I'd mess it all up, I'd never have believed it. I felt blissfully happy and completely content.

The next few weeks were taken up with letting everyone know. Jason didn't want to attract any media attention; we didn't want the whole Helen thing being brought up again, and although he wasn't really a victim of the paparazzi or the press in general, we both agreed we wanted to keep it all low-key and private.

Amber screamed down the phone. "If your ring is bigger than mine I'm going to kill you!"

"It's not," I told her, thinking of her huge diamond and cringing. I'd hate a ring like hers.

"It's smaller, but it's dainty and beautiful."

"Just like you," she said, laughing.

Mum and Dad were over the moon, as was Jade and all of our mutual friends.

We'd been engaged six weeks, when I met Dexter. If only I'd known then, what I know now.

Chapter Twenty-Nine

"So can you tell me where we're headed?" I asked, excited.

"To Cornwall."

"Lovely," I said, genuinely pleased. Jason had told me he'd booked a surprise long weekend away as a mini-celebration. Sian was holidaying in the Seychelles so she wouldn't mind me taking time off and the weather was bright and sunny so it looked set to be a wonderful break.

Jason was in a good mood; he'd created a playlist for the trip with all my favourite music, and he'd prepared a bag full of snacks. We munched on homemade crisps, chicken sandwiches, fruit and yoghurt covered raisins, and before I knew it we were driving through the countryside, past fields of sheep and cows, down narrow roads and then ... there it was. The cottage.

"This is where we're staying?" I asked grinning, as Jason pulled up beside a beautiful cottage. It was built in grey stone with a short stone wall all around it, enclosing a pretty little garden. I felt my face light up at the view behind it; we were half way up a hill with the sea on the horizon and the beach in full view only a short walk away. There were sunbathers on the golden sand and a few surfers in the turquoise sea. I stood and watched them for a moment, while Jason stood behind me.

"Who said holidaying in England couldn't be beautiful?" he said, putting his arms around my waist.

"It's gorgeous," I told him.

I turned back to the cottage and Jason pulled out a key and handed it to me.

"It's ours," he said, grinning.

I blinked a few times.

"For the weekend?"

"No, I bought it," he said, his eyes widening.

"What?" I swallowed hard, feeling happy, joyful tears brim up inside me.

"It's ours, Izzy. I know that we can't exactly move here, what with work and everything, but it can be a holiday home and I guess one day we can retire here, if you like it."

"Oh my God, Jason! You bought this cottage for us?!" I jumped into his arms.

"Yes. I remembered what you said about your sister and … well, you know, the story you told me. And we can get a dog at some point and paint the front door blue if you like," he said, holding me tight.

"Wow, Jason, it's so beautiful!" I said again, tears welling up in my eyes and falling down my cheeks.

"Let's take a look inside, shall we?"

We walked through the rooms holding hands. It was perfect. The front door opened into a little porch, and that opened on to the small but modern kitchen with granite work surfaces, a small dishwasher, oven, fridge and a small area for a dining table. I opened one of the cupboards; it was empty.

"I thought you'd like to go and choose all the furniture together," he told me. "All I've bought is a bed, for tonight. We need to stock the cupboards."

"Wow, Jason, this is so … wonderful," I said, kissing him on the cheek. He led me into the living room which had hard wooden floor boards and an empty fireplace.

"I thought we could buy a wood-burning stove for the fireplace," he said, "and a rug. Make it really cosy."

"Sounds amazing," I said. "I think it'd look nice with a wooden cabinet here," I said, gesturing to an alcove between the chimney and the wall, "and stack it with books and board games, and then come in the winter and just keep warm indoors while looking out at this." I walked to the window and looked out towards the sea.

"Amazing," I said, my eyes welling up. It was more beautiful than I had even imagined.

Jason just smiled, took my hand again and led me upstairs. There was a small bathroom.

"We need to re-fit all of this," he said, waving a hand over the old sink and bathtub.

"This is the spare room," he said, opening a door to an empty room. "Maybe we can have friends join us here now and then. And this," he led me to the next door, "is the master bedroom."

It had a huge window, again facing the ocean, letting in lots of light. Jason had bought a four poster bed and tucked underneath was a plastic box containing pale blue cotton bedding. Without a word, I pulled it out and we made up the bed. I lay down on it, and he grinned and then joined me.

"Jason," I said, turning on my side to face him, "thank you. This is just how I'd dreamed it. Really, I can't thank you enough." I felt a few tears run out of each eye.

"Don't keep thanking me," he said, sweeping a strand of hair from my face and dabbing the tears with his fingers. "Just be happy. That's all I want."

"I am. This is perfect."

"So you want to go shopping?" he asked, raising his eyebrows.

"Shopping?"

"For furniture and all that. We don't even have any forks."

So we went out and drove all over Cornwall, or so it felt, ordering sofas and buying everything from cutlery to a small, round, pine dining table with four chairs. We also found a double bed for the other bedroom; garden furniture; spare linen; towels, and some food for that evening. Jason threw some large floor cushions in to sit on until the sofas were delivered, and we got back just as the sun was setting on the horizon.

"I can't believe you bought this house!" I said, as we pulled up beside it again.

"We bought it," he said, kissing my forehead before getting out of the car.

I stood staring out at the sea while he unloaded, mesmerized by the view; taking it in. He'd gone and given me the one gift I could have desired most - the one thing I'd dreamt about for years. The house Helen wanted.

I looked up at the clouds. I'd never believed in heaven and had never imagined her hearing me or watching me, but quietly I sent a thought up to her, just in case.

I hope you like it, Helen.

"You okay?" Jason asked, looking nervous.

"Yes, just enjoying the view," I told him.

He stood behind me, wrapping his arms around my torso, squeezing me tight.

"You really like it?"

"Jason, it's perfect. I love it."

"You can decorate it however you want."

"I like it just like this," I told him.

"One day, we'll get a golden retriever, if you like."

He'd remembered every detail. I smiled and leant my head back against him, not taking my eyes from the sea. We spent all of Saturday and Sunday arranging things in the cottage, walking along the shore and paddling in the sea. We ate fresh fish and chunky chips on the sand and it was perfect. I kept grinning at Jason as if all my birthdays had come at once.

"You're incredibly romantic, thoughtful and absolutely wonderful," I told him as we packed up the car to leave on Monday morning.

"I'm not," Jason said, locking up the front door. "I told you, I just want you to be happy."

"I am," I told him.

"Good. Then I'm happy, too."

We drove home with more snacks and good music.

"We'll come back in a few weeks, if you like?" Jason suggested on the way.

"I can't wait!" I sighed happily.

On the Tuesday, I couldn't concentrate on work. I had a huge number of emails and letters of Sian's to get through but I kept thinking about the cottage. Eventually I opened up a new document on my laptop and began to type.

Dear Helen,

I want to contact you. I've always wanted that, but today more than ever. So I'm writing this letter, even though I have nowhere to send it.

So, were you there with me? Did you see it? Isn't it beautiful? I know it's what you wanted, and I have yearned to see it, to be there, to feel the sea breeze on my face and to wake up and gaze out at the blueness from my bedroom window. I can see now why you wanted it, why you felt it would be a good place to live, and one day I too will live there, and grow old there with Jason.

I feel like I need to enjoy the life that was taken away from you. I always try to live life to the full. I think I owe you that.

I hope you like it, Helen. I hope you can see the view through my eyes somehow.

Love, Izzy xx

Chapter Thirty

"Hello?" I said, feeling panicked. It was 2:34am. Who called at this time unless it was an emergency? The bed felt cold and I remembered Jason had gone away for the night to attend some sort of food event up north. The panic increased.

"Izzy, it's Dad. Now I don't want you to worry but your mum and I have been in an accident." His voice sounded distant and not like him at all. It sounded shaken.

"Oh my God, what happened?" I sat up and turned the bedside lamp on.

"Some idiot in a van, not looking where he was going. We were coming home from your Aunt Ruth's. You know how fast that main road is."

"Are you okay?"

"I'm alright but I don't know about your mother. She was unconscious in the car and they haven't told me what's going on. I'm waiting for a doctor to come and tell me." His voice cracked on the last few words.

With my heart beating fast, I got dressed and called a taxi to take me to the hospital. It only took half an hour but it felt like longer. Dad was sitting in a bed in A&E with cuts and gashes all over him, his leg at a funny angle. His eyes looked wide, worried and stressed.

"I thought you said you were okay?"

"Didn't want to worry you. Just came back from x-ray and I've broken my leg."

"Where's Mum?"

"She's having some tests. She's still unconscious."

"Bloody hell, Dad."

I sat with him for a while, silent but holding hands, and then they took him for surgery on his leg. I was shown into a waiting room where I tried to sleep in a chair, but couldn't. About 8am I got a coffee and asked a nurse to find out what was going on with each of them. I texted Sian and Jason the news and said I'd keep them updated. I sat sipping my coffee, wondering if the van driver was hurt, too.

All I could think about was Helen. When she was about eight years old, she was in a car accident with a friend. I don't remember the details, but her friend's mother had made a wrong turn and they all ended up here, at the hospital. Helen broke her arm. Mum and Dad rushed to her bedside and we sat there for ages, waiting for Helen to be seen. I was bored. That's all I remember, really. It was boring. Helen cried a few times. Eventually, we went home with her arm in a cast.

What would she make of this, I wondered? She was always more confident than me. Would she be hassling the doctors for answers? Is that what I should be doing?

And then I met Dexter.

I didn't know his name, but I recognised him immediately, I just couldn't remember where from. He was wearing doctor's scrubs and a white coat. He was carrying a file which he flipped open as he got to me. His dark hair was a little longer than before, but he still had the same cheeky grin and beautiful grey eyes, and he knew who I was straight away.

"Miss Swan?" he said, and then he looked down at me and we locked eyes. "Wow! Hello."

"Hi," I said, trying to place him. Had I met him at college? On my travels, somewhere?

"I'm Dr Williams," he held out his hand and I shook it, feeling some sort of current pass through us. "Would you like to come with me?"

I followed him into a little side office, and sat down. He made me even more nervous than I was already.

"Do I know you from somewhere?" I asked.

"I wasn't sure you'd remember," he said, blushing and looking down at his paperwork. "A beach in Wales. Pembrokeshire, I think. A good few years ago. We met by the shore?"

"Oh my!"

It was him. The Guy From The Beach, who I kissed while Ewan was asleep. My heart starting beating faster, remembering the intensity of the moment.

"Yes. I'm sorry we didn't meet again under more pleasant circumstances."

"Me too," I said, remembering the passion - the pull. I'd wondered for a while afterwards who he was, where he was. That I'd wanted to go back and do it again.

"Your mother has a subdural haematoma, Miss Swan," he began, becoming more serious. "Do you know what that is?"

I felt my shoulders drop. I'd watched enough medical dramas to know what he was saying. For the first time in several minutes I stopped staring into his beautiful grey eyes and looked down at the floor.

"A bleed of some sort, near the brain?"

"Yes. My colleague has just taken her into surgery. And your father is out of surgery. His operation went well and with some physio, his leg should recover pretty quickly. He will wake up soon, and I'll ask a nurse to take you to him so you can be with him."

"Okay, thank you."

"You're welcome, Miss Swan. Try not to worry." He squeezed my arm and I felt the current pass between us again. I looked at him in alarm and I saw that he noticed it too. He dropped his arm.

"Please call me Izzy," I said, feeling familiar with him for some reason. Perhaps because he'd put his tongue in my mouth. I remembered wanting to push him down on the sand and felt myself blush.

"Okay, Izzy. And I'm Dexter."

I nodded and got up to go back to the waiting area.

"It's really nice, actually, to see you again. I've thought of you often. That was pretty ... intense."

I smiled and nodded my head, but I felt annoyed. Did he really need to talk about this now, while a surgeon was preparing to operate on my mother's brain? The thought made me shudder. Actually, it was much nicer to think about him, than about what was going on in the operating theatre. I looked up at his lovely face and smiled.

"Thank you, Doctor." I stood up.

"I'm sorry about your mum. We will keep you posted," he said, his eyes making my heart thud harder.

"Okay, that'd be good. Thank you." I shook his hand. It felt hot and clammy.

I called Jason who insisted he'd come home but I told him to stay put. There was nothing he could do. I then called my Aunt Ruth and Jade, then Sian, who told me to sort out a couple of things later on when I had time and then take the rest of the week off. Ruth turned up at the hospital a while later with some bedclothes, toothbrushes and flowers. We sat with Dad all day. Ruth and Dad chatted trying to keep their spirits up. I mostly stared out of the window, trying to block out what was happening. Hadn't we been through enough as a family without this? It didn't seem fair. I kept trying to think of happier things. If I could block out what they were doing to my mum right now, maybe it'd be easier - maybe I'd get through it unscarred. I thought about making a nice dinner for Jason. Maybe Chloe could give me some tips and ideas and I'd make something really special. Maybe I could even make a nice meal for Mum, when she was better. But I couldn't think about Mum. So I thought about Dexter, instead. About the moment on the beach and how passionate it had been. About how he looked at me in that little office, like he'd been waiting for me all this time. Eventually the surgeon came and told us that Mum's operation had gone well and he'd let us know more as soon as he had news. We all sighed with relief.

Dad and Ruth insisted I go get something to eat, so I went to the cafeteria and bought an egg mayonnaise sandwich and sat down to eat it. I was just about to look at my phone to see if I had any messages when someone approached me.

"Do you mind if I join you?" Dexter asked. I looked up at his handsome face and nodded. "Sure."

"You should get some sleep," he said, probably noticing my tired eyes.

"I will," I told him.

"Are you close to your parents?" he asked.

I shrugged. "I guess so."

"I heard your mum's surgery went well." He said, taking a bite of his sandwich. I didn't really want to talk about her. I didn't want to think about her until I saw her and knew she was out of danger.

"Yes. Thank you."

We locked eyes for a few moments longer than necessary. He made me feel nervous - and excited and giddy. And guilty. Why did I feel guilty just sitting here talking to him?

"That day on the beach," I said, unable to stop myself and keen to change the subject from my mum, "that was maybe the most crazy thing I've ever done. My boyfriend, Ewan, was right there, but it was like this ... this power you had. It overwhelmed me."

He grinned and I took in his face again. I wasn't sure why I was being so honest. It was difficult to move my eyes away from his.

"I felt you were the one with the power, actually. It was like I couldn't resist you."

I felt myself blush again. "Strange, really. I don't know what came over us." I didn't know what else to say, but somehow this conversation was a good distraction from the alternative.

"It was like a magnetic force," Dexter said, making it sound quite simple.

"Yes," I said, feeling it again.

Jason. Jason. Jason. It made no difference. I wanted to kiss Dexter again. He made me feel like a teenager with a crush. I didn't even know him, but somehow I lost all control and rational thought.

"It was strange. I'm not sure why or how it happened, but it just felt right." He smiled and took another bite.

"Funny to meet again now," I said, feeling embarrassed and excited and guilty all at the same time. The canteen was noisy and I glanced around, taking in all the hospital staff, patients and visitors all going about their day, getting their lunches while we sat here in our own little powerful vacuum ... or so it felt. I looked back at Dexter and he was already looking at me. He smiled. I put my sandwich down, no longer hungry.

"So, this Ewan. Did you ever tell him?"

"No, of course not."

"Is Ewan the guy you're engaged to?"

I hesitated, not sure whether to be annoyed or flattered that he'd noticed. I glanced down at my ring. Jason's ring. The reality of the situation hit me and I told myself to stop getting carried away. Still, I looked across at his hand and spotted a ring on his finger, too. I felt disappointed and then ashamed of myself. It was a good thing he was married. Less temptation. And anyway, had I really expected a handsome, sexy, doctor with those amazing eyes to be single? Most unlikely.

"No, that didn't work out. I'm engaged to someone else." I decided to change the subject and keep it professional. "So you think my mum will recover quickly? Will there be any lasting effects?"

I wasn't sure I wanted an answer. Not thinking about her had worked for me so far, but now, suddenly, I needed to know.

"It's quite early to tell. I'll go and see how she's doing, after this, if you like?"

I nodded and smiled. I couldn't stop staring at him. He held my gaze.

"I'm sorry," he said, getting up, "if this is inappropriate then feel free to tell me so, but your fiancé is a lucky guy."

"You don't even know me," I said, feeling a little lightheaded.

He sat down again. "I know, but it's just..."

A group of nurses walked in, and he nodded at them. When they were out of earshot he continued.

"It's just something about you. You've still got it - whatever it was all those years ago on the beach. It's like—"

"A magnet?" I asked, feeling it yet again. So much for keeping it professional.

"Yes." He smiled. I smiled back. Somehow, I knew this would change everything, and maybe not for the better. But I couldn't stop myself.

"So you're married, huh? Your wife..?" I stopped, not wanting to know particularly but feeling it ought to be mentioned.

"Yes. Her name is Holly."

"Any kids?"

"One girl. Isla. She's two."

I nodded. What was I doing? Weighing up how wrong this was? He's a total stranger, I told myself. *You don't know what you're doing.*

"That's nice."

"I'm not happy with her, to be honest," he said quietly. This was quickly turning into the strangest conversation I'd ever had.

"I am. Happy, I mean. With Jason."

"Good," he said, smiling and turning his empty coffee cup round in his hands. "I guess that's my cue to back off." He laughed nervously. "I'd better get back to work. I guess I'll see you around."

He hesitated for a just a moment, waiting to see if I said

anything else. I looked at his lips and suddenly it was like I was back on the beach, feeling his arms around me; feeling my almost-naked body pressed up against his with the tide lapping at our feet; the sexiness of the whole situation plus the power he had over me. It was overwhelming. Now, in the hospital canteen, we stared at each other for a few seconds and that attraction was almost visible. Then he sighed and the moment was lost. We were just two people in a canteen again; two unavailable people who didn't even know each other. Strangers.

He stood up to go and I wanted to ask him to stay. I almost asked him to keep talking. I couldn't understand why. It wasn't just his beautiful eyes or handsome face. There was something about the way he looked at me that made me feel excited and pulled me in. I told myself it was just chemistry, just lust and a physical attraction. Animal instincts and nothing more. He said goodbye and was gone, leaving me feeling nauseous and confused. I should have asked him to stay, I realised, because now I'd have to go back and look at the worried, sad faces of Dad and Ruth. We spent another few hours sitting there with me trying to think of anything other than what was happening, and them making idle chatter, trying to keep it together.

I saw my mum briefly before I went home. She was still unconscious. She looked tiny, lying in the bed, pale and very frail, with various tubes coming out of her. I squeezed her hand and went home to sleep.

As I got into bed the panicky feeling had subsided but I wasn't sure I could sleep. I couldn't blank it out anymore and just kept thinking about my poor mum with her damaged head, and my dad with his broken leg. It was like everything in my relatively normal world had come to a halt and all that mattered was going on inside that hospital.

I felt miserable.

Eventually, I managed to stop worrying about them by

thinking of something else. And the only thing I could distract myself with, was Dexter.

Chapter Thirty-One

I hardly slept that night. My mind was busy, alternating between thinking about Dexter then thinking about Mum. She'd looked so weak and pathetic, and I just wanted her to recover and be back to her normal self. I called the hospital early to find out how both my parents were and a nurse told me they were both doing alright. I decided to stop by and see Amber on my way to the hospital. She made me a coffee and sympathised when I told her about the accident. And then I told her about Dexter. As I explained, her faced turned hard and cold and when it was her turn to speak she almost shouted at me.

"Izzy! What the fuck are you talking about?"

"It's like…" I tried to find the words.

"A magnet. You already said. What does that mean though?"

"I can't explain it, to be honest. There's just something irresistible about him. He pulls me in."

"The Guy From The Beach was another man to this one, Izzy. He was young and having fun, and you weren't hurting anyone. But this guy is married. He has a wife! And a kid! And you have a wonderful fiancé. And you've spent all of an hour talking together. Are you seriously entertaining this idea? Come on - get real."

"You don't understand," I protested. "I just get this feeling. It's like I know him already."

"All you know is that you are attracted to him. I mean, come on, don't you think he's a slime bag for flirting with you?"

"I know it sounds that way, but there's something there. I don't know what it is, I can't explain."

"You're just messed up about your parents. I'm sure you'll be feeling more rational in a few days. We all see attractive men in our daily lives. We can admire without considering cheating on our men to have a few moments with them."

"I just can't stop thinking about him, that's all."

"But you have to realise that it's just an infatuation. A crush or a feeling of lust. You are yearning for those few moments on the beach because they were spectacular. And I don't blame you for that, but that was then and this is now. Be realistic."

"Yes, I suppose you're right," I conceded. Although I wasn't sure that she was.

"How do you think Jason would feel if he knew about this?"

Hurt, betrayed, broken, angry.

"Amber, I can't help it."

"So many people would love to be in your shoes. You're engaged to a wonderful man!"

"I do know that."

We sat in silence for a minute. I sipped my coffee.

"You need to avoid seeing him at the hospital again, Izzy," Amber said calmly.

"What? It was just a harmless flirtation," I said, unwilling to agree not to see Dexter.

"This ceased being harmless the second he told you he wasn't happy with his wife."

"I don't even know him."

"Exactly. And he sounds sleazy to me."

"It isn't like that," I said, exasperated and regretting having told her. I hated it when Amber was right. I knew she was trying to help but I was just annoyed at the reality she was

170

setting before me. I didn't really want to hear it. And anyway, it wasn't as if I was going to run off with him. He was just a nice little distraction. He could be a little crush to think about while my mum got better.

"He's obviously looking for some excuse to leave his wife, and just because you had a silly thing on the beach once, doesn't mean you should risk everything with Jason."

"It wasn't silly. It was intense and romantic. And I'm not risking anything by talking to him. I'll tell him we can be friends."

Amber looked at me.

"But why would you be friends? There's no need to even speak, unless it's about your parents. And you really think someone who attracts you this much can just be friends with you?"

"Yes," I said, not sure if I believed it. She gave me another stern look.

"What? It's my life, Amber!" I picked up my things and stormed out.

I don't know what I'd been expecting. I guess I wanted her to justify my actions; to tell me that I should go with the flow and get excited about the feelings I was having. Instead, she did was she always did. She was my best friend and gave me the truth. I didn't appreciate it at that moment though and went on to see my mum and sulk silently about it all. Mum was doing okay and I didn't see Dexter that day. I wasn't sure if I was disappointed or relieved. Both, I think. Dad was fussing around Mum and she was just lying there, looking a bit hopeless and I tried to focus on her by making her comfy and worrying about her instead of myself. I went home with Dad and we ate fish and chips and talked about the old days - about Helen and our old house. It was nice, but the accident had clearly shaken him up. He seemed old all of a sudden.

Jason came back home but I told him to carry on as normal. He had lots of appointments and meetings and work to do. I went every day to the hospital. I caught a train to Dad's and then helped him hobble to his courtesy car (his car was wrecked from the accident). I drove us to the hospital, then helped him hobble some more to Mum's bedside. She had a private room which smelled of flowers; we knew she hated the clinical smell of the hospital and so Dad bought her a fresh bunch every day, and the room was getting full. This particular morning we had had to bring our own vase because the ward had run out. Mum was recovering slowly but didn't talk much and slept a lot. We sat and watched daytime television. Sometimes I left them alone together to go and read my book in the waiting area.

Dexter often walked past and I always sensed his presence and would look up. We locked eyes as he walked by and I'd try to read something behind the stare to discover what he was thinking and feeling. Sometimes he'd smile, sometimes he'd wink, other times he'd just stare at me without showing any expression at all.

On the second day he came and sat down next to me and asked about my mum and how she was getting on. On the third we started to talk about other things. I asked him why he'd wanted to be a doctor and he told me how he wanted to help people, to save and improve lives. He asked me about my work with Sian and made fun of me, suggesting I was a slave. I defended Sian, telling him I loved my job, which he said is rare and therefore he'd never tease me again. It became a little routine: drive Dad in, sit with Mum, leave them to chat alone, go chat with Dexter if he was about, go back to Mum, go home and eat microwave meal with Dad, go home, chat to Jason, go to bed and worry about everything.

One afternoon, about five days after the accident, I was just leaving Mum's room when Dexter was finishing his shift and he asked if I wanted to get a drink in a pub near the hospital. So I agreed to go, unable to refuse, wanting us to be friends at the very least. How I thought we'd manage that with all the chemistry and magnetism I don't know and I was a fool to think so naively.

So we walked along, smiling and talking, avoiding too much eye contact. Or I did anyway. Whenever we locked eyes it was like the rest of the world ceased to exist, which made me feel extremely happy and excited, but also guilty and nervous, somehow all at once. The mixture of emotions was making me exhausted. Our arms occasionally brushed against each other as we walked and I felt a little frisson of excitement every time it happened. I wondered what it'd be like to hold his hand, to feel that current running between us for more than a second.

Once in the pub we sat next to each other in a booth with a glass of wine each. There was an awkward silence as we looked at each other, smiled, and then I looked away. What were we doing here?

"Tell me about your wife," I said, taking a sip of my wine. I was curious about her. He sighed.

"Holly is … well, she's just a woman I live with, to be honest. I don't even know why we're still together."

"You must have loved her when you married her?"

"We'd been going out for six months when she told me she was pregnant with Isla. She was over the moon - thought it was the best thing that'd ever happened to her. I wasn't sure what to do; I love Isla now of course but at the time I didn't want a baby. I wasn't in love with Holly. But I figured I could maybe fall for her in time. She was nice and pretty. I know that sounds unromantic, but I wanted to do the right thing. So I proposed and we got married a few months before Isla was born."

"And did you fall in love with her?"

"No. I mean, I care about her, but she doesn't set my heart on fire, you know? She never has. Sadly."

"That's a shame. I'm sorry."

"Can I be honest?"

"Yes, of course," I said, scared that the honesty might be too much or could cause trouble, and yet at the same time hoping it would.

"No one ever compared to the feeling I had that day on the beach. I've been looking for it again, ever since. I want to feel compelled to be with someone. Compelled to kiss her."

I laughed nervously. "I didn't realise I had such an effect."

"What about your fiancé? Jason, right?"

I felt myself blush. Jason had come to the hospital to see Mum a couple of times, and I'd felt awkward every time Dexter had approached or walked by. I didn't want to talk about him with Dexter.

"He's great," I told him, because it was true.

"Are you happy?"

"I think so."

We locked eyes and for a moment I thought he was going to lean in and kiss me. I felt the blood rush to my chest and had no idea how to react or what I wanted, who I wanted, or how I felt about anything.

"Want another drink?" he asked, suddenly looking away.

"Sure."

He got up and went to the bar and I thought about his question again. Yes, I was happy with Jason. So what was I doing here? I had no idea. I watched the back of Dexter's head as he ordered the drinks and I hated him for a moment. Hated him for coming into my life and messing with my feelings. But then he turned and smiled at me and I looked at his lovely face and I was mush all over again. It's just a crush, I told myself. We'll just be friends.

I'm a light-weight. Two glasses of wine and I start to feel bold and invincible. So after drinking the second glass while talking about Isla for a while, I finally turned to look at him, after avoiding too much direct eye contact while we'd been talking, and blurted out:

"Why did you kiss me that day on the beach?"

Dexter turned towards me and looked at me that way

again. The way that made me feel like he might be about to kiss me. Like he couldn't take his eyes away from me. For a second, I thought he might lean in. I think he considered it for a moment, but then he leant back, away from me in the booth and sighed.

"You were just standing there, looking so beautiful and staring out to sea. I wanted to talk to you; wanted to come and say hi. I'm not normally that confident with women."

I choked on my wine.

"What?" he asked, frowning.

"You seem confident. With all your charm and the way you look at me. I mean the way you looked at me, then, on the beach."

He smiled. "Well, I was nervous. But then you put me at ease once we started talking and I felt comfortable, like I'd known you forever. And I figured if I didn't kiss you there and then, I'd never get the chance again. So I did."

"Yes, you did," I said, remembering it again. I wondered if his lips felt as good as I remembered.

"It took all my strength to pull away."

"Mine too. And I kept thinking about you, for days afterwards."

"Me too."

We looked at each other for a few moments again. We were further apart now so there was less chance of a kiss unless we shuffled along the seat. I finally took my eyes away and finished my glass of wine.

"I'd better go," I said, regretfully. Going back to the hospital to be with my mother, looking so sickly, and watching my father looking so stressed, wasn't appealing. It made me feel scared and powerless. The last time I'd seen them look so frail and weak was when Helen left.

Dexter reached out and put his hand on mine.

"Dexter, please don't."

"Just tell me you don't feel it too and I'll move my hand

away."

I couldn't lie. I turned my hand so that it was holding his and squeezed it. Then I closed my eyes and leaned my head back in the booth so that I didn't have to look at him. I felt him shuffle closer. Still holding my hand under the table, I felt his arm against mine. I could hear him breathing. It felt so easy to sit there and be with him - to pretend that there was no wife, no fiancé, and no vulnerable parents waiting for us. I let myself savour the moment for a few minutes.

Then I forced myself to think of Jason. My best friend, my fiancé, and the man I wanted to spend the rest of my life with. I pulled my hand away.

"I can't do this. I'm sorry Dexter," I said, without looking at him, knowing that seeing his face would be my downfall. I pulled my hand away and got up. I turned back and he was looking down at the table.

"I don't think we should talk anymore," I said. He looked up at me and the pain of what I was saying hit me. Could I really walk away from this man? And yet I had to.

"Please, Izzy, don't go. Can't we talk about this?"

"No, there's nothing to say."

I turned and walked out of the pub, half expecting him to follow me and then not sure if I was pleased or disappointed when he didn't. I went back to the hospital. Mum was asleep and Dad and Aunt Ruth were waiting for me outside her room.

"Where have you been?" Dad asked.

"Nowhere. Just went out for a walk," I lied, hoping they couldn't smell the wine on my breath.

Aunt Ruth invited us to her house for dinner and we went and ate cheesy pasta. They kept saying I was quiet, and I just said I was tired. I couldn't stop thinking about Dexter, about the way he looked at me and the way it felt when he held my hand. But I knew this had to stop, having already gone too far.

That evening, Jason was working late so I lay in bed alone,

forcing myself to stop thinking about Dexter. The trouble was, if he wasn't on my mind then all I could think of was my parents. I kept picturing their faces. How old they suddenly seemed. I kept picturing Mum back when Helen had gone. She'd been pale and had permanently red eyes; not just from crying but because she rarely slept. Something about the way she looked now, lying in that hospital bed, reminded me of the sorrow of those days. It didn't suit her to look so weak and vulnerable. I needed her to be strong.

Eventually, I fell asleep and I dreamt that Helen and I were walking home from school when a man approached us. He grabbed me and pulled me into the back of a van as Helen stood there crying and screaming and trying to reach out for me. The man closed the doors and it was dark. All I could hear were Helen's screams and I felt the van pull away.

The next day I drove Dad to the hospital once more. I was determined not to talk to Dexter and to tell him to leave me alone if he attempted to talk to me. Mum didn't seem very well and I went to tell the nurse, who said she'd come and see to her. As I was about to go back, Dexter came along the corridor. He smiled and I couldn't help but smile back. I forced myself to move my eyes away from his.

"Can I have a quick word in here?" he asked, gesturing to an empty patient room next to my mum's. I nodded and followed him in. He closed the door behind us and I sat on the bed.

"Izzy, I'm sorry about yesterday."

"I can't do this. This has to stop, Dexter," I said firmly. I was quite proud of myself for showing such amazing willpower.

"I'm sorry. I just can't seem to stay away from you."

A ripple of pleasure ran though my chest. How could what he was saying being so right and yet so wrong at the same time?

He came towards me as I sat on the bed, and stood so that our legs were almost touching. I put my bag on the bed next to me and looked up at him. I thought for a moment he might kiss me, and yet again I didn't know how I'd react if he did.

It all seemed so ridiculous, I almost laughed. He ran his hand through his hair and looked away, but still stood close.

"This is just an infatuation," I said. "It'll pass."

He looked down at me again.

"Not for me."

I looked up into his eyes. How did he do that? He looked at me like I was the most amazing thing he'd ever seen.

"Don't be silly. This is just a crush."

"This," he gestured his hands between us, "is more than a crush, Izzy."

I took his hands and squeezed them. I could feel the current running between us again.

"No, it's not. We don't even know each other very well at all."

"Tell me you don't feel it too and I'll leave you alone."

"I am attracted to you, yes. But I love Jason. Please, leave me alone."

His face fell and I wanted to comfort him. I wanted to clone myself, let one of me see how this turned out and the other return to my loving fiancé. As that was impossible, I walked out of the room without looking back and determined not to talk to him again and not to think about it him at all, if possible.

I went and sat with Mum for a while, wondering what she'd think if I told her, but she wasn't really up to talking and I didn't want to burden her with my problems.

Jason had a day off the next day and I didn't go to the hospital so we spent the day together, pottering around at home and going out for a walk. I avoided too much affection because it just felt too strange. When he asked me if everything was okay, I said I didn't feel quite well and was worried about my mum. Which I was, of course. I just couldn't be normal around him when all I could think about was Dexter. I thought about telling him but wasn't sure what good it would do; it'd only hurt him. I was irritable and quite short when Jason asked me questions, somehow thinking if I was mean to him he wouldn't love me as much. If he didn't love me as much I wouldn't feel so guilty all the time. But he was as nice and caring and understanding as ever, never biting when I snapped at him; just continued being lovely and no doubt putting it all down to the stress I was under with my mum.

"I keep thinking about Helen," I told him and then went into detail about my dream, and how my mum, lying in the hospital bed, reminded me of the days after Helen disappeared.

"You're linking the two because it's the only other time you've seen your mum so helpless."

"I just wish I could help her."

He gave me a squeeze and I sighed deeply and let him hold me there for a while. I felt safe in his arms. There was no sick mother, no missing sister, no tempting crush. Just me and Jason and, somehow, I felt better, if only for a short while.

I didn't see Dexter at the hospital for the next few days, and I concentrated on my parents and work. I went to see Mum every evening, but she didn't seem to be improving. I was worrying about her enough to stop thinking about Dexter too much. But at night, I'd lie in bed, listening to Jason's heavy breathing, and all I could see when I closed my eyes was Dexter's face, the way he looked at me like we were two halves of the same whole. I felt drawn to him, just like I had after our kiss on the beach. I wasn't sure I'd ever had a crush like this before.

I went to see Jade one afternoon while Jason was working, hoping that if I explained all my feelings she'd help me work out what I should do. But she was about as sympathetic as Amber.

"What's the problem with Jason? He's kind. He's totally in love with you. You should be happy."

"I was happy. I am happy. It's just ... I don't feel this burning desire, you know? I think I want more than this."

"More? What do you mean?"

"I want someone I feel passionate about. Jason is my best friend but I want someone I just *can't* keep away from. I want that ... obsessive, compulsive love. Like Romeo and Juliet."

"That's just movie-love, Izzy. Those characters don't exist. Being best friends is the finest foundation for a marriage surely?"

She put two mugs of hot coffee on the table between us and a plate of biscuits. I didn't take one; I couldn't eat when I felt so emotionally torn.

"Yes, I suppose, you're right."

"You've seen me do this time and time again. I meet men I have an amazing chemistry with. It's wonderful and full of lust and passion, and then a few months later it dies out and he moves on, leaving me lost and hurt. I'd give anything to find the kind of companionship you have with Jason."

I sighed and nodded. She'd had her hair cut shorter and dyed it bright red which suited her. I told her so and we changed the subject for a while. She got up to go to the bathroom and I decided I needed to talk some more. As she came back in, I mentioned Dexter again.

"Another thing. When I'm with Dexter he just looks at me and it's like we're meant to be together. It's just ... this connection we have. I don't understand it."

She took another biscuit.

"Dexter is the unknown. He's the forbidden. He's different and new and exciting. But after a little while together, do you not think it'd be the same between you and Dexter as it is between you and Jason?"

"I love Jason, but I never felt this compelled."

"You and Dexter have chemistry - no doubt about it. But

that's just hormones and lust."

"Yes, I guess so."

"Don't guess. You can't fall in love at first sight. You can't fall in love after only a few hours in each other's company. You can't steal a married man from his wife. You can't break the heart of the man you do love. Not for lust."

"Okay, I know you're right."

"I'm sorry, Izzy, I know it's hard. You just have to grow up. I know that's harsh, but you're too old for crushes, my dear. You're engaged to be married."

"You really think it's just a crush?"

"Yes. You've known him less than a fortnight!"

"I just don't know what I want."

"You need to stop seeing him. It's not fair on Jason, or Dexter's wife. No matter what she's like she doesn't deserve this. And what about his daughter?"

"You're right. I've already told him to leave me alone and he seems to have taken the hint."

"Good. Stop thinking about him now then. Distract yourself with something else and it'll all be fine."

"Thank you, Jade."

I relaxed a little and picked up one of the biscuits.

"Nice," I said, with my mouth full.

"I made them myself. Jason gave me a recipe when I came for dinner."

My phone beeped. I had a text from an unknown number.

I'm sorry, I know this is against the rules but I got your number from your mum's file. I need to speak to you. I finish work in an hour. Can we meet by the park near the hospital? Dexter.

I promised Jade I'd ignore him. But I kept wondering what he wanted and somehow, without consciously planning to - as if I had no will of my own - I texted him back to confirm I'd meet him. Then I told Jade goodbye, got on a tube and went to the park.

Dexter was sitting on a bench looking out at the water. He looked nervous as he glanced up at me. I spent the whole journey wondering what the hell I was doing and decided I'd listen to what he said and then tell him to bugger off. Who was he to come along and mess up my happy relationship? He couldn't just kiss me whenever he liked, on the beach with Ewan only a few metres away, and then try to lure me in while my mother lay ill in the next room and my fiancé was at home, none-the-wiser. How dare he? I was angry. But then I saw him sitting there and felt it again. That uncontrollable magnetic attraction, drawing me to him. Without saying a word, I knew he'd persuade me to do whatever he wanted. I hated it and loved it at the same time.

"Izzy," he said, reaching up and taking my hands in his as I sat down, "listen—'

"No," I said, pulling my hands away, although not without great effort. "Dexter, this can't go on. You're married! Married! And I'm with Jason and, really, we hardly know each other. This is just crazy. I can't see you anymore. Please delete my number and don't text me again."

I stood up but he grabbed my wrist. Our eyes locked and he looked like he might cry.

"Please don't go."

"Dexter, I can't." I swallowed hard. Be a grown up, I told myself. *This is just a crush.*

"I'm falling in love with you," he said quietly.

I looked into his perfect face and sat down again.

"What?" I said, half whispering. "But you barely know me."

I looked at his eyes, unable to draw my gaze away and hating myself for it.

"I can't be without you. I know I keep saying it, but you just draw me in. You and me. It's just ... we're two halves. You have to see that. When you're not around it's like half of me is missing."

I realised straight away I felt the same way too. This wasn't a crush. I had no choice. I couldn't stand the thought of not being with him. And yet I couldn't imagine how I'd end it with Jason. This is it, I told myself. Either way you get hurt, but you must choose now.

Dexter or Jason?

Jason or Dexter?

"I feel that way too," I said. "I just don't know what I want. I love Jason. I can't hurt him."

He smiled sadly.

"I respect that and I won't rush you. But can you really imagine going back now?"

"No."

"Can you imagine us not being together?"

"The thought is painful," I admitted. It'd be painful to leave Jason too, but I didn't say that. We sat for a long time, holding hands, looking out across the water.

"I better get home," I said after a while, realising it was past 7pm. "Jason will wonder where I am."

"If I said I needed you tonight - that I didn't want you to go - what would you do?"

"I'd stay," I said, feeling as if I had no power at all. I was at his mercy.

"What about Jason?"

"I'd tell him I wasn't coming home."

"How?"

I looked at his impossibly perfect face, at his grey eyes and the tiny smile appearing at the corner of his mouth. This is more than a crush, I realised. I love him. I love them both.

"I'd tell him I'm in love with someone else," I said quietly, looking away.

He placed his hand on my chin and gently turned my face back towards his.

"I know it feels wrong, and I wouldn't want you to feel good about ending your current relationship or hurting anyone. But this is beyond our control, Izzy. This is meant to be."

"You really believe in all that stuff? In fate? That things are meant to be?"

He sat back and looked out at the water.

"I'm a scientist, Izzy. I have never believed in soul mates and fate and all that stuff. There are billions of people on the planet so there has to be more than one person you could fall in love with. But when I'm with you I start to believe, because I've never felt like this around anyone else. It's like I feel whole and complete when you're here."

I put my head on his shoulder and leant against him. He put his arm around me.

"Sorry, that was pretty corny," he said, laughing a little.

"I like corny."

He squeezed my shoulder.

We sat for another few minutes.

"I guess we should both go home. When can I see you again?"

"I'm not going to cheat on Jason. I won't sleep with you or kiss you or anything, not while I'm with Jason."

"I wouldn't expect you to."

"You need to give me some time and space to think about all of this."

"Of course. Whatever you need."

He kissed me on the back of my hand and stood up to leave. I watched him walk to his car, smile at me and get in.

When I got home I felt guilty, sick, and nervous. I avoided Jason, using my mum as an excuse again, which I knew was an awful thing to do. I thought over and over again about how much I loved Jason, how well we knew each other, how little I knew of Dexter. I emailed Jade and asked if she thought it was possible to be in love with two people at once.

As I pressed 'send' I saw a text from Dexter:

I can't get you out of my mind. I just want to hold you. No pressure, take the time to make the right decision. But if you let me, I'll love you forever.

My heart did a somersault.

Chapter Thirty-Two

"So, in conclusion," said Jade, "despite my overall disapproval, I do believe that you can totally be in love with two people at once."

"That's great, but what should I do?"

Jade sighed. She'd called me up following my email and we'd met for dinner in a little restaurant close to the school she taught at. We had both ordered chicken salads, but I wasn't really eating mine. Between the trauma going on with my parents and my messy love life I'd not had much appetite lately.

"Didn't you always want to marry a doctor? Back in the day? Someone who cared for people and saved lives?"

"Yes, I suppose I did," I said, remembering the time before I'd met Ewan. "I'd watched a lot of medical dramas with my mum, that's all."

"Jason and you just know each other so well and you're so close, and you were happy, before. All we know of Dexter is that he's willing to cheat on his wife and leave her. That's not much in his favour."

"Just listen. When I'm with him, it's like ... all the pieces of my life fit together. I'm completely drawn to him and I can't help myself. There's all this chemistry. It's like we're two halves that fit together."

I felt like I was constantly repeating myself, trying to justify it somehow.

"You've known this guy for so little time, Izzy. How can you fall in love that fast?"

"I know. But it feels like longer. That time on the beach - that was the most passionate kiss of my life."

"Passion is overrated. I've had plenty of passion. You know what I want? A man who can be my best friend. A man who's reliable and trustworthy. You've got that in Jason."

"I know." I nodded, tired of hearing it all again, even though I knew I should listen. I sighed; something I seemed to be doing a lot lately.

"I'll tell Dexter it's not going to happen."

"Good. You'll get over him. Amber's right. I know it doesn't feel that way, but it really is just a crush. While you're crushing it feels like this might be the love of your life, but afterwards you wonder what you could possibly have been thinking."

I wasn't sure it was just a crush, but I knew I could never call it off with Jason. Lovely, understanding, encouraging, best friend Jason. He was an amazing lover and he was an amazing man and I wanted him forever. I knew that. I never doubted it, really. And I couldn't have them both. So, I chose him.

I sent Dexter a text:

This can't continue. I'm sorry. Please don't contact me again. Izzy.

The harsh light of a new day, watching Jason sitting there eating his cereal had also given me a reality check. I couldn't imagine not waking up next to him every day, sharing our news, talking and being together. I warmed up to him a bit and was quite pleased with myself for knocking the Dexter situation on the head. In the meantime, I had plenty of work to do. I got on with it, happy to be back to some kind of normality. A few days later, I was booking a flight from Toronto to Chicago for Sian when my mobile rang. I saw it was Dexter and ignored it.

My phone kept ringing and then Dexter sent a text.

It's your mum. Call me.

So I did.

"Just come down here," he said, sounding weird.

Jason had gone out to work. I managed to get a taxi pretty quickly. I wasn't sure if he was just trying to lure me to talk to him, using my mum as an excuse. I was worried either way and decided I'd slap him if he was faking it.

I met him in reception and my first thought was that I could never physically hurt him. He stood there talking to a receptionist, smiling and looking handsome and charming, like he always did. He looked up and our eyes locked and I realised I had missed him, these couple of days. But then his face looked full of concern and I realised something really was wrong.

Without saying anything, he led me to a small empty waiting room and told me to sit down.

"What's happening?"

"She passed out this morning, and then it turns out there was a complication..."

He started explaining, telling me the words, but I didn't hear them properly. Something about bleeding and her brain. It was all a blur.

"...we did everything we could but she's gone, Izzy. I'm so sorry. I wanted to tell you in person. They're trying to get hold of your father now, but he's not answering. Do you know where he is?"

My mother was dead? Did I hear that right? I looked at him and tried to take it in.

"My mum is dead?"

"Yes, Izzy. I'm sorry."

I stared at the floor for a moment and then I started to cry. Waves of grief flooded over me as big fat tears fell down my face. Dexter sat down and wrapped his arms around me. I leant into him and cried quietly into his jacket. "I'm so sorry,

Izzy."

We stayed like that for a few minutes.

"I love you Izzy," he whispered into my ear. I just cried.

Dexter called Aunt Ruth, who fetched Dad, who broke down and my heart almost broke all over again at the sight.

The next few weeks were a blur. Somehow, between us, we managed to start organising the funeral, and somehow I managed to put the situation with Dexter to the back of my mind. Jason was so kind and attentive, and I felt constantly guilty. He did everything for me; helped me organise everything, called relatives, held me in bed while I wept, and was more supportive, loving and caring than I deserved.

I felt terrible. Instead of spending those last days with my mum - checking she was recovering, savouring the precious time with her - I'd been running around messing up my love life and seeing another man.

I spent a lot of time thinking about her, about her life and the sadness she'd known. I thought about the accident, the suddenness of it all. I thought about my dad and how he'd get on with living alone.

I also thought about Fern, Helen's best friend at school. They spent a lot of time together over the years and Fern was often at our house. She'd sleep in Helen's bed with her and they'd giggle all night. I sometimes listened at the door and hear them talking about the boys they liked, fashion, makeup, girls they liked and girls they hated. I was envious of them, being two years older and able to do all the stuff that I wasn't, like wearing mascara and flirting with boys.

Fern's mother died when Fern was very young, and she often told Helen that she felt she had to look after her father, since he was alone. Funny, I hadn't thought of her for years. I wondered what she was up to and if she often thought of Helen anymore.

A week went by and I didn't see or hear from Dexter. I wanted to be with him. I wanted him to hold me and tell me loved me like he had on the day she'd died. But I wanted Jason, too. I spent most days in tears, flitting between thinking about my mum and thinking about Dexter.

Eventually, he texted me. Jason had gone back to work after taking a few days off to see me through. I was sitting watching *Casablanca*, contemplating who Ilsa really did love the most, when my phone beeped.

Dexter: How are you?
Me: Okay. How're you?
Dexter: Worrying about you. I miss you.
Me: I miss you too.
Dexter: Can I see you?
Me: I don't know if that's a good idea.
Dexter: Please. I'll buy you dinner. Just as friends. Tonight?
Me: Okay.

As usual, I couldn't resist him. But I also didn't see how we could possibly be friends. I decided I would thank him for being there on that awful day, but tell him this was the last time we could see each other. It had to be over and finished with because I couldn't cope with the deceit or the betrayal. Finished before we'd even begun, but so be it. I was a terrible liar and couldn't keep going like this with Jason. I wouldn't be going to the hospital anymore so we wouldn't see each other accidentally and I'd go back to how I was before. Or, I'd try, anyway. I figured there'd always be a 'what if' but I'd just have to live with that.

I got to the restaurant first; Dexter had booked a Thai place in Kensington that neither of us had been to before. He said he found it on the internet and figured the chances of seeing anyone we knew there were slim.

The waiter bought some spicy crackers over and I munched on one. I heard the door open and looked up to see Dexter walking in, looking handsome as ever. The waiter took his coat and Dexter's grey eyes scanned the room. His face lit up when he saw me and he walked over. He was wearing black trousers, a cream shirt and a dark brown v-neck jumper. I realised he was a good dresser. I had mostly seen him in his doctor's clothes up until now. I stood up and hugged him when he reached the table. His torso felt strong and he smelt good. He hugged me back and kissed my cheek lightly. I felt a current pass from his lips into me and almost shuddered at the thought that I'd never see him again after tonight. But it had to be this way.

We sat down, smiling at each other, not saying anything for a moment. I suddenly realised I might not be able to finish this after all. It should have come as no surprise really. How many times had I tried to end it so far? And yet here I was having dinner with him.

"How are you?" he asked, squeezing my hand on the table.

"Okay, yeah. Just getting everything organised for the funeral."

"It's awful, isn't it? My father died a few years ago. You expect your parents to reach old age."

"And you expect to grow up with your sister, but that didn't happen either. I guess I should be used to things not turning out how you expect them to."

I felt my eyes well up with tears and swallowed hard.

"Life's too short, that's for sure, and it shouldn't be wasted. You've been through so much, Izzy. It's no wonder you feel upset. It's okay, you've lost someone important. Well, two very important people." He squeezed my hand again.

I nodded and bit my lip. I didn't really want to talk about my mum or sister.

"Thank you," I said, "for telling me and for being with me that day."

"Of course. I wanted to be. It was no trouble."

"What did you tell Holly about coming out tonight?" I swallowed hard again and regained some composure.

"That I was meeting the guys for drinks."

"Do you find it easy to lie to her?"

"Yes. Is that bad?"

I shrugged. "Have you ever cheated on her before?"

"No. And I'll never cheat on you, if that's what you're wondering."

"You make it sound as if we're definitely going to be together."

"Well, you came tonight when I asked."

"I seem to be under some sort of spell. I can't say no to you. I hate that."

He smiled.

"This is it for me. I want you for life, Izzy. So, if and when you consent to let me be with you, I promise that I will never cheat on you."

"Aren't you cheating on me every time you get into bed with her?"

I know that sounded crazy but the thought of him going home after each of our encounters and being with her made me feel insanely jealous. I didn't want him to spend time with her anymore, even though I had no right to expect that.

He opened his mouth to speak but the waiter came over to take our order. We had a quick look at our menus, until this point untouched, and ordered a platter to share as a starter and two Thai green curries with jasmine rice. As the waiter walked away my eyes fell to Dexter who was already looking at me, of course. As usual I felt the wave of happiness pass over me as he smiled, and felt the magnetic pull to touch him and kiss him.

"So what do we do now?" I asked.

"I don't want to pressure you. You know I love you. You know what I want."

I shrugged. "I don't know. I don't know what you want, or what I want. I don't know anything."

"I just want you." He squeezed my hand again.

"We don't even know each other that well! We're risking everything we have - for what? For lustful hormones? Who knows what?"

"You love me."

"I love him too."

"Not the way you love me. You feel exactly the way I do. I can see it in your eyes. And I don't want to hurt anyone either, Izzy. I don't feel good about all this."

"Then why are you doing it?"

"Because sometimes things are meant to be. Sometimes you have to be selfish. Jason and Holly will move on and be happy with new people eventually."

I didn't want Jason to be happy with anyone but me. That was the trouble.

"And what about in a few months, when all the excitement of the unknown is gone? Will you fling me to one side?"

"Izzy, you know this makes sense. We're meant to be together. This isn't a fling. I'm not looking for a casual affair. I want you for the rest of my life."

I stared at him, amazed that he kept declaring himself like this. He was so certain. He stared back and smiled.

"You know you want me too."

"I do. I just can't lie to Jason anymore."

"So don't. Leave."

"Where am I going to go?"

"We'll get a place together."

The waiter brought our platter.

"Just like that? You make it sound so easy."

I realised I was starving. I picked up a wonton and started to nibble at it.

"It is. It's simple. We'll rent somewhere," he said calmly, picking up a prawn toast.

"We haven't even had time to ... to date ... let alone move in together. You sure we can do this?"

"Listen, it's all up to you. We can take it slower if you'd

rather. If this is all too much, just tell me to back off, and I will."

I couldn't and he knew it.

"I want to be with you all you the time, Izzy."

"I want to be with you too."

Somehow, being with Dexter suddenly seemed to be the only thing that did make sense. When I was with him, I wasn't thinking about my dead mother or my missing sister. I was just thinking about his lips and his eyes and the way he made me feel.

"Good. I know it'll be tough, but we'll get through it together and in the long-term all the hurt we cause them will fade, and they'll move on."

I kept eating, not knowing what else there was to say. We were silent for a while, just nibbling on our platter, looking at each other, smiling.

"So where would we live?" I asked after a while. Somehow my leaving Jason was becoming more and more inevitable.

We chatted for a while then, imagining a life together. Dexter said he'd like to live close to the hospital so we talked about living in North London. I thought it'd be nice to be close to my dad, anyhow. He said we could get a two bedroom house and rent it for the time being. Isla could come and stay at weekends. Our curries came and I picked at mine; the mixture of nerves, guilt and excitement had made me feel a little nauseous.

Dexter started talking about taking a holiday together, flying off somewhere warm to relax for a week or two. None of it seemed impossible. It all sounded perfect, in fact. Until I thought of Jason alone in our flat, wondering what he'd done wrong.

"You say these things and it makes me so happy and yet so scared at the same time."

"Scared of what?"

"Of making a change. Of the hurt we will cause. Of losing

everything. Of making a mistake."

"Izzy," he said calmly, taking my hand. "I love you. This is no mistake. We're *meant* to be together. I feel bad too but you have to stop feeling guilty. They'll get over it."

"We haven't even had sex, Dexter. How can we know that this is it? That we're compatible?"

"We can fix that," he said, grinning.

Suddenly, I didn't want to feel so conflicted anymore. I didn't want to feel the pain of losing my mother, the pain of lying to Jason every day, the guilt about everything that was going on. I just wanted to feel good, to feel pleasure, to feel his lips on mine again.

"Take me to a hotel," I told him, calling the waiter over.

"What? A hotel?" he asked, looking confused. The waiter appeared.

"Can we have the bill please?"

"Of course, madam." He walked away.

"A hotel? Seriously?" Dexter said, looking at me intently. I looked at his gorgeous grey eyes and thought, for the millionth time, about his lips on the beach.

"Yes, seriously."

"You sure about that?"

"Do you want to fuck me or not?"

He grinned again, paid the bill, and led me out into the street.

Chapter Thirty-Three

We walked away from the restaurant holding hands and, I admit, I thought nothing of Jason, busy at his restaurant, or of Holly, doing who knew what. Or of little Isla.

I didn't think about my mum or how my dad might be coping. I didn't think of anybody but Dexter and myself. I knew it was selfish and some part of my conscious was nagging at me that this was wrong, but I told it to shut up and pointed out a nice looking hotel down the street.

"It might be expensive," I said to Dexter as we went in. It looked quite posh.

"I don't care," he said.

"Do you have a double room available please?"

The receptionist gave us both the once over. No luggage. Him with his wedding ring, me with my engagement ring only. Walking in off the street wanting a room. I felt judged, but she smiled sweetly enough and booked us in. I suddenly felt very nervous and wondered what underwear I'd put on that day. I hadn't expected Dexter to see it.

We got into the elevator and stood facing each other only inches apart, looking into each other's eyes. Dexter smiled and I smiled back. He reached up and touched my cheek for a moment and then let his hand drop.

"You're so beautiful," he said as the doors opened. We walked in silence along the corridor, holding hands until we found our room. Dexter opened the door for me to go in first. I switched the light on, slid my shoes off and went over to close the curtains. It was a nice room with a large king-sized bed, cream coloured bedding, a fluffy dark green carpet, a wardrobe, a sofa and a desk with a chair. I turned back to the curtains and peeped out, looking down at the street below, unsure of myself, and not knowing how to proceed. I felt Dexter slide his arms around me and hold me tight as I leant back against him.

"We don't have to do this, if you don't want to."

I turned to face him and he kept his arms around me. Our faces were centimetres apart. I looked from his eyes to his lips and back again.

"Likewise, if you don't want to, it's fine."

"I do," he said, looking at me and moving his face nearer so that our noses touched.

And then our lips met again and it was even better than on the beach. He was stronger, firmer, more of a man than the boy he had been then. I put my arms around his neck and groaned as he started kissing my neck. I wasn't sure I'd ever wanted anyone more. I wanted to feel him inside me and I wanted him right now.

He unzipped my dress and I pulled my arms out, letting it drop to the floor and then in once swift notion, he undid my bra and started kissing my breasts.

And then I thought of Jason. My best friend. I owed him more than this.

"Stop, please stop," I said, hardly believing the words were coming out of my mouth.

Dexter released me instantly and took a step back.

"I'm sorry," I said, taking a deep breath. "I want you so much, but I don't want to cheat. We have to wait. I'll tell Jason. I'll end it. Can we just wait a little longer?"

"Of course," he said, smiling at me but obviously disappointed. I glanced down at his erection and giggled. He laughed.

"Do you want to just lie on the bed together and cuddle?" he suggested.

"I'd love to," I said.

I pulled my bra and dress back on and went to join Dexter who was lying on the bed, his head on the pillow. I put my head on his chest and my arm around his torso and he held me.

We lay like that for a few minutes and I started to cry.

"Don't get upset, baby," he said softly, squeezing me tight and holding my head. "It's all going to be fine, I promise."

Chapter Thirty-Four

When I got home at 4am I burst into tears again. Jason thought I'd been out for dinner and drinks with some girls I worked with at one of Sian's companies. I had been out late with them a few times before, so he hadn't suspected anything out of the ordinary. I'd sneaked in, thinking he was asleep already but he was sitting up in bed watching a film.

He figured I'd had too much to drink and was upset about my mum, and the fact that this should have been the case just made me cry harder. I got into bed and he held me in his arms and I didn't want him to let me go.

"You're my best friend," I told him more than once as he held me there. Dexter and I had left the hotel and agreed that we'd tell Holly and Jason we were leaving them in a few weeks. I wanted to get past the next few days first, survive my mother's funeral without having to explain to Dad why Jason wasn't there. Plus I wanted him there to hold my hand - selfish though it was.

My mother's funeral was surreal and emotional, but went as well as it could. Everyone wore black and grey and offered words of comfort. Everyone was very nice but no one could make me feel better about losing her. I sat between Jason and Dad, holding both of their hands. I stared at the coffin and I forgot about my upside down love life and just wept for my mum. For the sadness she'd suffered in life and the sadness of her death.

I leant against my dad and he gave me a tissue. We both wiped our eyes. Then we all went outside and Jason put his arm around me. I saw Dexter in the crowd. He smiled at me and I smiled back, before watching him turn and leave.

I hugged aunts, uncles, cousins and family friends all afternoon in my parents' local pub. They'd put on a little buffet and I was first to get a large glass of wine. As I came away from the bar I saw Amber standing there smiling sadly, her hand on her hip, her big red curls falling over her shoulders. I hadn't noticed her at the crematorium.

"That was lovely," Amber said, giving me a hug.

"Thank you for coming. I'm so sorry about before."

"It's okay. I know I wasn't supportive."

"You were trying to help."

"I wanted to call as soon as I heard about your mum from Jade, but I wasn't sure if you'd want to hear from me."

"Of course I would, Amber. I love you. Thank you for coming."

We went and sat down at a table while all the other guests bumbled into the pub and queued up for drinks.

"So how's it going?" Amber said quietly. "I think I saw Dexter. He was there, wasn't he?"

"Yes. And I have tried to keep away from him Amber, but it's been so hard."

"You're going to leave Jason aren't you?"

I felt my eyes brim with tears.

"Amber, please don't judge me. I just can't give Dexter up."

She hugged me again.

"Dexter had better not hurt you," she said in my ear. I told her quickly and quietly about what had happened, about the hotel and where we were at now.

"Well, sounds like you've shown some amazing restraint. You should give yourself credit for that at least."

That didn't really make me feel any better as Jason came and sat with us and gave me a comforting squeeze. The rest of the day was all about my mum, though. Friends and relatives said some wonderful things and I played the hostess as best I could by supporting my dad and thanking everyone for coming as they left.

Later that night, I lay in Jason's arms and cried yet again. I cried for the sister I lost when I was twelve. I cried for the mother I'd lost two weeks ago. I cried for the relationship I was about to lose any day now. I cried because I felt guilty and scared and selfish. I realised I didn't like myself much anymore. But Dexter did. Dexter knew everything I'd done and he still loved me and still wanted me. That gave me some sort of comfort.

"I love you," Jason whispered as we fell asleep.

"I love you too."

And I did. I loved Jason so much. Giving him up would be the hardest thing I ever had to do.

Chapter Thirty-Five

"This is for you," said my dad, handing me a small box the day after the funeral. It said 'Izzy and Helen' on it.

"Where did you get this from?"

"It was in your mum's cupboard. She told me, when she was in the hospital, that if something went wrong I was to find it for you."

"Do you think she knew something would go wrong?"

"Maybe." He looked sad and tired. The past few weeks had aged him.

"I've been trying to remember the last thing she said to me," I told him. "I think it was something about the book she was reading."

"Last thing she said to me was 'Don't bring flowers tomorrow, I've got enough,' and I just laughed at her."

"Maybe she did know," I said, sighing.

"She's with Helen now," he said.

I swallowed to keep from crying. I had figured my mum was a rotting body in the ground, and that was that. But again, just like when I was at the cottage in Cornwall thinking of Helen, just for a moment, I believed. I saw them together, reunited; the fourteen year old who never grew up with her mother, and I felt happy for them. Maybe mum was at peace, finally.

"Do you mind if I go up to my old room to open this?"

"Of course not. Have a minute alone."

I went and sat on my old bed and slowly lifted the lid. There was a pile of Mother's Day cards, a book mark I'd made her when I was about fifteen and a few photos of Helen and me together when we were small.

Resting on top of all this were two crisp envelopes. One said 'Izzy', the other 'Helen'.

I took a deep breath. Should I open Helen's? I held it for a few minutes and decided to save it for later.

Dear Izzy

If you're reading this then I must have died, and so I'm sorry for not having been tougher and stronger to battle whatever it was that got me.

It may seem strange to you, to write a letter when I'm young, fit and healthy. But if losing my eldest daughter has taught me anything, it's that life is short and fragile. And I didn't get to say goodbye to her. So I want to say goodbye to you.

Izzy, you are my pride and joy. I love you so much. Follow your heart and go with your instincts. And always, always do the right thing for you.

I've written a letter for Helen, which I know might seem strange. But I can't imagine my girl being dead in a shallow grave somewhere so just in case, one day, she comes back to you, please give her my letter, too.

Be happy, my dear daughter.

I love you.

Mum

I sat there, tears streaming down my face feeling shocked, touched, emotional, fearful. I suddenly felt unsure again and wished I could ask her what to do about Jason and Dexter. I wished she could tell me what to do, who to pick, how to handle this whole awful mess I'd got myself into. I wanted to confess my sins, to redeem myself, yet somehow it was too late. She was gone. Follow your instincts, she said. The trouble was, my instincts were telling me to stay with Jason, the safe bet, my best friend. But at the same time somehow they also told me to run to Dexter, kiss him and be with him.

"You okay?" Dad peeped around the door.

I showed him the letter which he sat and read quietly on my bed.

"I'm so selfish," I said, out of the blue. And then it all came out. About Dexter: on the beach, in the hospital, in the restaurant, in the hotel. About Jason and how he was so perfect for me in every way. How I loved him, but how I loved Dexter too; how I couldn't get him out of my head; how I couldn't imagine giving either of them up.

My dad just sat and listened, looking concerned and yet calm.

"And I just feel so awful. I know I should be thinking about Mum, and I am. I miss her so much. It's just all too much to cope with. What am I going to do, Dad?"

He took a deep breath, took my hand and said:

"Tell Jason."

"Really?"

"Yes. Tell him everything. He deserves to know. And then work at it. Because he's an amazing guy and he loves you. I suppose I should tell you now that I had an affair once."

"What? Really?" I was so shocked my mouth actually fell open.

"Yes, it was years ago. You were about seventeen. I was completely infatuated with a woman. Her name was Shirley and we worked together. I thought I was in love. It lasted a few months and then I realised I didn't love her. It was new and exciting and wonderful, but she didn't really know me like your mother did. Your mother was my best friend and I couldn't be happy without her. So I told her everything. And she hit the roof, as you'd expect. But then we looked at our marriage and improved it. She said she realised that she had neglected me a bit since Helen disappeared and that maybe we should both put in more effort. We built trust again and, to the day she died, she was still my best friend. Just like Jason is

204

yours. You just need to spice it up with him, somehow, and I bet you'll feel happier. Stop seeing this Dexter fella. He needs to sort things out with his wife. That's my advice, anyway. I know you'll do your own thing and I love you either way."

"Thank you, Dad," I said, giving him a hug. I couldn't quite believe all he'd said. He put my letter along with Helen's in the box with all the other stuff and went downstairs. I cooked us some dinner; a chicken and asparagus recipe Jason had taught me and we watched it in front of a film.

"You'll do the right thing. Even if you want to be with Dexter, it'll all turn out okay," Dad said as he walked me back to the tube station that evening.

I hoped he was right.

Chapter Thirty-Six

"How can you be so confused?" Dexter asked me the following afternoon as we ate lunch at a café near the hospital. "I know I want you."

"He gives me security, you know? I feel safe with him. He's a wonderful person and he'll do anything for me. I feel like he'll love me forever, if I let him."

"Security? I'd rather feel vulnerable," he said, holding my gaze intently. "I'd rather feel that I had to prove my love every day, to earn it."

"Is that how I make you feel? Vulnerable?"

"Yes," he said, taking a mouthful of food.

Another moment passed.

"You want the truth?" he said. I looked up. He looked emotional now, his eyes were slightly red. My heart was beating fast and I had to will myself to sit back, to not lean in and kiss him.

"Of course," I said. "I want you to be one hundred percent honest with me."

"Sometimes I think about what it was like to kiss you and I think I'll go crazy if I never get that chance again. If you end this, if you choose him, I'll just go mad."

"But what if you just want what you can't have?"

"Izzy, I don't just want you tonight or tomorrow. I want you for life."

"I know, and I want you too."

"Please don't hurt me, Izzy. This is so right. We're meant to be." He took my hands.

He looked desperate, lost, scared; his eyes were wide, his face grew pale. I pulled my hands away. We sat like that for a few minutes, staring at each other, when he finally looked away. I leant forward and kissed him.

"Eat your lunch," he said, eventually pulling away.

I realised something that hadn't occurred to me before; either way, people were going to get hurt. We'd passed the point where no one lost out. If I chose Jason, I hurt Dexter. If I chose Dexter, I hurt Jason. Either way, I had to lose one of them, so I would be hurt too. There was no win. I had to make a decision and I had to do it soon before I lost my mind. Jason was already worrying about me as I'd been acting distant, and we hadn't been intimate since before my mum had died. This couldn't go on.

"I can't keep doing this," I told Dexter, getting up. "This is too intense. Give me a few weeks."

"I'm sorry Izzy."

"Two weeks. No contact. Please?"

"Okay," he nodded. "Whatever you want."

The intensity of his feelings for me was getting too much. I hated lying and avoiding Jason and knew the time had come to be honest. I wanted to be a better person than my behaviour over the past month had been.

Chapter Thirty-Seven

The next few days I tried to act normal at home, but I knew I was different; I was irritable and snappy and moped around in a semi-trance. Jason kept asking what was wrong and I kept saying I was tired and busy with work; or if I'd been quiet for a while and he asked me what was the issue, I'd say I'd been thinking about my mum; or that I'd had a busy day with Sian.

Most of all, I was angry. I was angry with life and confused about who I was or where I was going anymore. How could my mother die so young, when I'd already lost my sister? How was my father supposed to cope now? How was I supposed to make a decision between the men I loved? Between the passion I felt for Dexter and the companionship I had with Jason? I didn't want to think about any of it anymore. So I just shut down. I worked hard and called my father regularly and avoided everyone else. Despite me being a depressed, irritable madam, Jason was as patient, calm and kind with me as always, which just served to make me even more confused about what I wanted.

Then one evening, after a week apart from Dexter, we had dinner, cleared away and then Jason sat down with me in the living room and said:

"What's going on?"

"Huh?" I said, trying to look him in the eye but unable to.

"Come on Izzy, I'm not stupid. You've been distant for weeks. You're not affectionate, you don't want to have sex. You seem depressed. What's going on in that head of yours? Is it just your mum or is something else bothering you?"

I hesitated. I had no idea what to say or how to be fair to him when I knew hurt was coming eventually. How much longer could I really delay this? I thought about what my dad said and considered confessing all. But then, where would I sleep tonight if I broke it off now? I glanced at the clock, it was gone 10pm.

"Nothing. I'm sorry, I've just..." I hesitated. I wanted to say: I'm just the most selfish, horrible person imaginable.

"You've just what? Fallen for someone else?"

"What? No!"

"Do you love me?"

I hesitated again.

"It's that doctor, isn't it?"

I put my head down, stared at his stripy socks.

"How do you know?"

"I'm not stupid. I think I know you well enough by now." He sighed. "I was just hoping I was wrong."

"I'm sorry, Jason," I said, because I didn't know what else to say.

"Don't you think this is partly down to losing your mum? Your emotions are all over the place right now, that's all."

"I started having feelings for him before that. I met him once before, a long time ago, when I was with Ewan." I felt the relief flood out of me as I explained.

"Why didn't you tell me?"

"I've been so confused," I admitted. "I didn't know what I wanted."

"And I assume he knows how you feel?"

"Yes. He feels the same way."

"How bloody wonderful for you both." He shook his head and stared down at the carpet.

"I think I'm in love with him," I said quietly.

"Fucking hell, Izzy!" I'd never heard him swear before. He leapt up and his face turned red. He continued to shout at me, his eyes blazing, full of anger and pain. "Why couldn't you have talked to me about this? Why didn't you come to me, tell me how you were feeling before it got to this - to you breaking up with me without actually saying the words! For fuck's sake, Izzy! I thought we *communicated*. I thought we were beyond all the bullshit. I thought we were honest with each other ... but ... I thought wrong I guess!"

I watched his eyes fill with tears and I almost hugged him and told him we'd work through it, that I'd made a mistake. But the rest of me still felt that magnetic pull; that thread that tied me somehow to Dexter. It was impossible to ignore.

So I whispered something of an apology and he watched me with a horrified look on his face as I told him that I loved him, that I'd always love him, but there was something else, something stronger with Dexter that I couldn't ignore.

"I'm just trying to work out why you'd throw away a four year relationship to be with someone you hardly know. Do you not think losing your mother has just made you messed up in the head?"

"I am feeling messed up," I said, starting to cry, "and no, it doesn't help that I've just lost my mum. I don't know what I'm doing and I'm scared. But I can't ignore the way I feel about him."

"Bloody hell," he said, sitting down. He bit his lip but the tears were falling. I didn't know whether to go and hug him or not.

"I am so sorry. I would like us to be friends, Jason."

"We can't." He let tears fall and I watched with horror as he sat down on the sofa and fell apart, crying hard and putting his head in his hands.

"Why not?"

"Because I love you so much, Izzy. I'll never move on if I see you."

"I love you too," I said, moving closer and putting my arms around him.

"Then stay," he said, holding on to me as we wept together.

"I can't. I love him."

He pulled away and we looked at each other for a moment, water in our eyes and on our cheeks.

"Have you screwed him?"

"No."

"Honestly?"

"No, I couldn't cheat on you. I told him I had to make a decision and he's giving me some space."

"And your decision is made? You want him?"

"Yes, I think so. I'm so sorry."

He cried for a moment and I held him. He didn't deserve this. I hated myself. After a while he sat up and took a deep breath.

"I think it's best you leave now."

It was almost midnight. I got up, nodding, packed up a bag and left for Amber's house.

"His face will haunt me forever," I said as I burst into tears on her front door step.

"Oh Izzy," Amber said, hugging me into her arms.

Chapter Thirty-Eight

Thursday. Two days before my wedding.

Ewan was there before me, sitting in the pub, looking at his phone. I stood back and watched him sip his beer. He was wearing a black leather jacket and blue jeans. Looking as gorgeous, and as sexy as ever.

"Hello stranger," I said, putting my bag down on the floor beside him.

He stood up and hugged me tightly. "Wow, Izz, I've missed you!"

"I missed you, too." He smelt amazing.

He went to get me a drink, a glass of rosé of course, which made me smile, and then we sat. Wow, he really was gorgeous. Those blue eyes. He was smarter, now, though. Tidier hair, clean shaven, nice clothes.

"I couldn't believe it, when I saw you last week. What a coincidence!"

"Well," he said, looking down and then back up at me. He really was still gorgeous. "I admit I have been looking for you."

"What?" I wasn't sure whether to be happy or annoyed.

"My brother told me you were living in Notting Hill."

I remembered bumping into Alex years ago and nodded.

"And so I've been in the area and I always keep an eye out for you."

What did that mean? I looked away, took a deep breath and decided to change the subject.

"So tell me what you've been up to. All these years. All the places you've been."

He took a sip of his drink and seemed to relax a little.

"Well, of course I went to Australia, as you know. Then travelled through Asia, to Japan, Vietnam, Thailand. Then I went to Africa."

"Wow."

We ordered lunch, both opting for pasta as a reminder of our time in Italy together, and he told me some stories about the places he'd been, the people he'd met, the food he'd eaten. Occasionally he'd say "you'd have loved it" and I wondered if I would have, and if in some parallel universe maybe I had, or maybe I'd gone but hated it. I told him about my job and he took a keen interest and asked lots of questions. We chatted more than we had on any one occasion during our relationship. Then there was an awkward silence for a moment. I sipped my wine and looked at those blue eyes again and grinned at him.

"It's so good to see you," I told him. "I like your hair shorter."

"You look great," he said. "I should never have let you go."

I laughed. "Thank you. You look good too."

"I mean it, Izzy. Why did we break up? I loved you. I know I didn't say it often enough. I was young and foolish but I was broken when you went home."

"I loved you too. I almost didn't go home. But I didn't want to travel. I wanted to be settled, near my parents. I didn't have that same travel bug as you."

He nodded. "Well, I'm cured! Been home and working for a year now as a sales manager, in an office."

"Wow. I never thought I'd see the day."

"Me neither. Funny. I'm happy, though. I like it."

"That's great."

"Except for one thing."

"Oh yes?"

"You."

"Me?" I was astonished.

"I want you back, Izzy." He leant forward and looked at me seriously, his blue eyes penetrating mine. "I've never stopped loving you. I know it's been a long time and you're with someone else and getting married on Saturday and that this is the worst time to do this to you, but I want you. I met girls while I was away but none compared to you. I only thought of you every time I slept with someone else. I am still in love with you."

I stared at him. How I'd wanted to hear these words when I'd first come back from Verona. How I'd longed to see him again. Back then, I'd loved him so much more than I loved Greg now, I realised.

So much more.

Was it possible to go back to that? Had I changed too much? I sat there staring at his gorgeous face and remembering how he used to make me feel.

Now what was I going to do?

Chapter Thirty-Nine

The day after leaving Jason, I woke up in Amber's spare room and had a little cry. I picked up my phone and texted him to ask if he was okay. I didn't expect a reply and none came.

Then I texted Dexter and arranged to meet him at the hospital. I hung around in the reception area for about twenty minutes before he came and gestured for me to follow him. He found an empty room and we went inside.

"You look awful," he said. "Are you okay?"

I was aware my eyes were red from all the crying and I was tired after little sleep. I nodded and smiled at his grey eyes.

"I left Jason." Three words. If only it'd been as easy to do as it was to say.

"Really?" his face lit up and for the first time since my conversation with Jason began the day before, I felt happy.

"Really."

He picked me up and spun me around and kissed me hard until Jason and the tears and everything else disappeared. I was where was I meant to be. Dexter had to get back to work but told me he'd meet me wherever I wanted him to after work and we'd talk more.

I went home when I knew Jason would have gone off to work and got a few more of my things, and packed up all my work stuff. Then I called Sian and asked if I could stay in her apartment. She was never there and she was very happy for me to borrow it for a while. I had a spare key so I took Fred and as much stuff as I could fit into a taxi and went round there. It felt funny for Fred and I to be around her furniture and belongings again, but strangely safe at the same time.

As soon as I had my stuff installed, I sent Dexter a text giving him Sian's address. He said he'd come round straight after work. I lit candles and prepared some dinner for us. When I opened the door to him he looked happy. His eyes were bright and he flung his bag on the floor and wrapped his arms tightly around me.

"So how did it go?" he asked as we sat on Sian's sofa sipping wine. "Start from the beginning."

"I told him. It was hard. We both cried. But I was honest about us. It's funny. Just one conversation was all it took in the end. I mean, how can it be over, just like that?"

"It just is."

This isn't a game, I wanted to tell him. Didn't you realise this was going to happen? How could he be so flippant? I bit my tongue.

"Okay. So, you're staying here for how long?"

"As long as I need, really. Sian's never here. I guess once you've told Holly, we'll look at getting a place?"

"Yes, yes of course."

"You can stay here," I said, "whenever you want."

"I won't tell Holly about you," Dexter said. "Just that I'm leaving."

"Okay. Fair enough."

"There's just one thing," he said, coming over a little cold and serious.

"Okay..."

"It's her thirtieth birthday in two weeks. She's planned this big party. I'm not sure it's the decent thing to dump her right before that."

I felt a surge of jealousy and anger race through me. He'd been the one so certain and now the time had come, he was delaying.

"I suppose..." I said. He grabbed my hands.

"I'm just trying to play fair, really. Two weeks and then I'm all yours."

"All mine?"

"Yours and no one else's."

I put my arms around him. "I can wait two more weeks."

"Thank you." He kissed me slowly and then more passionately, causing us to fall back on the sofa.

"Stop," I said, pushing him away.

"What now?"

"When was the last time you had sex with Holly?" I asked, not sure that I wanted the answer.

"Over a year ago."

"Really?"

"Yes. Really."

This suddenly made things better. I pulled him to the bedroom where he undressed me and this time I didn't tell him to stop. I felt his naked body moving on top of mine and I knew this was right, that this was what I'd wanted. All the intensity of the kisses we'd shared was mirrored in our love-making. It was like no two people had ever fit together so well.

He left around midnight, promising me that it was only another two weeks, and then he'd be able to stay with me all night, every night.

The next day I went back to Jason's for the rest of my things. I texted him first, asking if he'd rather be out but didn't receive a reply. I was planning to get the last of my stuff, put the key through the letter box and go. But when I came in, he was waiting in the hallway. He looked pale and tired.

"I thought you would try to be out."

"You want me to make this easy for you?" Jason asked.

"I know I don't deserve anything from you," I said. "I thought it'd be easier for you, that's all."

I pulled the engagement ring out of my pocket and held it out to him.

"What am I supposed to do with that?" he asked.

"I don't know. Sell it?"

"Keep it," he said. "Something to remember me by. Every time you look at it, remember how much I loved you and how much you hurt me."

I sighed.

"I didn't want to hurt you Jason. And believe it or not, I'm hurting too."

"I think I'd be better off leaving, actually," he said, pulling his jacket on. "Leave the key, will you?"

"Yes," I said, biting my lip. Please don't let this be the last time I see him, I thought to myself.

"Have a nice life, Izzy," he said without looking at me and slamming the front door behind him.

I gathered my things quickly, being careful not to take anything that might be deemed joint ownership - only my books and other personal items. Jason had paid for anything we shared, anyway.

I left him a note, scribbling as I cried a little:

Jason,
I'll ask my dad to come and get my office furniture, if that's okay with you.
I am so sorry. You are a wonderful person and you'll find someone else, someone better than me.
I do love you, you're my best friend.
Take care,
Izzy

I left it on the dining table, shuddering at the thought of him finding someone else but knowing I had no right to expect anything else. I slipped out, posted the key through the letter box and went to Sian's apartment.

Chapter Forty

Dexter took a few days off work and we spent them together, mostly at Sian's place. He told Holly he was attending a medical conference up north somewhere.

The sex was as amazing as it had been the first time. Any fears I'd had about not knowing each other well evaporated. We connected on every level; we talked about the future, about renting a house and eventually buying one. Dexter suggested we go on a holiday somewhere warm to relax in the summer and talked about introducing me to Isla one day. He said he thought she'd love me, as would his parents and friends.

He told me he loved me all the time. He was affectionate and tender; passionate and intense as ever. One night we lay naked in bed in a post-coital haze, staring at each other. I thought I could stare at those grey eyes forever.

"Good night, soul mate," he said, kissing me on the forehead. I turned to face the other way and he held me from behind.

Still, I did miss Jason. I missed his jokes and little things he had done, like cooking me dinner, asking me about my day, bringing me little gifts and finding news articles he thought I'd be interested in. All the talking and sharing. I missed my best friend, when it came down to it.

Dexter became busy in the days leading up to Holly's birthday and I spent the night of the party watching chick flicks and eating chocolate, knowing it wouldn't be long now.

The date was set and he would tell her two days after her

birthday. But the day after her birthday he turned up at Sian's place unexpected, his face white and his hands shaking.

"What is it?" I asked, thinking he might be ill.

"Come and sit down," he said, walking to the sofa.

"What's wrong?"

"I told her. Not about you, just that I was leaving her. I couldn't wait any longer," he said, blurting it out quickly. At last! I felt instant relief.

"That's great!" I said, putting my arms around his neck. He carefully removed them.

"Dexter, you're scaring me, what is it?"

"Holly's pregnant."

I let it sink in a moment; let it settle.

"What?"

"She's about six weeks pregnant. I had no idea. And I'm a doctor!"

"But you said you hadn't—"

"I know what I said."

"You liar!" I said, furious and scared at the same time. I slapped him hard around the face. He recoiled and looked shocked. My hand stung. I was pretty shocked myself.

"I'm so sorry, Izzy. I said that because I thought it'd hurt you if I told the truth."

"So you were screwing me and screwing her at the same time?"

"I had to ... keep up appearances, and honestly, did you not sleep with Jason since all this started?"

He had a point. Jason and I had slept together once since it all started. But I hadn't felt good about it and had cried afterwards. Poor Jason had figured it was because of my mum, when really it was because I felt guilty towards Dexter. Still, I hadn't been the one who lied and claimed that we hadn't done it for a year.

"Okay," I said, calming down. "It's okay, I understand. This doesn't matter, Dexter. I still want you. Two children, one child, what does it matter?"

"I told her..." he paused, his voice cracking a little, "I told her that I'd give it another go."

"What?" I said, hardly believing what I was hearing and feeling a little faint.

"I said that I'd try to make our marriage work. It's a tiny, innocent baby, Izzy. How can I leave her now?"

"Isn't Isla innocent?"

"Yes, of course, but I can't just walk away from a pregnant woman can I?"

"Do you love me?"

"Yes, of course."

"Do you love her?"

"No. But I'm going to try. I owe her that."

I thought I might explode with anger and despair. The tears came – big, fat, fast tears rolling down my cheeks.

"I can't believe I'm hearing this," I said, breaking down.

"I'm sorry, Izzy. I have to stop seeing you. I'm so sorry."

"I gave up everything for you! I loved Jason! I hurt him so much! For nothing!"

"Izzy, I'm sorry."

"Get out!" I screamed.

"You're my soul mate, Izzy, you have to understand, this is breaking my heart," he pleaded.

"Get out!"

"We'll be together in the next life. I really do believe that."

"What the hell does that mean? Get out! Get out!" I was hysterical.

He left then. I felt myself fall to the soft cream rug where I lay all night, crying, and then staring up at the ceiling. Then crying again. I think I was almost wailing at one point.

How had this happened? How had I lost so much in such a short amount of time? I'd lost my mother and Jason, and now Dexter too.

Eventually, I stopped crying and sat up, trying to figure out what was happening. And that's when it hit me: my mum was dead. She really wasn't coming back, and this was all real, not a dream but real life. My mother was dead. My sister was dead. And my relationship with Jason was dead.

Three months. That's all it took for Dexter to ruin my life.

Chapter Forty-One

Thursday. Two days before my wedding.

"So what did you tell Ewan in the end?" Jade asked as she sat beside Amber, their mouths hanging open. It was seven p.m. and we'd just shared an Indian take away. I'd only picked at mine, having had pasta with Ewan for lunch and, lately, I was too emotional to eat much anyway.

"I told him I'd think about it."

"What?" Amber almost shouted.

"I loved him, once. I miss him, even now. I loved him more back then than I love Greg now. That has to mean something."

"Oh God, we need drinks," said Jade, getting up and going to her kitchen. Amber just stared at me in disbelief. Jade returned with large glasses of red wine.

"How do you measure love?" Amber asked me.

"What do you mean?"

"Well, you said you loved Ewan back then more than you love Greg now. How are you measuring it?"

"I just know," I said, sounding like an annoyed child, "I know that when I was with Ewan I loved him unconditionally and I would have been thrilled to marry him. With Greg, I'm marrying him because I got swept up in it all but I don't feel that passion or spark that I felt with the others."

It felt good to finally admit how I was feeling, to realise what the problem was and to get it all out in the open. Jade and Amber glanced at each other and Jade was just about to speak when my mobile phone buzzed. It was on the coffee table, nearest Amber. She glanced at it, picked it up and then said: "Holy shit!"

"What?" said Jade and I in unison.

"It's from Dexter."

"Let me see," I said, getting up to take the phone.

"No, I'll read it out."

"Okay," I sat down again. I'd only tell them what he said anyhow. What could he want, anyway?

"Izzy, this is Dexter. I need to see you. ASAP. Call me," she read out.

I got up and snatched the phone and typed a reply.

It's too late.

Dexter called me straight away but I didn't answer. Jade and Amber were standing with me, looking at my phone.

"He's the one I really thought I'd have to hold you back from," Amber said, shaking her head. "That bastard screwed up your life and now he wants to screw it up again?"

Another text.

Please answer

I shook my head and typed a reply.

Leave me alone. I'm getting married on Saturday

"Stop replying," said Jade, sitting again and taking a big mouthful of wine.

Another text.

Then I need to see you before then. Explain a few things. Please.

Amber snatched the phone and typed my next reply.
This is Izzy's friend Amber. Fuck off. She doesn't want you

anymore.

I frowned at her but shrugged my shoulders. My phone beeped again.

I love you, Izzy. We're soul mates. You know this.

Between the wine, the declarations of love from my ex-boyfriends and the pre-wedding nerves, my head was swirling. I wasn't sure how much I could take in one day. Ewan had been shock enough. How is a person supposed to know who they'd be happiest with when given so many choices?

Now Ewan was far from my mind. He was nothing compared to what I felt with Dexter. But he hurt me beyond belief. I wasn't sure I could ever trust him, and I was pretty sure I'd never get over it if he broke my heart again.

I typed a reply:

Regardless, it's too late.

I closed my eyes for a minute. Amber picked up my phone.

"Regardless? So you agree that you're soul mates?"

I opened my eyes again. "I've never felt as intensely about anyone; never connected as well as I do, or did, with Dexter. You know that."

"But you don't want him?"

"No. I can't get hurt like that again."

"But if he's your soul mate, Izzy..." Jade started.

Amber nudged her. "Don't make her even more confused."

My phone beeped again.

Please, just let me see you. I'm at the pub opposite the hospital. Please, Izzy. I'll do anything.

The thought of seeing him again made my heart skip a

225

beat.

"I never thought I'd say this," Amber said, "but Izzy, if you really think he's your soul mate ... if you really still think that, after all the hurt ... then maybe you shouldn't marry Greg."

I watched her, hardly believing what I was hearing.

"I agree," Jade said.

"So you think I should meet him?"

"I think you should call off the wedding."

"I'm so confused," I said, putting my head in my hands. "What if Dexter hadn't text me, would you have let me marry Greg?"

"It's just when you talk about how you loved Ewan more than Greg ... and then you still, even now, feel this connection with Dexter. You shouldn't marry Greg if you're really not sure."

I looked up. Amber was biting her lip. Jade was smiling sadly.

"Jade?" I asked.

"I think she's right. You should be honest with Greg. Maybe take some time out."

"You've both been telling me all week to focus on the wedding and how wonderful Greg is."

"We thought you had cold feet," Jade said. "But this is more than that."

I sighed. "I'm going home," I told them.

"It's only seven thirty. You don't want another wine?" asked Jade.

"No thank you. I think I should be alone. I need some time to think."

They hugged me goodbye and I walked to the tube station. When I got there I had a choice to make. One direction would take me home, to Greg's place. He was out with his friends this evening so I could sit at home for a while and think about all this. Or I could take the tube in the other direction, which would take me to Dexter.

But really, there was no decision to make. There never was with Dexter. I knew the minute he texted me that I'd give in. He took away my freewill. The magnet was pulling me once again.

I gave in.

I'll be there in half an hour.

He replied straight away.

Great. I'm waiting x

Chapter Forty-Two

One of my memories of Helen was when she lost her pet rabbit, Bouncer. My parents and I didn't care much for Bouncer. He was an evil little thing with black fur and sharp claws which he was quite happy to scratch you with. He liked to nibble on your fingers and clothes, too. But Helen loved Bouncer, and she was the only person he could tolerate. She'd faithfully clean out his hutch every week and cuddle him. She and Dad built him a little run out of chicken wire and she'd feed him carrots while sitting on the lawn with her dolls.

When Helen was eleven, Bouncer died.

Helen couldn't handle it, I suppose and she went into denial. She watched Dad take him and bury him, and she helped to clear away his hutch and all the chicken wire and put it all in the garage. But she didn't shed a tear or seem affected in anyway.

Then, one day, a few weeks later, she had a really bad cold and was feeling pretty ill and she just burst into tears as we sat eating breakfast and said she couldn't believe that Bouncer was dead.

I sat eating my breakfast the day after Dexter broke my heart and told me he wasn't leaving his wife and that she was in fact pregnant. Somehow, I felt like a haze had lifted. This strange dream-like world I'd been in had faded away and now I was back to myself.

However, nothing was like it was before. I was back to being in Sian's house. I'd lost Jason and I'd lost my mum and I wasn't even sure how it'd all happened; just that it had. When

I looked back on the time since the day of the accident, it was like it wasn't really me, just a surreal, abnormal version of myself. I kept staring at Sian's white walls taking it all in. How could it have come to this? How could Dexter say all those things and then just take them back, just like that? Did he have no concept of what he'd made me give up for him?

Most of all, I kept thinking: had I really been so stupid, to throw away my relationship with Jason for a man I barely knew? I considered this over and over again. Something must have been wrong with my feelings for Jason, but what? When I thought of him, I was filled with nothing but warmth and happy memories, and then the pain that I'd seen on his face, the hurt I'd caused. Caused for what? For nothing.

On the second day, I was lying in the dark about to call Amber and tell her when Dexter texted me.

This is so hard. I miss you.

I replied straight away. Maybe this hadn't all been for nothing, after all?

Me: I miss you too. Come over.
Dexter: I can't.
Me: Please. We can work this out.
Dexter: I'm sorry.

I didn't reply again. I just sat and wondered if I'd ever feel happy again. A few hours later, he knocked on my door. I opened it slowly, thinking it might be a parcel for Sian. I almost collapsed into his arms but he held me away, firmly and his face was different - cold somehow.

"I just wanted to check you're okay," he said, taking my hand and leading me in before shutting the door.

"I'm fine," I said, trying to mirror the cold exterior. "Brilliant. Never better."

He turned to look at me and looked like he might cry.

"I know this is hard, Izzy. I am sorry. I have no choice."

"You have a choice," I said, hoping I wasn't about to start begging. "Choose me."

"I want to, but I also need to do the right thing by my family."

"Then why did you come here today?"

"I just wanted to check you're okay. But from now we shouldn't talk or text or anything. I think we should just ... forget that anything happened. Clean break and all that."

"Easy for you to say. You didn't give up anything for me. I gave up my fiancé and my home."

"This isn't easy for me, either Izzy. I love you and this is a hard choice for me."

"Oh, I feel really sorry for you."

"I'm sorry, Izzy, I really am. I didn't mean to be so cold."

He wrapped his arms around me and for a few moments I thought he'd changed his mind and was going to leave her, after all.

He leant in to kiss me and as our lips met I couldn't believe what was happening. He started pulling at my clothes and before I knew it we were on Sian's rug, naked, having fast, delicious, amazing sex. He was mine, after all. I was elated.

Then he got up and helped me to get dressed. He pulled his clothes back on and then he kissed me again.

"I'd better get home, sorry baby," he said, kissing my forehead. I felt anger soar through me.

"So that was just a goodbye fuck?"

"Izzy, please."

I felt tears appear in my eyes and willed them not to fall, but they tumbled over and ran down my cheeks.

"Don't cry, Izzy, please," he said, putting his arm around me. He sounded like he might cry too. "I can't leave her. I told you that yesterday."

"I wish we hadn't met! I was happy. I loved Jason," I said,

breaking down in his arms.

"I know. I'm sorry."

"I don't understand. If you love me - if you think we're soul mates - then why can't we make this work?"

"I don't love you," he said quietly.

I pulled away, horrified. "What?' I almost screamed.

"I was in love with the idea of you, Izzy. Of something new and exciting," his face was cracking and tears were appearing.

"Don't say that!" I said. "That's not true, look how upset you are!"

"I love Holly," he said, looking away. "I was just confused. I'm sorry."

"Liar. Look at you, you're crying."

"I know. I'm sorry. I'm just trying to make it easier for you."

"Get out!" I said, almost screaming at him. "Leave! Now!"

He tried to hug me again, crying harder this time.

"Look at you, crying! You do love me!" I screamed, moving away from his arms.

"Izzy, I love you, of course. I'm stupid. And I'm so sorry."

"Get out! And don't come back again!"

"Izzy, please—"

"Leave! I never want to see you again."

And he did. Just like that, he was gone from my life.

I felt rage ripple through me and, turning back into the living room, I groaned loudly and dramatically, trying to let all the pain out, but it was still there. So I sat on the sofa and cried uncontrollably for what felt like hours. Eventually I texted Amber.

I need you.

She was at the front door within an hour. I repeated the conversation.

"He loves you so he's just trying to help you get over him,

set you free."

"I don't want to be free," I said quietly, leaning against her on the sofa.

"I know."

"You can say 'I told you so' if you like."

She didn't though. That's one of the things I love about her; she knows when to be silent.

Chapter Forty-Three

I dreamt about Dexter a lot after that. Mostly we would be arguing. I'd shout and scream and break down in tears. Sometimes he would come and put his arms around me, kiss me and tell me he loved me, and that he was going to leave Holly after all. Other times he'd leave me standing there, shouting and I'd wake up with a jolt and lay there staring into the dark, wondering if I'd ever get over this. I dreamt that we were having sex, too. On the sofa; on the rug; in my bed; in that hotel where it never happened. It was always intense and passionate, and much better than it had been in reality. I'd wake up feeling horny and start crying.

In my head I wrote Holly at least a dozen letters, always anonymously, telling her that she deserved to know that her husband had cheated on her. I think I thought if she broke up with him he'd be mine again. Then I realised he was never mine to start with. I think the children are the only thing that stopped me. I imagined them in bed together, him touching her stomach as the baby grew. Did he ever think of me or wish it was me lying there? Or did he wish we'd never met? Did he still feel the pull that I couldn't seem to let go of? Did he have an empty, cold hole inside him?

I thought about Jason a lot too. I'd wish he was there to hold me, comfort me, and tell me he loved me, despite all the hurt I'd caused. I sometimes wondered if I'd loved Dexter at all, or was it just a crazy, obsessive crush like Amber had said in the beginning. Something silly that had got out of control. When I thought of Jason, I realised I hardly knew Dexter at all. With Jason I knew everything, and the thought of him in bed with someone else hurt even worse than the thought of Dexter with Holly. Still, I couldn't bring myself to call him. It seemed too late, now. I couldn't erase what I'd done.

After receiving some life insurance inheritance from my mum, I could afford to buy a small one bedroom house not far from Jade. I pulled myself together, somehow, and I moved on with my life.

I kept watching Jason on television. He still had the nervous energy and seemed to have lost yet more weight, now looking a little too skinny. I tried calling him a few times but he never answered. I contemplated going to his house or the restaurant to talk to him, to beg him if necessary, just to be friends - but I was scared of the rejection.

Although I was quite lonely and low in general, I loved my little house and I settled in quite quickly. Sometimes I wished I'd gone to Australia with Ewan. Surely none of the other crap would've happened then? I'd be blissfully happy, wrapped up in his arms somewhere warm, with only a bar job to go to instead of having to run someone else's life. Instead of being alone.

Other times I wished that I'd never set eyes on Dexter. In fact, I thought that a lot. If only that stupid crazy van driver, who, as it turned out had also died in that accident, hadn't driven wildly, my mum would still be here and I'd still be with Jason.

Two months had passed by, and slowly. Somehow I was beginning to not feel quite so depressed about how things had turned out. Amber and Jade came over for cocktails one evening and we sat on my little red sofa talking about the way things had gone.

"Sometimes," I said, after a handful of olives and a sip of Mojito, "I wonder where I went wrong. I was so sure that Ewan was the one, then Jason and then Dexter."

"I don't think there's only one," Amber said matter-offactly.

"Really? I never used to think so, either. But I can't imagine being with someone new now, having loved those three so much and having felt so hurt in the end."

"There's six billion people on the planet," said Jade. "There must be hundreds, if not thousands, of people you could fall in love with and be reasonably happy with. The thing is the timing. Maybe Ewan wasn't ready to settle. And maybe you weren't, either, when it came to Jason. And Dexter ... well he just turned out to be a sleazebag."

I laughed. It seemed she'd summed it up pretty well.

"But this is what you need to do. You need to go and live your life. Enjoy it and eventually, another Jason will come along and you'll be happy," Amber said.

"Why Jason?" I asked, confused.

"Because he's the one who I liked the most," she said, grinning.

Me too, I realised. Although I didn't know who I loved the most, I knew he had been the one I was most content with for longest. I missed his companionship most of all.

I put my all into my job. Sian had slowly given me more and more responsibility and I was now making executive decisions on her behalf, becoming more involved with the business as well as her personal life.

Jade started dating a guy who was only 21; he was adorable but seemed so immature to me. He made me think about what I was like at that age. I was young and impressionable, following Ewan around like a lost puppy. How I'd changed. I thought I knew what I wanted now; what was good in a relationship and what was bad. I knew what I wanted, for when the next man might come along. I felt wise, mature and confident that I wouldn't get into a mess ever again.

As we both know, that wasn't the case. Somehow I learned nothing.

Chapter Forty-Four

"Jade didn't tell me how cute you are."

"Thank you."

I smiled at Greg, trying to determine whether he was cute or not myself. He was conventionally handsome, everything was in the right proportion; nose, ears and eyebrows neither too big nor too small. He had a chiselled chin and nice brown eyes and a decent hair cut. He dressed well and he was polite and charming so far.

Amber and Jade had both insisted I needed to move on and get out there again, to date men and have some fun, and as Jade put it: "It's been too long since you got laid." So they tried setting me up on a few blind dates. Amber had set me up with one of her colleagues, but he was kind of goofy and I wasn't keen. Then Jade had mentioned Greg, who she knew through a friend of a friend and here we sat, at a little restaurant in Covent Garden, sipping wine and making small talk.

"Nice place," I said, desperate to avoid an awkward silence. I smiled, glancing around the restaurant. It was up-market, quite posh. The sort of place that Jason would know about and Ewan could never afford. And Dexter ... but no - I must stop comparing them, I told myself. I'm here with an attractive man, with a splendid menu and I'm moving on. Stop thinking about the others and have a nice time.

"What are you going to have?" Greg asked me.

"I'm considering the lobster. How about you?"

"Waiter!" he said, raising his arm and clicking his fingers in a very pompous fashion.

A waiter appeared immediately, although looking a little put out. "Yes sir?"

"Two lobsters please."

I couldn't be bothered to point out that it was only a consideration, not a firm decision and let the waiter take my menu with a smile and a nod.

"So let's get the life stories over with," he said after the waiter was gone. "I've been single for three months. Got dumped by a redhead with a cold heart. My mother hated her, so she was pleased. I am in business, got a few small companies that I own. I've got a family so big even I don't remember all their names. My parents own three homes and I was a spoilt child and am fully aware I can be pompous and a snob. But I try really, really hard not to be, because I hate that in other people. You go."

I smiled at him. I liked his openness.

"Okay. I've been single for about two months. I have been in love three times, and each time I've somehow screwed it up. But I'm hopeful about the future. I've matured, you see." He grinned and raised his eyebrows. "And I work as a personal assistant, which I love, and I own my own little house, which I also love."

The date really went very well after that. He asked me more about the other guys and I told him my sad little tales and he was sympathetic and said Dexter obviously didn't deserve me, which made me feel better. I asked him about his girlfriends too, and we joked about what crazy women they must have been to have let him go. It was light-hearted, despite the topic of heartbreak, and I had fun. At the end of the evening he kissed me goodbye on my doorstep and walked back to the cab with a backwards glance and a smile.

The next day he sent me roses. None of the others had done that. I called him to say thank you and he asked when he could see me again. He was almost too keen, but it was nice to feel wanted again and I arranged to see him again the next day. I was starting to feel normal again. Human. He was fixing me, somehow, and I liked it.

I offered to make him dinner and invited him to my house. I was planning on making my own pizza and dug out a recipe Sabina gave me back in Verona, which I'd scribbled on a few times since with some of Jason's suggestions. I bought some wine and decided after a few drinks, I'd surely feel more attracted to him and maybe even seduce him and, finally, I'd be moving on. It seemed like a good plan, at the time.

Greg showed up early, again proving how keen he was, which helped boost my wounded ego rather a lot. The pizza wasn't as good as Sabina's, or Jason's, but it turned out pretty well. I put olives, mozzarella and spinach on top and we drank the wine and fell into easy relaxed conversation. This time we talked about work, mostly. I told him about working for Sian, living in her place, and how my work had changed over the years; I was now working on corporate presentations and business plans with her, putting together proposals at the same time as finding her a manicurist in Tokyo or booking her a chiropodist appointment in Madrid.

"Sounds like she keeps you busy," Greg mused.

"She does. I know it sounds like a bit of a nothing job, but I enjoy it."

"Not at all. How many people say they enjoy their job? I think it's great that you do."

"Really?" I was pleased.

"Yes. At least you're helping to support a business that makes money and puts something back into the community."

Sian was patron of several charities and sponsored various initiatives, so I figured that was what he was referring to.

"True," I said, sipping my wine.

"I'm sure she appreciates your loyalty, too. I've gone through no end of personal assistants; a good one is hard to find."

I smiled, feeling proud of myself.

Greg continued to tell me a bit about his businesses, most of which went over my head. I watched him while he was talking, still unsure if I found him attractive or not. He was good-looking, I decided. I really wanted to fancy him, but I wasn't sure if I did.

The small talk continued. I told him about my family, not mentioning Helen, trying to keep it light-hearted. He told me he had a sister and that his parents lived in the south of France. Eventually, we moved to the sofa and he kissed me soon afterwards. I'd had enough wine to just close my eyes and enjoy the moment. He was an excellent kisser, and soon I was dragging him into my bed. I felt human again and it was nice to just be natural and myself.

When I was with him I wasn't thinking about Jason or Dexter, or the mess I'd made. So I let him swoop in and take care of me. Before long I was receiving roses on a weekly basis. He took me to Rome for a long weekend. He kissed me on a moonlit walk. He took me dancing to a '90s night at a club. We ate out a few times a week, always in amazing restaurants; a few times we went to the cinema or the theatre. He was Prince Charming and I was no longer the damsel in distress. He rescued me from the despair and pain Dexter had left me with, by providing some fun.

I just forgot to actually fall in love with him.

Chapter Forty-Five

Then one day Greg told me he loved me and asked me to marry him. We had only been together for three months. They were three very romantic months. But I wasn't convinced he was the one for me. I was just enjoying the time we had together, without giving much thought about the future, yet. He was wonderful and kind, but I wasn't sure I was falling in love. He was fun to be with, but I didn't feel that same fluttery feeling I got when I met Ewan, or that crazy, intense magnetic pull I had with Dexter. He wasn't my best friend, like Jason. We just had a nice time and I was enjoying myself

So how did I end up engaged to him?

Well, I was drunk. It was New Year's Eve and we were at a party Sian had thrown. It was a big affair and I'd been rather stressed dealing with her appointed party planner every day during December that I'd been pretty keen to get tipsy and enjoy the event when it came around.

There had been no hints. We'd been seeing each other a lot, but we hadn't even said 'I love you' yet. I wasn't even sure I wanted to, and I hadn't even given it that much thought. I'd gone to my Aunt Ruth's for Christmas with my dad and Greg had in turn gone to stay with his family in the South of France. By New Year's Eve, we'd not seen each other since Christmas Eve. And I was pleased to see him, but more because he was a fun date to have around than because I was hopelessly in love.

So the party started off well. People arrived in their posh frocks and tuxedos and Sian wafted around the room greeting her friends, family, colleagues and acquaintances. I wore a simple black dress I'd picked out just the day before with Jade, after a panic about what I'd wear. She'd helped pin my hair up and do my make-up. Greg had collected me in a limo, which is where the drinking started; there was a bottle of champagne in the back which I drank quickly, out of nerves more than anything.

When we arrived, the hotel had laid out canapés, but I didn't eat anything. I was still nervous about the whole thing going well. But then I saw the room all decorated and saw the planner who assured me all was fine, and then I saw several guests had already arrived, and I relaxed. And had some more wine.

Now I'm a lightweight. I get drunk after a few glasses. Amber said I'm a fabulous drunk, because I get all happy and giggly and fun. And I started telling people I love them. Usually friends and relatives but I have been known on occasion to tell a stranger I love them. What larks! What fun! But it's dangerous when you're with a man who likes you more than you like him. Anyway, so I was wandering around with Greg on my arm, chatting and laughing and drinking and it was fantastic. I was having a lot of fun.

Then, as the clock was nearing midnight and Greg and I were counting down, I decided to tell him I loved him. Because, really, I did care about him a lot and although I wasn't sure I was falling in love, I was happy he was in my life. And he really did look so handsome in his tux.

"Four, three, two, one!" we shouted. "Happy New Year!"

I threw my arms around Greg and shouted in his ear:

"I love you!"

"I love you, too!" he said, pulling my arms away and kissing me on the lips. He got me all turned on ... I get horny easily when drunk, too.

And then Greg said:

"Marry me?"

And I said:

"Yes!"

And we went up to our hotel room and had lovely, fun, drunken sex. It was only the next day, when sober, that I realised what I'd done.

Oops.

But it'll be okay, I thought. We'll have a long engagement. Plenty of time to decide for sure if I loved him. Plenty of time to pull out if I don't really want to go through with it.

Then his mother got involved and Greg was all enthusiastic, and they said 'Why wait?' Why wait indeed? Especially when there was a cancellation at this 'fabulous' hotel in a 'fabulous' location in Surrey, and she knew the owners, so why not get it pencilled in? The date was set for just six months time and, before I knew it, it was my hen night and I had one week to go.

Chapter Forty-Six

Greg's mother had seemed disappointed initially, I think, when we told her. We had only met once before and she had been nice to me but I don't think she liked me that much. But she had the good grace to hide it reasonably well. She offered to plan, pay for and organise the wedding, and I accepted gratefully, back when I still assumed I'd have at least a year, or hopefully more, to get used to the idea before it went ahead.

But she thought we were so lucky to get this spot due to this cancellation, when usually you'd have to wait three years (three years!) to book this hotel. So Pamela went ahead and pencilled us in, telling us about it only afterwards.

Even Greg looked surprised as she told us over a delicious fish dinner at a restaurant in Soho. He looked at her smiling face, then at me sitting there expecting him to explain that this was too soon. Then he looked back at his mother. And to my ultimate surprise, he said:

"Well, why wait, right?"

And I grinned and went along with it, foolish girl that I am. His mother told us how fabulous the hotel was; about this three year wait we would be avoiding; about her friend the pianist who would play for us; about the three hundred guests she wanted to invite, and finally, she said:

"So what do you think?"

Well, it's all a bit much, actually.

But instead I said: "Pamela, that's wonderful, thank you so much."

Because what else could I do? This woman wanted to plan

an amazing wedding for her son. Who was I to stop her or to hold back the fun? And really, he was a wonderful man and the wedding did sound like a lot of fun. She was even talking about having fireworks. Apparently Greg's friend Tim had had them for his wedding and she'd thought they looked 'just fabulous' in the photos, so I smiled and nodded and went along with it all, thinking that it really was going to be quite a fancy big shebang, when it came to it. And I'd be the bride. Lucky me.

Whenever we had a free lunch time or evening or weekend, Pamela, my darling mother-in-law to be, would whisk us off to food tastings and to look at cakes, and to browse flower catalogues. No expense was being spared and I often wondered where all the money came from.

"Family money," Amber told me. "His parents probably own a huge estate the size of Pemberley."

Actually they did own a large stately home in Yorkshire. The National Trust managed it for them, letting tourists come and visit. They mostly lived in a villa in the south of France but Pamela set up home in an apartment in Kensington to be closer to the wedding arrangements, which meant I saw her every day. I started to get to know her better than I did Greg.

We had champagne tastings one afternoon, and then I went off with my dad, Amber, Jade and Aunt Ruth to pick my wedding dress straight afterwards. I'd gone for a simple, ivory, strapless dress with a little beading around the top and bottom.

Then there was the buying of the rings.

"What about this one?" Greg pointed to a plain gold band and I tilted my head to the right, considering it. It was just a gold ring, plain and simple.

"Why don't you try it on?" I suggested, wandering over to the ladies' rings.

I'd suggested that we pick our own rings - mostly because of my disappointment over my engagement ring. It wasn't ugly by any means, and I'm sure it cost a fair amount, which made me feel guilty about disliking it, but I couldn't help it. It just wasn't me. My first issue was that it was gold. I didn't own any gold jewellery and hadn't ever planned to. I like platinum, as Jason had known. He'd picked the right ring because he knew me better than Greg did.

The second issue was that the diamond was huge, almost embarrassingly so. I would have chosen something small and dainty and subtle for myself. In fact, I'd have happily chosen the exact same ring that Jason picked out for me. I'd not allowed myself to think about this too much; after all, Greg had known me for very little time and we didn't even live together. Jason had a good few years to figure me out. Yet he'd still got it wrong, hadn't he? He'd thought I was trustworthy and caring when I'd turned out to be a selfish adulterer. But enough of those kinds of thoughts, I told myself. This is meant to be a happy occasion.

I realised very soon though that it was going to be hard to find a ring I actually liked or that would match my engagement ring. Surely it had to be gold, too. Most of the rings were similar; gold bands – either plain or with a pattern. I stared at them wondering if I should have just been honest with Greg from the start and asked to exchange the ring. I think if he'd offered to, right from the start, I'd have done that happily. But he didn't. He just assumed I'd love it. I wasn't sure if this was arrogance or just lack of consideration; he was confident in his choice and he liked it, and the sales women had no doubt told him how beautiful it was, so why would I think any differently? Maybe it'd grow on me.

I glanced at it on my finger and then back at the wedding bands in the window.

"Seen anything you like?" Greg asked, putting his hand on my shoulder.

"It's like choosing a tattoo, isn't it?" I said, finding the analogy funny and thinking about Ewan's tattoos. And then I thought more about Ewan and his lovely, sexy self. I shook my head lightly to snap out of it.

"I'm not sure I know what you mean," said Greg. "Surely this is a little more romantic?"

"I just mean I'm choosing something that I'll wear for the rest of my life. I might have different tastes in ten years or thirty years or whatever."

I couldn't ever imagine liking my engagement ring, though. I glanced at it again and felt guilty.

"How about this one?" Greg pointed to a slim gold band, which was just as good as any other on display. He called the assistant over. I tried it on and figured it'd just have to do.

"I love it," I lied.

Ten minutes later we were sitting in a quaint little cafe eating sandwiches and Greg was chatting about his speech.

"I need to raise a toast to the bridesmaids, right?"

"Yes. Say something about how beautiful they look."

"Okay."

"I'd keep the speech short, if I were you. Wedding speeches get boring fast if they last too long."

"Already thought of that."

"You'll be great," I said, wondering if he was nervous.

"Thank you. I'm sure it'll be fine," he said confidently before taking a bite of his lunch. He grinned and I grinned back. I felt silly about my disappointment with the rings. Did it really matter? All that counted, really, was that Greg wanted to marry me. He was a nice, charming, confident, successful person who would take care of me. I was finally settling down and no manipulative doctors were going to stop me. Or so I thought.

Chapter Forty-Seven

Thursday evening. Two days before my wedding.

I walked into the pub with sweaty hands and feeling a little light-headed and dizzy with anticipation. But I felt calmer as my eyes fell on Dexter sitting in the corner with a bottle of beer in front of him. He was looking down and as I approached I saw he was playing with a beer mat. He put it on the table and looked up. Once more those grey eyes were on me, pulling me in. I stopped as I got to the table and hovered, not wanting to sit.

"Izzy. I'm so glad you agreed to meet me." He got up and we had a quick hug. The magic was still there. I still wanted him.

"Hi Dexter."

"How are you? Sit, please. What can I get you to drink?"

"Have you got your car here?" I asked in as monotone a voice as I could manage.

"You want to go for a drive?" he asked, and I nodded. We left his bottle on the table and went out to the car park. He had a new car; a shiny, black BMW.

"Nice car," I said, getting in the passenger side. He got in next to me. It still smelled new, too.

"I've missed you," he said.

"Just drive," I said, trying to sound cold and putting my seat belt on.

I tried to remain calm; I didn't want him to see how nervous and conflicted I was. I realised he'd always made me feel that way: conflicted and confused. I had no idea why I wanted to drive. I just didn't want to sit in the pub. There were too many memories of moments we'd had there. Moments that had only led to bad things; horrible, painful memories.

Dexter drove and we sat in silence for a few minutes. I glanced at him a few times but he was watching the road. He looked good. He'd recently had a haircut. I looked at his left hand. No wedding ring. I'd imagined seeing his hand with no ring so many times. Now that it was empty, I looked down at my own hand and realised I'd left my engagement ring in Jade's kitchen; I'd taken it off while I'd helped her do the washing up.

He pulled into a narrow street and we sat for a few minutes. He turned the engine off and suggested we get out. It was a warm evening. I leant against the car and he came around and leant beside me, our arms almost touching.

"Well?" I asked, turning towards him.

He suddenly put his hands on my neck and drew me towards him. As always, I couldn't resist, and I let him kiss me.

I was cheating again, I realised. I'd kissed Dexter while I was with every other man I loved. And now it was less than 48 hours until my wedding. His lips felt the same - hot and sweet. I forgot everything around me and just put my arms around his neck.

So, Dexter wanted me, after all.

Chapter Forty-Eight

When it came to sex, Greg was pretty good. It wasn't as fun as with Ewan or as earth-shattering as with Jason, or as intense as with Dexter. But he knew what he was doing, what to do, what not to do. This is more than can be said of many men, according to Jade, who once told me she'd slept with over thirty - the hussy.

The only thing was he didn't like to do it that often. Now I'm not the kind of girl who needs to get it every day, by any means. Ewan and I, after the novelty of each other wore off, did it about three times a week, maybe more when we were travelling. With Jason it was at least once a week, and that was for a good couple of hours (what with that skilful tongue...), and of course I'd never actually been in a relationship with Dexter, so we didn't really have a chance to get into a regular sex routine. Now, Greg, despite seeming to enjoy it very much, never ever initiated sex.

He was affectionate and loving, and never made me feel like he didn't want me. He got turned on just as soon as I started kissing him or touching him, or if I appeared in some sexy lingerie or whatever. He never turned me down. But he never made the first move. And this bugged me.

I mean, isn't it supposed to be the other way around? Isn't it supposed to be the guy who is gagging for it and the woman who rolls her eyes and says "Okay but make it quick, dear?"

After a lot of debating with Amber and Jade, we decided I had to confront him about this. Amber seemed to think it might be the source of all my trouble; that the lack of sex initiation had led to the lack of passion, and therefore my lack of conviction that I should marry him. Jade was just concerned that he was 'frigid' and said I needed to find out why.

So about six weeks before the wedding, just after I'd moved in and while sitting eating biscuits in front of *Mock the Week*, I took a deep breath and turned to Greg.

"Why don't you ever seduce me?"

"What?" he said, frowning and pausing the television. Hugh Dennis' face was frozen on the screen.

"Why don't you ever make the first move when it comes to sex?"

"What about the first time?"

Admittedly, the first time we did it he pulled my top off. But only after I invited him in for coffee after our date, and started pulling him towards my bedroom. It was hardly his idea.

"Since then," I said.

"Well, I don't know. I never think of it."

"We haven't done it for two weeks. Did you realise that? Do you think that's normal?"

"I don't think it's a big deal. Do you want to do it now, then?"

"Only if you want to. I thought men thought about sex about a hundred times a minute, or something like that?"

"Well, not me."

"So it seems."

"Is this a problem?" He looked concerned and I wondered if this might be our first fight.

Not that I like arguing, you see, but sometimes I wanted him to show a bit of passion for something, if it was something he disagreed with. If only his right to never seduce me, ever, if he didn't want to.

"It'd just be nice, sometimes, to think you wanted me."

"I do want you! And the sex is amazing, I just don't feel I

need it that regularly, that's all."

"Do you masturbate often?"

He looked surprised at that one. I wasn't sure where that had come from, but I wanted to know.

"No, never. Not since I met you."

"Oh come on Greg, surely now and then you do?"

"No, I don't ... you know ... feel the urge."

"Well, I do," I told him, blushing but hoping that might prompt a little more honesty.

"Really? When?"

"I don't do it all the time but just occasionally, if you're out and I feel in the mood."

He raised his eyebrows. "Well good for you."

"So it's really fine if you do it, too."

"But I don't."

"Hmm ... okay," I said, turning back to Hugh Dennis and un-pausing it.

So that was the end of that. I decided to leave it, to see how long we could go without having sex if I left it all to him. Jade told me about an interesting vibrating toy that went a long way to making sure I was more than satisfied, and I figured I'd just wait for him to make a move.

And so just before our wedding we hadn't done it for two months. We'd been together less than a year so we should have still been in that honeymoon stage where it's all kissing and sex and fun.

I wasn't sure if that sounded like a couple who ought to get married.

Chapter Forty-Nine

Thursday night. Two days before my wedding.

Dexter leant me against the car, kissing me hard. I wondered for a second if he was thinking we'd have sex here in the street. He started kissing my neck and whispered: "Tell me if you want me to stop."

Hadn't I heard that somewhere before?

"Stop," I whispered.

He pulled away immediately and we both leant our backs on the car again.

"I'm sorry," he said. "I just couldn't stop myself. I've missed you so much."

Had I missed him too? I'd been angry mostly; angry that he'd let me ruin things with Jason. I pictured how good Jason looked earlier in the week, then realised I should be thinking of Greg. I suddenly felt angry.

"What the hell is going on?" I almost shouted, shocked at myself.

"Izzy, come on."

"I'm sorry. I just don't know what we're doing here."

"Shall we go somewhere to talk? My hotel is only ten minutes drive away."

I got into the car again and we drove in silence. He tried to put his hand on mine but I moved it away.

"Why are you staying in a hotel?"

"I left Holly. Been staying there for a few weeks. I'm going to get my own place."

"You actually left her?"

"Yes and I've been trying to track you down. I forced myself to delete your number after it all went wrong between us, but I managed to get it again from the hospital database."

"I'm pretty sure that's illegal."

"Well I didn't know how else to find you."

I'd wanted this so much. For months I dreamt of him leaving Holly and being with me. But then when I thought about it now, it was Jason I was regretful about, not Dexter. Now that Dexter was here again I just felt angry. Yet I wanted to kiss him. Oh, it was all so confusing. Ever since that day on the beach he'd been able to kiss me without my consent, and I'd let him. I had kissed him while with all three of the men I'd loved yet he'd never once made me as happy as any of them. All the time we'd spent together had been emotional and stressed.

I said as much as soon as we were sitting on the bed in his room. He offered me a drink. I refused, and we sat down to talk.

"It's been emotional and stressful because we were never truly together. But I can be all yours now. You can see for yourself: I'm single, available. Just like you wanted."

"But I'm not!" I said, losing my temper again. "I'm getting married on Saturday!"

"I know, and I know I should've realised how much I love you and adore you and can't live without you sooner. But I'm here now."

"What about your children?"

"I'm still going to see Isla all the time."

"And the baby?"

"Oh, that wasn't true."

"What?" I felt anger rise inside of me again.

"Holly was faking it. She knew I was seeing someone else and thought it might make me stop. She was going to pretend she had a miscarriage, but confessed."

"And you just left her, like that?"

"Yes. Not straight away, of course. I tried to make it work for a while. It was actually quite easy, in the end. She told me she wasn't sure she loved me anymore."

I took a deep breath, trying to take this all in.

"Izzy, I'm sorry for all the pain and stress and hurt. But … Izzy, look at me, please."

I'd been staring at the floor and I looked up, swallowing hard.

"Izzy, we're two peas in a pod, you and I. You know that. We are like magnets; soul mates."

"Stop throwing clichés at me, Dexter."

"They may be clichés but you feel it too, and that's why you were so hurt when I ended it. I'll never hurt you again, Izzy."

He moved in and kissed me again. I let him, just like I always did. He started to push me back on the bed and for a split second I thought: I'll cancel the wedding and I'll be with Dexter.

Then I had an epiphany.

How dare he do this to me two days before my wedding? How dare he assume I'd come back to him, despite the fact I'd obviously moved on? Did I really want to be with someone who could so easily cheat on his wife? Did I even know him *that* well? If I thought of one word to describe his actions and his personality it would be … selfish.

So was it just a physical attraction, this pull?

Time to grow up, Izzy. He isn't the one for you.

I sat up with a jolt, pushing Dexter away from me.

"It's too late," I told him, standing up. "I shouldn't have come here. I'd like you to take me home."

He grabbed my arm, a little too firmly. "Izzy, come on, you know we'll be together eventually. We're soul mates."

"No," I said, sighing. "I don't know that. I know that I ruined the best relationship I've ever had because of you. I know that you caused me nothing but pain and I know that I

254

don't love you. Maybe I did, but I don't anymore."

"Izzy, please," he stood up too, and I saw tears in his eyes. "I love you."

"It's too late," I told him.

"You'd have let me leave Holly, even though I thought she was pregnant?'

"Well, you said you were no longer having sex with her. Perhaps if that had been the case, we wouldn't have had an issue."

He nodded, and with a heavy sigh picked up this car keys.

"You're really going to marry this guy?"

"Yes. I love him."

Well, he didn't need to know I wasn't sure.

"You just said that Jason was your best relationship."

"Well, I didn't mean it. I'm happy with Greg. He's the one for me."

"Well I hope he deserves you. I hope he makes you happy."

"He's never made me cry. That's a good start."

Dexter nodded and bit his lip.

"I'd better get you back then."

We drove in silence once more; me wondering if I'd ever forgive myself for this. Two days before my wedding. Could I not get through any relationship without kissing Dexter? I decided not to tell anyone, not even Amber or Jade. I only wanted to forget and to imagine it was a dream.

"I'm sure I'll see you in the next life," Dexter said as I turned to say goodbye.

"Yeah, whatever," I said, finally tired of his bullshit.

"We're soul mates, Izzy. We just fucked it up this time around."

"No, you did."

"Okay, it was me."

I smiled at him.

"I don't believe in soul mates," I told him.

"We'll see," he said, swallowing hard. He looked away and

at his steering wheel. His eyes were watery. I had no sympathy.

"Take care, Dexter. Have a nice life."

"If you change your mind..."

I didn't reply. I had a little vision of me slapping him around the face. I figured it'd be quite satisfactory. But instead I just smiled, got out of the car and quietly closed the door behind me. The spell had finally lifted.

As I looked up at Greg's house, I saw that Jade was just approaching the front door. She turned around and looked at me walking away from Dexter's car, which slowly moved off. I didn't glance back.

"I knew it!" she said, hands on hips.

Chapter Fifty

Greg and I were getting married so fast that an engagement party didn't really seem like a worthwhile endeavour, but Greg had suggested we invite our parents out for a meal and drinks about a month before the wedding. I told him if he organised it, then to go right ahead and plan whatever he liked. I was busy with work and his mother was calling me every day with wedding questions and ideas, most of which I told her, "Whatever you think". I didn't have the energy to plan an engagement party/meal out as well. I was so busy with it all, I hadn't had time to even stop and really give it all enough thought. Not even to think about whether I really wanted it to happen. Or not until about a week before, anyway.

The engagement meal had become much bigger than I'd anticipated, however. Greg had taken 'plan whatever you like' to the extreme. We arrived at the restaurant and, along with our parents, there was Amber and Tristan; Greg's best friend Tim and wife Libby; Jade and her current beau, and Greg's sister Adele with her boyfriend Niall, who I hadn't even met yet. I took a seat next to Amber and watched nervously as my dad and Greg's mum chatted at the other end of the table. Mixing families up like this seemed kind of strange.

"Why didn't you tell me you were coming tonight?" I asked Amber. "We spoke just yesterday."

"Greg wanted to surprise you," Amber said. "He's quite the romantic, isn't he? Very sweet."

"Yes. He is," I glanced at him; he was deep in conversation with Tim, sitting opposite him.

"I thought you were, too. You always liked the romantic gestures before."

"I know ... I just want to be married without all the fuss."

"You must be the first bride I know to resist all the fuss."

"I know." I sighed. "I guess I just don't want too much drama. Isn't the getting married part the important thing? Actually saying 'I do' and then getting on with life together?"

"Yes, I suppose," she said, picking up her menu. I did the same.

**

A few hours later, our mutual friends and families were riding a champagne high and chatting happily as if they'd all known each other for years. Jade had struck up a conversation with Greg's mother, and our fathers were talking business. Greg had his arm around my shoulder but was chatting to Jade's date. I made a little small talk with Adele, who was lovely and told me how excited she was about the wedding.

I looked around the table, hearing snippets of the various conversations and realising this was my world now; these were the people who made up my life. I wondered who Helen would have chatted to if she'd been here. Me, I decided. She'd have been quizzing me about Greg. Because she'd know. Without me having to say to her, she'd be able to tell that I wasn't one hundred percent sure.

When I was little, I used to go to ballet lessons. I loved it for a few years, but then slowly I got bored. I kept going, though, because my mum was so proud of me. She'd tell me over and over again how I was a lovely dancer and how I should never give it up; how one day I could be a professional dancer. I'm pretty sure she was biased or trying to make me feel good, because I'm not particularly coordinated. But, anyway, I kept going for her sake, although by the age of eight I hated it.

Then, one day, Helen said to Mum;

"Izzy hates ballet, Mum. You should let her give it up."

Mum was surprised and quizzed me. I admitted it was the truth and that was the end of my ballet days. I wondered for a while afterwards how Helen knew, because I'd managed to keep it from my mum, who was older and wiser and usually knew much more than Helen. So I asked her and she told me that she always knew when I wasn't sure about something.

"I know you better than you know yourself, Izzy," she'd said.

Seeing as Helen wasn't here at the engagement party, I realised I'd have to voice my concerns to Amber, who up until this point hadn't really known I wasn't sure. I had to get them off my chest before I exploded with emotions and ran away or, worse still, told Greg how I was feeling.

I looked at him, animatedly talking about his job while his mother listened proudly, and tried to find a fault in him. He was so nice, so lovely, and there was no reason why I shouldn't marry him. So what was missing?

The rest of the evening was pleasant enough. I made an effort to get to know Greg's best friend's wife, Libby, and she told me all about her wedding to Tim and I smiled and gave her the required enthusiasm.

"It's so much fun, planning it all, isn't it?" she asked, beaming. I nodded my head, trying to be agreeable. I didn't mention that my future mother-in-law had actually planned everything for me.

"My sister Amy got married in Vegas," she told me. "Missed out on all this. Still, everyone's different."

I lay in bed that night thinking about Libby's sister and wondering if maybe Greg and I could just run off to Vegas before I had any more doubts. It would be simpler, and then we could just get on with our lives. But I knew he, and especially his mother, would hate that idea.

Three days later, I was sitting in Amber's living room while she prepared us drinks. We'd gone out to a Japanese restaurant and I'd managed to get through the evening without worrying too much, but as soon as I was on my own I worked up the courage to talk about it.

"I'm not sure," I blurted out as she came through the door with two glasses of wine.

"I've got red, if you prefer?" she offered, looking at the glasses of white in her hand.

"No. I'm not sure about Greg."

"Oh, that's natural. Wedding jitters, cold feet, whatever you want to label it."

"I've just been swept along with all this and sometimes I wonder if I actually want to be his wife. I don't even know if I want to be his girlfriend. I'm completely overwhelmed by his love for me and I don't know if I feel the same way about him."

"But you seem so happy when you're together. Why did you agree to marry him?"

"I was drunk, and then I thought it'd be a reasonably long engagement."

"And his mother got involved and you got swept up into it?"

I was glad she got it.

"Exactly. And what's not to love? He's funny and handsome. He's smart and charming. He just … takes care of me like I'm a princess.'

"True," Amber nodded. "All those things are true and I think you've just got cold feet. This is a big commitment and you haven't known him long. So it's natural to be nervous and unsure."

"I guess so," I smiled.

"You'll probably feel better as the time gets nearer."

"It's just—"

"Oh God, don't compare him to Dexter, please. That was an unhealthy obsessive crush that got out of control."

I felt a little frisson of pain at the sound of his name and almost corrected her that I'd been crazily in love with Dexter, but held my tongue.

"It's Jason," I told her. "I know, I left him and I hurt him. But before I met Dexter," I tried not to wince, "I was so happy with Jason. I just loved being around him, and I kind of missed him when he was at work or whatever. I felt so close to him, and we'd share everything and talk all the time. It's not that I'm still in love with Jason, I'm not. It's just I don't feel as strongly about Greg, as I did about Jason, during the peak - if that makes sense?"

"Listen, every relationship is different. Don't compare them."

"I suppose it's just cold feet, like you said. Anyway, I can always get divorced, can't I?" I laughed.

"What it comes down to is this: do you love Greg?"

"I think so."

"Let's write a list of reasons why you love him," she said, "and I'll remind you of it if you feel nervous again."

"Good plan."

Chapter Fifty-One

Thursday. Two days before my wedding.

Jade and I went to the pub across the road and I decided to confess the kiss and the drive with Dexter. She listened without passing judgement or comment.

"Wow," she said, when I finished. "I just had a feeling when you left that you were going to meet up with him."

"Yes, you know me so well."

"You have amazing will-power."

"Well, I went and saw him in the first place."

"Yes, but I remember how you used to talk about Dexter. He was like … a god to you. You could never resist him and you defended all your feelings and actions. You're stronger now, obviously."

"I still kissed him."

"It was just a kiss. Don't worry about it. Important thing is you made the right decision."

"Yes," I said with a sigh.

"So, are your feet warm now? I mean, what are the chances of seeing Ewan, Jason and Dexter in the same week? Ewan and Dexter both made you offers but you're still here, and the day after tomorrow you're going to marry Greg. I think that tells you something."

I nodded slowly and looked at her face. She was smiling; optimistic; hoping it would work out. I didn't want to disappoint her. She looked like her mum, my Aunt Ruth, when she smiled. My dad had the same smile too. I sighed and shrugged my shoulders.

"What? *Really*? You're *still* not sure?"

"It was just a crazy few days," I told her. "Seeing them all again bought back a lot of memories."

"I know. For me too actually. I was remembering how you followed Ewan around like a lost puppy."

I laughed. "Yes I suppose I did."

"And the Dexter thing was almost a little obsessive."

"Yes. I suppose so."

"Well, I'd better get you home and to bed. You need your beauty sleep."

"What about Jason?" I asked, unsure it was a good idea to bring him up, but I wanted to talk about him.

"Jason? What about him?"

"Well, you said I followed Ewan around and obsessed over Dexter. What about Jason?"

"Jason was just ... normal. He was perfect for you. You know Amber and I wanted you to stay with him. We felt he was the one you'd stick with. But things don't always work out the way you expect them to."

"He was perfect for me. You're right," I said, sitting back and finishing the last of my drink.

"Come on Izzy, none of that." She put her arm around me and I leaned on her shoulder. "Jason has moved on and so have you. Greg is perfect for you as well. You know that. You just have to relax and enjoy yourself. Please. I hate seeing you like this."

She was right, I realised. Anyway, what was I going to do? Tell Greg it was all off on the morning of the wedding? Jilt him at the altar? No way could I do that to anyone, let alone a man who'd been so good to me.

"You're right," I told her. "This has all just been about crazy hormones and nerves, that's all."

"That's my girl. Let's go home. I'll see you tomorrow for our manicures."

We walked back to my front door.

"Thank you, Jade."

"No problem, darling girl. Sleep well, okay? Love you lots."

"Love you too."

We hugged, and then she was gone. I snuck into the house and found Greg reading in bed. We talked a little about our day and I felt bad lying. He seemed a little on edge himself, but I didn't ask why. We turned out the lights and I cuddled into him and for the first time that week I felt calm and content. I was going to marry Greg, and that was fine. So it wasn't full of passionate sex and lust and adventure and best friendship. But it was still pretty great and he was certainly wonderful. Really, I was a very lucky lady to be marrying him.

"You awake?" I whispered.

"Just about," he whispered back.

"Why do you want to marry me?" I asked him.

"Because I love you. Do you love me?"

The question threw me. Why would he ask that now?

"Of course. Goodnight."

"Goodnight," he whispered and turned onto this side, putting his arm around me. We fell asleep like that after I'd lain there for a while wondering if I'd imagined the nervousness in his voice. Was he unsure too?

I woke up with a start. It was almost 7am and Greg was asleep beside me. I watched him for a moment and decided that this was where I ought to be and, anyway, everyone had put a lot of effort into making this wedding special, so I was darn well going to enjoy it.

So I got up, got ready, and went downstairs to read my book. My phone started to ring and I answered it in a whisper, so that Greg couldn't hear me.

"Hello?"

"Did you think about what I said?"

Ewan. His voice made me nervous. And then it hit me. Suddenly, it all became clear: Yes, I had loved Ewan, back in the day, much more than I loved Greg right now. But I didn't want him - not anymore.

"Yes, I did," I told him, "and I love you too, Ewan. But it's too late."

I heard him sigh

"Okay, Izz. Fair enough. It was worth a try."

I laughed, despite the awkwardness.

"Take care of yourself, Ewan."

"Do you think we could be friends? Maybe meet for a drink now and then? I'd like to meet Greg, too."

"Actually, yes," I said, wondering if it'd be weird but willing to give it a try. "That'd be lovely."

"Great. Well I'll call you sometime then. Good luck for Saturday."

We said our goodbyes and I hung up. Now I knew clearly what I wanted, and I also knew for sure what I would do. Finally I felt calm.

Chapter Fifty-Two

I was determined to show Amber and Jade that I was happy and doing the right thing. They'd both seen me up and down, sure and not sure, and I just wanted them to enjoy the wedding without any concerns or lectures or questions. I didn't want, or need, any more pep talks or advice. So I acted the part of the happy bride and they went along with it, no questions asked.

First, we went to have our nails done. I opted for a French manicure and Amber and Jade had theirs painted silver. Then we went for lunch in a trendy restaurant recommended by Greg's friend Tim where we had champagne cocktails and fancy food. We talked a lot about the men in my life and how they'd shown up this week, and laughed. Amber's jaw dropped open when I told her about the incident with Dexter and shook her head, giggling from the champagne.

"I'm proud of you," she said, laughing. "You were unsure, but you figured it out. And now you're going to marry the aristocrat and live happily ever after."

I smiled and nodded. It really would work out fine, because how could I not be happy with Greg? Surely getting along well was the thing we needed most and we certainly got on brilliantly.

After that we had facials and pedicures and then we went and checked into the fancy hotel that I was going to get married at the following day. We ate dinner, and Jade and Amber checked into their rooms whilst I went to the huge, beautiful, bridal suite, and got into bed, staring at the ceiling.

And then I began to cry.

There was a knock at the door. I threw the duvet back, dabbed my eyes on a corner of my nightdress and looked through the peep hole.

"Greg!" I said, shocked, and opened the door. "This is unlucky, you know."

"I'm sorry," he said, smiling sadly, "I just had to talk to you. In person. Before the wedding." He looked pale and tired.

"Okay," I said, worried that he was going to jilt me. I felt more embarrassed than anything and then realised with horror that I might actually not mind if he did. He walked past me into the living area, and sat down on the sofa.

"What's wrong?" I asked, sitting beside him.

"Have you been crying?"

"Yes," I admitted. "Just worrying about tomorrow."

"I thought so."

"What's wrong? Why are you here?"

"You."

"Me?"

"Yes. Izzy, are you sure you want to marry me tomorrow? Because it's okay if you don't. We rushed into this relationship and I'm very aware that my mother and I pushed the whole wedding thing along. I just don't want you to feel pressured or do something you don't want to."

He really was too nice. I hesitated, unsure how to reassure him.

"Izzy?"

"I'm sorry, I'm just surprised, that's all. Of course I'm sure," I looked away from him and down at the floor. "Maybe I didn't expect us to get married so soon, but everything has been so wonderful." I smiled and looked back at him. "You take care of me and I feel safe with you."

"But are you truly, deeply in love with me?"

I swallowed.

No, I am not.

There it was, right before me. But I couldn't stand the thought of being alone, so I lied.

"Of course I am."

"Then why did you go out the other night with a man who I assume was Dexter?"

I gasped. I let my mouth hang open for a few seconds, unsure where to begin or how to start.

"Answer me, Izzy. I need the truth, please."

Chapter Fifty-Three

My last conversation with Helen.

It was lunch time and we were in the school playground. Some of our friends were sitting in a circle playing some sort of card game that Maria, a girl from my class, had taught them. I didn't feel like playing and had sat outside of the circle, reading a Roald Dahl book my parents had bought me for my birthday.

I looked up and saw Helen talking to Mr. Broom, the Drama teacher. I looked back at my book, and felt her come and sit beside me.

"It's good, isn't it?" she asked.

"Yes," I said. "What were you talking to Mr. Broom about?"

"He wants me to audition for the school play."

"Are you going to?"

"Maybe."

"How's Mark?" I asked. She'd spent break time talking to him, sitting beneath a tree.

"He's fine. I told him I don't want to be his girlfriend anymore."

"Why?"

"I fancy Simon."

Simon was the cutest boy in our school. We all fancied him.

"I thought you fancied Mark."

"Well. I did. But he's a bit boring."

"He's kind to you, though," I said, remembering he'd bought her a Twix yesterday.

"Yes, I suppose so." She seemed distracted, distant. I'd spend the rest of my life wondering why.

"Remember I've got a flute lesson after school," she said, getting up to join the other girls.

"Okay," I said, looking back at my book.

And there it was; the simplest of conversations. Nothing worth remembering had the day gone as planned. Had she come home as normal, I'd probably never think of that day again.

Sometimes I'd wish that I'd told her to skip flute and that we'd take my remaining birthday money from Nana and go to Woolworths and spend it all on sweets. Or go to the cinema, if we had enough.

Other times I wished that I'd taken flute too. Maybe together we could have fought off her abductor. Maybe he wouldn't have bothered even trying if there had been two of us.

But I couldn't change the past. I couldn't find a way to bring Helen back. Just as I couldn't find a way to erase Dexter from my past. I couldn't undo the wrongs which had pained Jason, and which would now pain Greg.

What I could do, was seize every moment. Because every year that passed by was another year that Helen had never had. I owed it to her to stop being confused and unappreciative of what I had. Greg was a wonderful, kind person and he deserved my honesty.

So I told him the truth.

Chapter Fifty-Four

The night before my wedding.

"Start from the beginning," he said, smiling sadly. "That's probably best."

So I started off telling him about Jason. How I'd seen him at my hen night. Then I told him about Ewan, and how he'd told me he loved me and wanted me back.

"Well, I can't blame him for trying," he said. I smiled. Greg didn't.

"It was also very strange seeing them both," I told him. "It was like ... I couldn't remember why Ewan and I weren't together anymore. And I couldn't remember why I'd hurt Jason, and I just felt weird, you know, seeing him with someone else."

"You were jealous?"

"I guess so."

"Well, that's natural. You shouldn't read too much into it."

"I know. So then I got a text from Dexter."

"Right. I knew it. When are you going to realise he's a pig, Izzy? He cheated on his wife and promised you the world, and then he hurt you. You were broken when I met you, Izzy. Don't let him do that to us."

"Just let me tell you what happened."

So I did. I told him I couldn't resist the urge to see Dexter. I told him I'd never had any closure, that there seemed things left unsaid. I told him about the kiss and watched his face. He didn't frown or wince; just nodded and let me carry on with

271

the story.

"But I realised that I didn't want him at all. I was angry with him and that's why I'd wanted the closure, I think. I wanted to yell at him because he allowed me to break up with Jason, and what I had with Jason was amazing and I didn't even realise how amazing it was until I'd ruined it."

He was studying my face, but showing no emotion on his.

"Go on," he said gently, squeezing my hand.

"I know it was my own fault and I know that I really shouldn't have let myself be so easily influenced by him, but he hurt me and the person I loved most. I just wish I'd never met him. Jason and I were so good together, and I was so happy and everything was perfect until I met Dexter. And I hate him for that. He parted me from Jason forever and I'll never forgive myself."

I was crying by this point, and hadn't even thought about what I'd said. It just came tumbling out. Greg put his arm around me and I leant into him.

"I'm so sorry that I kissed him, but you have to believe me - I hate him. I wish we'd never met."

"Because then you'd still be with Jason?"

"Yes, exactly!"

I felt the shock wash over me and held my breath for a few minutes. Had I really just said that? Did he hear? Did he realise what I was saying? Of course he did.

"Izzy, you need to stop feeling guilty." He said this slowly, quietly, holding me in his arms as I rubbed my wet eyes and cheeks.

"Okay," I said, sniffing and sitting up.

"We can't get married tomorrow."

"I know," I said, nodding.

"I love you," he said, tucking a strand of hair behind my ear.

"I know," I said, nodding again.

"But you don't love me."

I bit my lip. No. He was wonderful and everything I should want, and yet I didn't want him. I wanted Jason. Why didn't I realise this sooner? Why didn't I know how much I loved Jason when I had him? I thought back to the night I'd met Dexter and wanted to slap myself in the face.

"I do love you," I said. "I'm just not in love with you."

"Well, maybe we're both in love with the idea of each other. We seem to get on so well. I'd like to remain friends."

Was I hearing this right? Was he really letting me off the hook?

"I want you to be happy, Izzy." He squeezed my hand. "Keep in touch, yeah?"

We both stood up and he gave me a brief hug. It felt awkward somehow.

"So it's over? Just like that? What about all the guests and the money spent?"

"Don't worry about anything. Why don't you just go home and I'll take care of everything."

"Greg, you're too nice. I feel so ... horrible."

"Enough of that. Stop feeling horrible and guilty and down on yourself. You need to figure out what you want, Izzy. Go find yourself. Be Izzy for a while. Go find Jason, if you want. Just make yourself happy. Because you of all people know that life is short. So... go. Enjoy it and don't ever have a moment's regret about you and me. We both learned something, I think."

I stared at him in disbelief. Even when it came to my betraying him, he was the perfect gentlemen.

He hugged me again and then he was gone. I wanted to get out of here before he told anyone, so I texted Amber and Jade, grabbed my bag and was just throwing everything into it when they knocked on the door.

"What the hell is going on?" Jade asked as they came in, seeing my bag packed.

"I don't love him," I said, "and he knows me well enough to

tell."

"It's all off?" Amber put her hand to her chest.

"Yes," I said, breathing a sigh of relief.

"How's Greg?"

"He's okay, actually. I think in a way he's relieved, too. He knew I wasn't sure."

"So where are you going?"

"Home," I told them. "My house."

It had remained empty since I'd moved in with Greg.

"I'll come with you," Jade said. "Just let me pack my things."

"No, really," I told them. "I want to be alone for a while. I think I need to figure some stuff out."

Amber and Jade filled me in later that Greg had spoken to my dad, who'd informed the rest of my family, and they'd all slowly spread the word around that the wedding was off. Greg told them all that we'd just realised we didn't want to get married. He'd made it simple and easy for me, proving once again just how perfect and kind he really was.

Chapter Fifty-Five

It was three months to the day since the wedding day that had, in the end, turned out to be just a day without a wedding. Greg had, as one might expect, been wonderful. He'd cancelled all the plans, informed all the guests, and even helped me move my stuff back to my own house. My family and friends were quite shocked, but supportive. Dad and I had a long chat the following weekend and he'd suggested I take some time to be alone for a bit. He said I should think about what I wanted and not rush into another relationship until I knew myself a bit better.

I thought about Jason every day but didn't dare approach him. He'd moved on, and was with that super-beautiful, super-skinny, super-model Anna now, and I couldn't cope with the rejection I was pretty sure I'd receive. I didn't expect to enjoy living alone again but I didn't mind it too much. Sian kept me busy working and I fell into a routine. Greg and I remained friends; he met me for lunch once a week and we'd chat about old times and the future and he was quite philosophical about our failed relationship. One time he even told me that it was the best thing that could've happened, us breaking up. He felt the first few months of our relationship were fantastic but since we'd got engaged, he'd not been one hundred percent sure either.

Occasionally, while we were together, I wondered if we'd get back together eventually. As if the rushing into it had just ruined our chances, along with all my doubts and the fact that I hadn't got over any of my ex-loves, of course. But I still didn't fancy him, really. Being friends was good. I liked having him in my life.

So, one sunny Saturday afternoon, three months on, I was at my dad's house with Jade and Aunt Ruth playing scrabble in the dining room. Jade was winning, Ruth was yawning a lot, and I was mixing the letters S P O and O around and around, wondering if I could put down 'oops' or 'poos'. The phone rang and Dad got up to answer it.

"Oh, hello," he said, a look of concern spreading across his face. He walked out and I couldn't hear his voice. I decided to go with 'oops', and Jade decided to look it up in the dictionary.

"Shall we just declare Jade the winner anyway?" Ruth suggested. She had almost twice my score.

"Yes," I said, clearing away the mugs of tea. I took them into the kitchen.

"Well, thank you," Dad was saying in a strangely high-pitched voice. "I'll speak to you later then. Good bye."

"What's wrong?" I asked, his white face frightening me.

"Ruth! Jade!" he called. They came in, looking confused.

"What's wrong Dad?"

"That was the police," he started to explain. I held my breath. "They've found a body, which they believe to be Helen's. They should be able to confirm within the next 24 hours."

I gasped. Ruth went to Dad and put her arms around her brother. Jade took my hand. We all stood there, taking this in.

"Where?" I whispered.

"Buried in the garden of a teacher from your school. A Mr Yates."

I couldn't remember a Mr Yates. I said so, still trying to take this in. "He died a few months ago and the people who bought his house found her."

"How awful," Ruth said.

"Intact?" Jade asked. I suddenly realised what she'd meant.

"Yes, I believe so. They didn't say otherwise. It looks as if her legs are broken, pelvis shattered. He said it might have been a car accident and a cover up."

My mind was racing. All I could think was that I hoped she didn't suffer. That this theory was true, and that he'd just hit her with his car and buried the evidence. That she hadn't been raped, or tortured, or in any pain before she died.

"I hope she didn't suffer," I whispered. "That's all I hope. I hope she was rendered unconscious immediately."

"It might not be her," Jade said, tears on her cheeks. "We don't know for sure."

"It is," I told her. It had to be. Something like relief washed over me. It was a tragic accident. Nothing more. Nothing quite as horrific as we'd all imagined.

Lying in bed that night, I tried to picture a corpse that'd been rotting for all these years. Would there be anything left of her, apart from bone? I pushed the thoughts from my mind and decided to get up and call Amber. It was the middle of the night but she answered straight away and listened as I tearfully told her about the phone call.

"Oh, Izzy," she said.

Chapter Fifty-Six

Of course, it was Helen's body. The DNA tests proved that. They were also pretty sure she'd been hit by a car, probably speeding, and that Mr. Yates had obviously decided to hide the evidence. I had so many questions, like where had the accident taken place? Had she died instantly? How could he have possibly taken her body so easily without anyone seeing him? The police had opened up a whole new investigation but had warned us that no definitive answers may ever be found.

So my father finally planned the funeral for the daughter he'd lost almost twenty years ago. It was like some great weight had been lifted and we could finally mourn and get over it.

The day before the funeral, I asked Dad if we should open Mum's letter to Helen. I didn't really want to read it and Dad agreed. It would only make us sadder. So we arranged for it to be put inside her coffin, along with a photo of the four of us together.

I wasn't sure which I felt more strongly: anger, relief, or sorrow. I stood holding my dad's hand in the service as we both wept. I was glad my mother had been spared this. Ruth was our rock; she handled the flowers and the food and everything, really. She organised us. Jade helped.

We went back to our house for sandwiches and cake afterwards. A bunch of Helen's school friends came and it was a bit of a reunion; not too sombre in the end. Dad said he wanted to bury Helen and Mum's ashes together somewhere, which seemed a nice idea to me. Greg came and helped to clear up afterwards, too. He was just as amazing a friend as he had been an amazing boyfriend.

And then somehow, we got back to normality again. But things were different. I was no longer unsure about my future. I felt calm. I felt like I knew what I wanted. I had made stupid, awful mistakes in my life, but I knew I wouldn't make them again. For the first time in my life, I felt like a grown-up.

I continued to work hard, although it hardly felt like work because Sian and I were such good friends now. Amber got pregnant and I was thrilled. Jade actually moved in with a man called Ash and seemed happy. I didn't date, or flirt, or even contemplate meeting another man. I was okay on my own.

And anyway, what man would ever live up to the love of my life? No one could. And I'd lost him forever.

Chapter Fifty-Seven

It was a Tuesday. I was in Sian's apartment and it was raining. We'd had a little meeting and she'd gone off to the airport. I liked working at her place, and had carried on. I had four phone calls to return, a restaurant to book for her in New York, and her niece to find a birthday present for. I was distracted in all of that and didn't look at my emails for a while, and then, when I did, my insides felt lit up.

To: Izzy Swan
From: Jason Edwards
Subject: Cottage

Hi Izzy
Congratulations! I'm sorry that this email is almost four months overdue. I hope you had a special day and that you have a long and happy marriage. I wanted to do this in secret, as a surprise, but it's tricky as I'm not sure how to get in touch with Greg...

Why on earth did he want to get in touch with Greg?

...You see, I'd like to offer you both the cottage in Cornwall. I haven't used it, and I bought it for you. I know how much you loved it and if it wouldn't be too weird, I'd still like you to have it. I know what it means to you. So, if you're interested, I'll sell it at the price I paid for it. If you could just let me know. I think you're the only person I could sell it to.
Regards,

Jason

I re-read the email several times. I had thought about the cottage a lot since Jason and I had broken up, but I didn't know how I could possibly afford to buy it off him, and I wasn't even sure I wanted it without him, anyway. I was sure he'd have sold it by now, and was surprised he still had it.

It was four months since I'd seen him, that week before the wedding that never happened. I wondered if he was still with Anna. I googled him, looking for information but there was nothing new. He'd lost touch with Tristan pretty soon after we'd broken up; Tristan being forced to be on my 'team' as Amber and I had been friends for so long. I considered calling Chloe, or Harry, or his parents for information, but it seemed kind of cowardly.

Then I wrote about ten different texts out before finally sending one:

Hi Jason. Got your email, thank you. How are you? How's Anna? Hope all is good. Maybe we could meet up to talk about the cottage? Izzy x

I decided not to tell him about Greg. I wanted to know about Anna first. After what felt like hours, but was really only twenty minutes, he replied:

Hello Izzy. I'm well, thank you. No longer seeing Anna, only went on a couple of dates. Hope all is well with you too. I'd rather not meet, if that's okay. Maybe you can just put me in touch with Greg? Sorry, it's just difficult for me. I wish you all the happiness in the world. Take Care. Jason x

I kept re-reading it, and then re-reading the email and debating. I wanted to ask Jade and Amber what to do, but they were both working and I wanted to deal with this quickly. In the end I took a deep breath and went out, hoping my courage wouldn't fail me by the time I got there.

As I knocked on his front door, I wondered for a second if he might have moved. Or he could be at work. I guessed I could go to the restaurant. But then I heard movement, and then there he was, opening the door.

"Izzy, hello," he said. I saw the nervous look across his face, just like when we first met.

"Can I come in?" I asked, not sure where to start.

"Of course." He stepped to the side and I brushed past him into the hall.

"I'm sorry. I know you said you didn't want to see me."

"It's okay. Can I get you a cup of tea or something?"

"No thank you."

I went into the living room and sat down. He followed behind me and sat opposite. Everything was just as I'd left it, just over a year ago now. It was so familiar, it felt surreal. Like all the bad stuff hadn't happened.

"How are you?" I asked, glancing around the room for any sign of a girlfriend. A nail file or a photo frame; girly books or chick flick DVDs. I couldn't see anything and relaxed a little.

"I'm good. How're you?"

"I'm well. They found Helen," I told him.

"I heard. I'm so sorry, Izzy."

"Don't be. At least we know now."

"So you got my email?"

"Yes, thank you."

"And Greg, what did he think?"

"I've no idea. I didn't marry him."

His expression changed for half a second and then went back to normal. I couldn't tell what he was thinking. Was he pleased, relieved, happy? Or didn't he care? Was he just annoyed because that meant I probably couldn't afford to buy the cottage on my own?

"I'm sorry ... do you mind me asking why?"

"I don't love him," I said, speaking quickly now, trying to get it out, "Jason, I love you. I've always loved you. I had a stupid, silly crush that got out of hand, but I should never have let it."

His face was blank, showing nothing. We stared at each other for a few seconds. What should I do now? So I continued, telling him how I felt.

"Dexter and I, we never had sex until I'd broken up with you because I loved you - even then. I never stopped loving you. I was just pulled into some sort of crazy, stupid attraction that didn't really mean anything, in the end. I've learned so much since then. I'd never be tempted again because I realise what we had was so special. Dexter ditched me and I cried because I missed you, and I realised how stupid I was. I've missed you every single day since."

I started crying, softly. He looked at me, expressionless, and I continued talking. "I was a mess when I met Greg. I didn't think you'd take me back and I was afraid you'd reject me, so I went along and let him be kind and nice to me. I think I was trying to replace you in some way, but I didn't love him. I love you. I've always loved you and I was just hoping you maybe still loved me enough to give me another chance."

I took a deep breath. He was staring at me; his eyes misty but still with little expression. I stared back, taking in his dark eyes and his lovely, lovely face and I thought about how amazing it felt to lay in his arms, to talk to him about my day, to hear about his life, to be a couple. And I knew with absolutely certainty that he was the one I wanted. He was the one I loved and, really, it had been Jason all along. I'd just been too wrapped up and over-analytical and stupid to realise it. Eventually, he looked away and down at the carpet.

"Say something, Jason."

"I'm not sure what to say," he said slowly, still staring at the carpet. "You hurt me, Izzy."

I moved over to sit next to him, putting my hands on his.

"I know, but I'll spend the rest of my life making it up to you if you let me. Don't you still have any feeling for me at all? I read the email and I just thought ... maybe there was a chance..."

He looked up at me then and I looked into his dark eyes wondering how I could ever have left him. He stared back at me, and I felt a moment of elation. Surely this was it. He was going to kiss me and everything would be just as it should.

"I'm not sure," he said, looking away again. "I need to think about it."

"Right. Sure, of course," I said, getting up. Had I really expected a better reaction than this? At least it wasn't an out and out rejection.

I walked into the hall. "Call me, if you'd like to talk."

"I'll be in touch," he said. "Just give me some time to think."

I nodded, wondering how long I'd have to wait. I went out into the street and started walking towards the tube station. I thought about what it'd been like to live there and how much crap I'd put myself through since then.

"Izzy!" I heard Jason's voice just as I was about to go through the turnstile in the tube station. I turned and he was running towards me. I walked towards him and we met at the station entrance.

Without a word he put his hand on the back of my head, pulled me to him, and kissed me. I threw my arms around his neck and as our lips moved against each other, I realised he was a hundred times better kisser than Dexter. What had I been thinking?

After a few seconds he pulled away.

"Thank you," I whispered, with my hands on his face. His dark eyes looked into mine.

"Forever, this time, okay?" he said.

"Okay." He kissed me again.

It felt as if I'd come home.

Epilogue

"To you, Mrs Edwards."

We clinked glasses.

"To Helen, and the house she always wanted," I said, smiling.

Coming here for our honeymoon had been Jason's idea. We'd spent the months before our wedding visiting at weekends, painting the walls, putting furniture in, making it perfect. The bedroom now had wardrobes with wellington boots and raincoats stored in them. The spare room was all made up, ready for when welcome friends came to stay with us.

The living room was painted a deep red colour and had a good stock of books and board games on the unit we'd bought years ago. We'd had to dust it all off when we arrived a few weeks after getting back together. The kitchen cupboards were full of ingredients for the delicious cooking we'd both partake in; Jason had resumed my cooking lessons and I was getting pretty good. We'd stocked up with herbs and spices and all sorts of yummy foodstuffs, so that we'd always know if we came at short notice there'd be plenty to eat.

There was a vase on the dining table and each time we came I bought fresh flowers with us. It was a home away from home; a retreat; a romantic love nest which I adored almost as much as my new husband.

In the end, my wedding day was fairly low-key. Jason and I got married in a registry office surrounded by our parents; Amber, Tristan and their baby girl Amelia; Jade and Ash;

Chloe and Harry. Then we went to Jason's restaurant, which they'd closed for the day. It was decorated with white lilies in tall vases, twinkly lights and lots of candles. Chloe organised most of it. It was beautiful and perfect, and I had absolutely no doubts whatsoever leading up to the big day. Then we spent the night in a luxurious hotel, paid for by Sian, and were driven to Cornwall the next morning.

It might not have been a tropical island in paradise, but it was ours. Our little cottage; the one I'd dreamt about since I was 12 years old. Perfect for our honeymoon.

We stood looking out at the sea from the living room window. I looked down at my wedding ring and smiled smugly to myself.

"All we need now is the golden retriever," Jason said, putting his arm around my waist.

"This is enough," I said, smiling.

Can you see through my eyes, Helen? Can you see that view?

THE END

Fantastic Books
Great Authors

Meet our authors and discover our exciting range:

- Gripping Thrillers
- Cosy Mysteries
- Romantic Chick-Lit
- Fascinating Historicals
- Exciting Fantasy
- Young Adult and Children's Adventures

Visit us at:
www.crookedcatbooks.com

Join us on facebook:
www.facebook.com/crookedcatpublishing

Printed in Poland
by Amazon Fulfillment
Poland Sp. z o.o., Wrocław